ROBBY

COOPER CONSTRUCTION SERIES
BOOK 3

By Jen Davis

ROBBY

Copyright © 2019 by Jen Davis.
All rights reserved.
First Print Edition: May 2019

Limitless Publishing, LLC
Kailua, HI 96734
www.limitlesspublishing.com

Formatting: Limitless Publishing

ISBN-13: 978-1-64034-602-4
ISBN-10: 1-64034-602-3

Dedication

To everyone still struggling to love themselves.
You are beautiful just the way you are.

CHAPTER ONE

Robby

The smell of fresh pepperoni pizza mingled with the new-construction scents of drywall and sawdust as Robby set the delivery boxes onto the just-installed island in the nearly finished kitchen area. The countertops wouldn't come in for a couple of days, so a piece of heavy plywood served as a flat surface in the meantime.

His buddy, Kane, sniffed out the food first. "Hot damn. What did we do to deserve this?" Pizza was usually a treat reserved for the beginning or end of a build, not a random weekday lunch.

Robby grinned. "You can thank your wife for this one. Something about it being your birthday?" He tore open the top box and held it up. "Why didn't you tell us?"

With a careless shrug, Kane plucked a piece from the offered pie. "Birthdays were never really a big deal in my family."

Brick, Robby's best friend and surrogate older

brother, pulled out two pieces at once and folded them together with his big hands. "Not sure I'd advertise being born on April Fools' Day either." He winked as he took an enormous bite.

"Whatever. You're just jealous because my lady takes such good care of me." Kane punctuated the pronouncement with his own hefty bite, the movement pulling the shiny scar taut across his cheek.

"Don't get too ahead of yourself. Not only does my beautiful wife take care of me, she's looking out for your dumb ass too. She's cooking a big dinner again, and she wants to make a birthday party out of it."

Kane stopped chewing and swallowed, shuffling his feet.

"What?" Robby laughed. "Haven't you ever had a birthday party before?"

Brick gave Kane an appraising look. "I don't think he has," he murmured. He flashed a small smile. "Can't say I've ever had one either, but Olivia's real big on celebrating. First time we ever met was at a birthday party she threw for Will."

Robby let Brick's words sink in. "You guys have never had birthday parties?" No matter how bad his final memories of home were, his childhood had been full of laughter and love.

A birthday never passed unremarked in the Jordan home. His mom had always said each of her children was a miracle worthy of rejoicing. Of course, those were the days before his father kicked him out. But still, the idea no one had ever celebrated the birth of his friends…it was all kinds of wrong.

The strange thing was, neither Brick nor Kane seemed bothered by it. Kane shrugged. "Don't sweat it, brother. We just didn't do things like that." He paused. "Well, we did stuff for my dad, but for Dad it was different. I guess it's hard to miss something you've never had."

Robby instantly saw the statement for the lie it was. He'd never had a real relationship, and he sure as heck missed having one.

John didn't count. If the man had ever loved him, he would have never…No. He wasn't going there.

Still, he understood what made Kane want to ignore the hurt, so he didn't call him out for the fib. "Maybe you didn't celebrate with your old family, but this year, things will be different. I, for one, am very happy you were born, and I'm going to be at this dinner with bells on." He turned to Brick. "Who else will be there?"

"I was just going to invite the guys from the crew. I already texted Will, Cy, and Evan. They're coming. Xander can't make it; he's got something at his kid's school. Which leaves Matt." Brick kept his voice free of any inflection.

Kane wasn't quite so considerate. "Matt, huh?"

Robby scrunched up his face. "Stop teasing me over my stupid crush. I'm more than aware he doesn't feel the same way."

"C'mon, Robby." Brick wiped his mouth with the bandana he always carried in his back pocket. "You can't control how someone else feels."

Kane rolled his eyes. "Yeah, if you're gonna feel

stupid, maybe it should be because you've convinced yourself you're in love with a man you barely even know."

Pfft. What did Kane know about how he felt? Robby looked to Brick for some backup, but the big man wouldn't meet his eyes.

"Look," Kane softened his voice, "I'm not trying to bust your balls, but really, what *do* you know about the guy? What makes him laugh? Is this his dream job? What did he want to be growing up? Hell, do you even know his kid's name?" He sighed. "I get it. He lights your fire. I'm just saying, maybe get to know him before you decide he's the man who hung the moon."

Robby wracked his brain, hoping to find the answers to any of Kane's questions. Surely, he knew the little boy's name.

Nope.

He had to know *something* about Matt.

Quiet. Kind of shy. Lean and muscular with dark brown skin Robby had dreamed countless times of touching. His black hair was neat and trimmed tight to his scalp, and it was just one of a dozen ways he always looked put together. Always clean shaven, always in khakis and a polo shirt. About the same age as Robby, the guy looked like he belonged more on a college campus than a construction site.

So, the sum total of Robby's knowledge: Matt was reserved…and hot.

Apparently, Kane knew what he was talking about.

"Guess I'm pretty shallow." Robby winced.

Before his friends could answer, the man in

question came in from where he had been working in the master bedroom and swiped a slice of the pizza. He drifted to the corner of the room before he took a bite.

Brick cleared his throat. "We're, uh, having a little party at my house tonight for Kane's birthday if you want to come."

Matt kept chewing, his eyes trained on the floor.

"Matt?"

The man's head shot up with a confused expression that was almost comical. "You're talking to me?"

To Brick's credit, the big man didn't laugh at Matt's confusion. "Yeah, man. It'll be fun. My wife is making fettucine. Come reap the benefits of her pasta of the week."

As they waited for an answer, Matt seemed to shrink a little under the weight of their attention. He bit into his slice of pizza without answering.

There's no time like the present.

Robby took a step toward him. "There won't be anyone there you don't know. Besides," he grinned, "I'll need someone to talk to while these two are making cow eyes at their wives."

Brick must have been slouching because, somehow, he seemed to stand taller than his normal six-feet-and-change. "I've never made cow eyes in my life!" he sputtered at the same time Kane scowled and muttered something unflattering about Robby's anatomy.

A hint of a smile flickered across Matt's handsome face, but he didn't say anything.

"You don't even have to talk much," Robby

coaxed. "And Liv's a good cook, so at least you'll get a nice meal out of the bargain."

Brick elbowed Kane in the side. "And birthday boy here can convince himself there are people in the world who don't think he's a complete asshole. At least for one night."

The glower on Kane's face gave way to a slack jaw. "What the fuck, brother? If this is what birthdays mean to you guys, I'll take a pass."

It was impossible not to laugh at his outrage. Even Matt chuckled. As the laughter died out, he nodded. "Okay. Sure. I'll be there. It's the house on Burgundy Street we finished last year, right?"

"Seven o'clock." Robby beamed.

Kane didn't share his enthusiasm. "I hate to break up this love-fest," he groused. "But none of us are going anywhere unless we finish up here for the day." He muttered under his breath about birthdays being bullshit as he stalked out into the garage, signaling everyone it was time to get back to work.

***

Every time Robby stepped into Brick and Liv's house, he felt a ripple of pride. Not for anything he'd done necessarily, but for the amazing craftsmanship put into building the place.

It was a Cooper Construction original, built by his own crew. Well, technically, Xander's crew, but same difference. No one had any idea when they were building that Brick would eventually buy the place.

The investment had helped the company at a time it really needed it.

Now, whenever he walked into the living room, he remembered sharing a pizza with the guys during the sheet rock process. Or in the kitchen, the time Xander, the foreman, remembered his birthday and gave him one of those birthday cards that played a little song when he opened it. This was also the build where he and Brick had become friends.

Brick's wife, Liv, welcomed him inside after he rang the bell with his elbow. "Robby! I'm so glad you could make it. Here, give me one of those." She took one of the two bottles of wine he carried and ushered him inside. "Leave the other one there on the table. Jonathan is with Kane in the garage."

He smiled at her use of Brick's given name and left the wine where she'd indicated before seeking out his friends. He thought he'd find them playing darts with the board on the garage wall. Instead, they were side by side, staring at a small square of paper in Kane's hand.

"—the size of an avocado right now. I still can't believe it's real." The former biker glanced up as Robby entered the room, a shell-shocked expression on his angular face. Just a hint of a beard shadowed his jaw these days. His once-long dark hair now barely touched his collar, but it was a tousled mess, like he'd been running his hands through it a dozen times or maybe tugging it out at the roots.

Brick, on the other hand, was all smiles. He slapped Kane on the back, then rose to his feet. "Kane here's gonna be a daddy!"

Kane held out the paper in his hand, a

gobsmacked expression on his face. When Robby took it, he realized it was an ultrasound photo. Happiness for his friend warmed his heart, and he sent up a quick prayer of thanks for the blessing. "Congratulations. I'm really happy for you."

Raking his fingers through his hair, Kane blinked rapidly, his expression giving no sign he'd heard a word Robby said. "We're having a baby." He launched to his feet. "A baby!"

Brick chuckled. "We got it, brother. When is it due?"

"What?" Kane's eyes focused on his friend. "Um, October. Looks like we had a shotgun wedding, and we didn't even know it." He froze. "She got a tattoo. Christ. That's bad, right?" Without waiting for an answer, he rushed past Robby, back into the house.

It was hard to imagine Kane as a father. Granted, he was usually more together than this, but it had only been a few months since he was all grungy and snarly. Still, the guy had offered him the gift of friendship—of family—which was no small thing. Maybe he could help out and babysit every once in a while. He loved kids.

"I think the news is going to take some time to sink in." Brick smirked. "We'd better get out there before he trusses her up in bubble wrap."

In the kitchen, Kane's wife, Amanda, read aloud from her phone about the risks involved with pregnancies and tattoos. Apparently, there was a small chance of Hepatitis or HIV infection but only if the needles weren't sterile.

Kane nodded, lost in his thoughts. "I trust Gerry.

He's been my ink guy for years. But you should talk to your doctor." He looked at her like she was the sun. "Nothing is more important than your health and our baby."

Setting her phone on the counter, Ms. Griffin wrapped her arms around his waist and rested her head against his shoulder.

Robby shook his head. Not Ms. Griffin. Yes, she kept her maiden name, but he was supposed to call her Amanda now. It was hard for him to think of her outside the parameters of being his boss.

She ran Cooper Construction with her step-brother, Mike, and for a while, she'd been a lot more hands-on with Xander's crew. But since Mike was back from medical leave, Robby only saw her in social situations like this one.

It was still a little awkward.

Tonight, Amanda wore nice jeans and a pink sweater, which helped separate her from the pencil skirts and silky tops she usually wore on the job. She had her red hair in a ponytail and showed no sign of the pinched expression she wore when heads were about to roll.

Despite Amanda's more casual appearance, he was far more comfortable with Liv and her perpetual smile.

She flashed one now as she linked arms with the other woman. "I'm so happy for you both. The baby, the wedding. You both waited so long to be together. I know how amazing it is to wake up every morning next to the love of your life."

Brick covered the hand she had resting on the counter with his own.

Nodding, Amanda glanced at Kane. Her face took on a dreamy quality. "There's nothing else like it. You couldn't pay me to be single again. It was so lonely. I made work into my whole life. It was empty." She shrugged. "Life is meant to be shared, you know?"

Oh, yeah. Robby knew. How many nights had he borne witness to their domestic bliss? Burned with shameful jealousy over it? He wanted the same kind of life for himself more than Midas wanted gold.

But wanting someone to share his life with had never been a problem. The problem had always been finding someone who wanted him back.

Not for sex. Finding sex had always been easy. In the early days, it was the only thing that kept him clothed and fed.

But those men didn't want the real Robby. They never knew him.

No one did.

CHAPTER TWO

Matt

Matt stared at his feet as he knocked on the door at the familiar house where Brick and his wife lived. It had been their team's work site for months. He knew every nook and cranny of the place like the back of his hand, and now it was someone's home.

Weird.

With a deep breath, he shook off his discomfort—or at least he tried. He was an invited guest, after all. If it got too awkward, he could just focus on the food then get the hell out of there.

Nothing ventured, nothing gained.

It still kind of surprised him Brick had issued the invitation. He had never been part of the inner circle the big man maintained with Kane and Robby. But the crazy thing was, they really seemed like they wanted him to come. He couldn't ignore this kind of opportunity. Not when his only friend these days had yet to master potty training.

Screwing up his courage, he rapped twice on the

door, and it opened before his nerves could get any worse. Brick's wife—Will's sister—greeted him with a warm smile. "Matt! I'm so glad you made it." She motioned him inside. "We missed you at Christmas."

Right. They'd invited the whole crew for the holiday. He'd shared a small turkey breast with his mother and his son, Jimmy. Mumbling, he thanked her for the invitation, and in a cheery voice, she chattered charmingly about how her door was always open and something about how any friend of her husband was a friend of hers.

They passed through the foyer with its shiny wood floor into the family room where Will lounged on the sofa beside Cyrus and Evan, watching ESPN. All three held longnecks.

Will lifted his beer in salute when Liv led Matt inside. The man had tan skin and blond hair, his coloring very similar to his sister's. He was obviously at home in her space. "Hey, buddy. They told me you were coming, but I thought they were shitting me. Grab yourself a brew. I've stocked up the fridge."

Cy just grunted, and Evan didn't say a word. He never did. Matt didn't think he could—a side effect of whatever military accident had caused the burn scars on one side of his body.

Matt waved at the men and followed Liv into the kitchen. Brick stood at the stove, stirring something in a big silver pot. Liv stepped behind him and kissed his shoulder blade.

Feeling like an intruder on their private moment, he looked away and saw Kane and his wife,

Amanda, sitting at the table in the breakfast nook. He paused, his eyes lingering on Robby beside them. Dark, wavy hair that was forever falling into his eyes, like it was right now. Fair skin, rangy shoulders.

He looked so comfortable here. Must be nice.

Matt never had many friends growing up. Not until Patty came along freshman year: a comrade, a confidant, and an avenging angel all in one petite package.

How many times had the guys in school called him a pussy? A pansy? A loser? Because he kept to himself. Because he didn't want to play football. Because he hated jeans and T-shirts.

How many times did his classmates accuse him of thinking he was too good for everyone else?

Patty had stopped their shit quickly.

He shook off thoughts of his son's mother.

Robby was lucky. There was no chance sex was going to ruin his friendship with Kane or Brick.

The guy was nice, even if he always seemed a little nervous. He wasn't like anyone else Matt had ever met. He brought to mind spun sugar: a sweet, beautiful thing, but one with an underlying brittleness. In the wrong hands, he could be easily broken.

Matt rolled his eyes at how ridiculous the idea sounded in his own head. He could just imagine how dumb it would come across if he said it out loud. One of many reasons he kept most of his thoughts unspoken...less chance of embarrassing himself.

Robby scrambled from his seat and hurried

toward him. "Thank goodness! I need a break from baby talk."

"Ain't nothing wrong with talking about my baby," Kane grumbled, and his wife laughed at his cranky tone.

"Sorry, Robby. I forget my pregnancy isn't quite as exciting to other people as it is to me." She tilted her head toward Matt. "You'd better make your escape while you can, though. Liv and I were just about to catch up on *Sons of Anarchy,* and you know how it gets Kane all riled up."

"M.C.s are not like that," he gritted.

Matt scratched his head. "I thought they canceled *SOA* years ago."

Robby leaned into the fridge and pulled out a beer, offering it to Matt. "Oh, they did. These two are binge watching it on Netflix just so they can talk about it in front of Kane and get under his skin."

Amanda laughed and laced her hand with her husband's. "Yes, well, that and Charlie Hunnam's abs. Jax spends an inordinate amount of time without a shirt on. Must be very hot in Northern California."

Liv fanned her face with her hand in an exaggerated wave. "I get very hot just watching!"

The women were still laughing when Robby tugged Matt back toward the living room, where the other guys stayed glued to the screen. "I'm not really into sports," Robby murmured, "but if you want to watch, I don't mind."

Matt shook his head. He didn't even know what sport was played this time of year.

Robby led him out to the front porch, to a swing

he hadn't noticed when he'd arrived. It was made of heavy wood, which made sense if it had to support a guy like Brick.

Taking a deep breath of the night air, Robby closed his eyes briefly, then took a sip of his iced tea. "I'm not really much of a beer fan, either. Maybe next time, they'll let me make a batch of Rum Punch. I don't drink these days, but I'd be happy to make them for everyone else."

Matt had never tried Rum Punch before. He wanted to ask what was in it, but the question seemed dumb. He took a swig of his beer instead. It was bitter and crisp. Whatever was in Rum Punch had to be better.

"I always loved trying new mixed drinks back in the day. My ex used to keep a fully stocked bar. When I was there by myself, I used to go on 1001-cocktails-dot-com to find random stuff to make. It passed the time." Robby shuddered. "I only tried one with Jägermeister, though. Once was enough."

Matt made a mental note. He'd heard of Jager but had never tried it.

As promised, Robby did enough talking for both of them. "I liked to take the crazy-sounding drink names to the bar and try to stump the bartenders." He sipped his tea. "I got a few weird looks, but they always came back with the drink I asked for. And they always got a good tip for their trouble."

They sat in companionable silence for a couple of minutes, rocking gently on the swing. This was the best time of year for weather in Atlanta, the nights just cool enough to remind folks summer hadn't arrived yet. The neighborhood was quiet;

only the faint sound of the TV hinted they weren't alone.

Robby's usual nerves seemed muted, and strangely, it helped Matt relax a little too. "I've, uh, been meaning to ask, I mean—you think there's any way I might be able to earn to some extra cash at work?"

Robby tilted his head to the left. "You need money?"

His face burned. "Yeah, I was hoping there might be some extra shifts I could pick up, since we're moving into the spring season."

The tight lines on Robby's shoulders relaxed. "Oh, yeah, that makes sense."

"I, uh, have a little boy." How much should he say?

Robby rubbed the back of his neck. "I know. I've, uh, heard you on the phone with your girlfriend a few times."

"She's not my girlfriend." The declaration came out sharper than he intended.

But instead of making Robby flinch, it made him grin. He held one of his hands up in supplication. "Sorry. Ex-girlfriend."

He didn't bother to correct him. It was a fair assumption. "Yeah, well. Things are tight. If there are any extra shifts—"

"I'm sorry. No overtime, man." Robby paused and rubbed his chin. "If you're looking for some extra cash, though, maybe you should look into a side job…like bartending."

Just the idea made his beer go down the wrong way. He broke into a coughing fit, and when he finally came up for air, Robby watched him with a half grin. When he was able, he choked out, "Are you kidding?"

Robby rolled his eyes. "Why? Because you're shy?" He didn't wait for an answer. "The best bartenders only have to do two things: listen and make drinks."

"I can't make drinks." The most he had ever done was mix a seven and seven for his mom.

"Weren't you listening to my story?" Robby pulled out his phone. "Every drink ever created has the recipe online." His fingers flew across the screen before he lifted the device and turned it outward. It had links for drink recipes from top to bottom.

Matt shifted uncomfortably. "I don't know."

"Well, I think you'd be perfect, at least in a smaller place on a slow-shift to start. Follow the directions, flash your gorgeous smile now and then, and you'll barely have to say a word." Robby shrugged. "Just my two cents. Think about it."

He would.

A few more minutes of silence. A cricket chirped somewhere near the porch. The smell of garlic bread meant dinner would be ready soon.

Robby inhaled deeply. "I love eating here. Liv can really cook. It's a nice break from my TV dinners in front of the PlayStation."

Matt perked up. "You're a gamer?"

"Am I a—heck yeah. My PlayStation is my baby. I'm online all the time." Robby caught the interest on his face. "What about you? You play?"

He nodded. "Yeah, but not so much online,

though."

"That's half the fun! What do you do? RPGs? First-person shooters?" Robby squinted his eyes, giving him an assessing look. "*GTA*?" He tacked the last one on the end, almost like an afterthought.

"I like the first-person shooters these days. *Battlefield* and *Call of Duty*, mostly." This was something he could talk about. "But when I was younger, I was all about the RPGs. *Final Fantasy* and stuff. The bigger the world, the better."

"Have you tried the VR? It's just like being inside the story." Robby's voice was a cross of wistfulness and awe.

He chuckled. "Did you catch the part where I told you I'm strapped for cash? I can't afford a VR headset. I don't even have a regular headset with a microphone."

"What?" Robby clutched some imaginary pearls. "We can't have that. Look, I have an extra headset—two, actually. They're not in perfect condition, but they'll get the job done. I'll bring one to work tomorrow."

Oh, no. How had he become a charity case? He shook his head. "I can't accept."

"They're not the fancy ones. I'm talking the nineteen-ninety-nine variety from Walmart. They're just collecting dust in my apartment. The backup headset to my backup headset." The breeze rustled a lock of Robby's brown hair into his eyes.

Robby had great hair. Dark and thick with just a little bit of wave.

He blew the hair out of his eyes and kept talking. "To tell you the truth, it's kind of freeing to just talk to people I'll never meet in real life. Or you don't have to talk at all. Either way, it's a lot less lonely than sitting by myself in my apartment for another night, you know? And, hey, we could totally play together online. I think it would be a blast."

For sure. There was no time to decide whether to say so out loud, though, because Will poked his head out the door.

"Dinner's ready. Liv says there'll be cake too, so get your asses in gear. She won't let us start without you." He didn't wait for an answer, just disappeared back inside the house.

With a grin, Robby saluted Will's back. "Guess we've got our marching orders."

The fettucine and garlic bread tasted every bit as good as they smelled. Butter dripped from the bread, and the garlic gave it a little bit of bite. Plus, Liv had broiled some parmesan cheese into a crispy top. The alfredo sauce coated the pasta and small pieces of chicken inside. Matt couldn't remember the last time he'd enjoyed such an amazing meal.

Though he'd never tell his mother.

Laughter and conversation drifted all around him. He felt included but never pressured to talk. It was…kind of perfect.

Liv served cake, as promised, rich and chocolatey. By the time he finished eating, all he wanted to do was crawl into his bed and sleep for a year. He rarely went anywhere after work, other than his Tuesday evening computer science class.

He bowed out after half a piece of cake and a chorus of warm goodbyes.

On the way home, he scrolled through the night

in his head, reliving Kane's bad jokes, Amanda's toast to her husband, and the easy camaraderie among Robby, Brick, and Kane.

He envied the simple friendship the three men shared. He'd never made friends easily, especially with other guys. The only person he'd ever really clicked with had been Patty, and their friendship had soured after they fell into bed together. He might have connected with his college roommate, Shawn, if he'd paid a little more attention and acted like a friend when the guy had needed it most.

But he couldn't turn back the clock. Couldn't fix either of those mistakes now. He could only move forward.

Maybe tending bar. Robby thought he could do it, but could he really? It's not like he could walk away if people expected him to talk too much.

But what had he said?

Just follow directions and flash your gorgeous smile.

The train of his thoughts came to a crashing halt, and the words *gorgeous smile* kept repeating over and over again. His heart sped up.

Surely, it was one of those things people said.

Right?

It had to be.

He reached for the radio and cranked the volume, bobbing his head to the music. Stupid to let his thoughts drift this way. Robby was his co-worker. Maybe he could even be a friend.

God knows I need one of those.

Matt's phone buzzed, and he gripped the steering wheel, stuffing down the anxiety the familiar ringtone always inspired.

Patty. It was only ever Patty who'd call him this late.

Dangling their son in front of him like a carrot on a string.

The thought stilled his hand for a second as he reached to pull the phone from his pocket, but only for a second. Even if she only called him at the most inopportune times, he wouldn't risk missing a chance to see Jimmy.

His son always came first. So he always answered when she called…and he always would.

She didn't even wait for him to say hello. The moment he swiped to answer the call, she was already talking. "You need to come pick up the baby."

"This late?" He kept his voice neutral.

She sighed into the phone. "Yes, this late. They called me in to work."

Ah, the new job. She'd been cryptic about her new gig when she started a few weeks back. Said talking about it would jinx it. More likely, she took pleasure in holding out on him.

"Are you coming or not?" She asked it like his answer didn't matter. "If you're too busy, my mom will be more than happy to take him, but don't expect her to hand him over when it's more convenient for you."

True story. The only person who hated him more than Patty these days was her mother. If he missed this chance to pick up Jimmy, there was no telling when Patty would offer again.

"I'm on my way." He hung up quickly and

turned the car toward her apartment.

For the millionth time, he imagined how much better his life would be if he could just get custody of Jimmy all to himself. He'd let Patty see him, of course, but no more of this twisted back and forth where he could only see his son when it was convenient for her.

A judge would make the decision soon enough.

He'd saved every cent he could. Paid an attorney to force a paternity test to legally establish himself as Jimmy's father. Then, he'd paid even more to file for primary custody.

Mr. Bolton was the best lawyer he could afford, but the man had warned him not to get his hopes up too high. He'd said, in most cases, a judge would side with the mother.

Poor Patty. Had a baby with the man she thought was her best friend, the man who not only let her think they'd get married and backed out but wanted to take their child away from her to boot.

She turned on the tears, and everyone wanted to comfort her. And, somehow, he became the villain in this piece. He'd loved Patty once, but never the way she wanted, and she'd never forgiven him for it. He blamed himself for the destruction of their friendship, but he couldn't let it excuse her behavior.

Pulling to stop at a red light, he squeezed his eyes closed.

He'd lost things too.

Three and a half years on scholarship at Georgia Tech had left him so close to his dream. He needed only nine more credit hours—basically, three classes—to finish his bachelor's degree in architecture. The dumbest part: they were all electives. He'd already finished with the core curriculum, but he needed a full-time job to pay for diapers and food and daycare.

The scholarship he'd earned had only applied if he was a full-time student, and he couldn't carry a full course load while working forty hours a week. Off scholarship, it cost hundreds of dollars to take an individual class at night. He'd finally saved up enough to take one this semester. The computer science class required very little studying or effort. Math and sciences had always come naturally. After this, he had only two classes left, and really, they could be anything. If his life hadn't taken a turn, he'd be finished by now. A familiar pang of regret thumped in his chest.

Not for having Jimmy, but for the timing of it all. Just a few more months and he could've been safely ensconced in an internship instead of hefting beams and nailing up sheet rock.

He shook his head against the familiar thoughts as he turned onto Patty's street. His dreams weren't over. They'd just slowed down. It wasn't a question of *if* he'd finish school…but when.

Jimmy had to be his priority, though. The custody battle meant he needed money for the lawyer, a good home, and a steady income. His dreams had to take a backseat, and it would be worth it if it meant more time with his boy.

When he pulled up outside the apartment complex, two minutes remained in the fifteen-minute window it usually took him to get there.

Still, she already stood in the parking lot, a crying child perched on her hip.

The little boy reached for him the moment he stepped close. Tears stained his chubby toddler cheeks.

"What's wrong?" Matt swept Jimmy into his arms and rocked him gently.

Patty rolled her eyes. "He's teething, Matt. Stop overreacting." She thrust the diaper bag at him and flipped her braids behind her right shoulder.

His heart lurched at her venomous tone, and he wished for the thousandth time he could've been the man she'd wanted him to be. Her life—their lives—would be so different now if he could be like everyone else. If he could just feel some attraction, some desire for her…for anyone. But he never felt a spark. No matter how hard he tried, he couldn't force it, not beyond the one night that had resulted in Jimmy. And trying to fake it afterward had only made things worse.

He sighed. "You ever going to tell me about this new job of yours?"

"Back off. We're not friends anymore. My life is my business." She turned and headed toward the curb where the bus came to a stop. Not so much as a second look at him or the little boy, whose cries had mellowed to an occasional hiccup.

It wasn't that she didn't love Jimmy. Matt knew she did. It was the boy's father she hated.

"Da!" Jimmy proclaimed, his sticky hand patting Matt's cheek.

He hugged the baby close. "Yeah, Jimmy. Daddy's here." His heart settled, breathing in the smell of his son.

He strapped Jimmy into his car seat and headed back to his apartment. There, he'd have everything to meet his son's needs, from a bath to a sippy-cup to his favorite stuffed giraffe.

Jimmy whined from the backseat—a telltale precursor to more unhappy tears.

"Hey, buddy." Matt put as much cheer into his voice as he could. "Wanna sing with Daddy?"

The whining stopped.

Singing was never one of his favorite pastimes, but he'd run through Piedmont Park in a chicken suit to make his son laugh. Being Jimmy's father was the most important, most rewarding, thing in his life. "Old MacDonald had a farm."

Jimmy joined in with an off key "ee-i-ee-i-oh."

He'd have enough time to get through all of Jimmy's favorite animals between here and home.

Then, he needed a plan.

No problem.

Tomorrow, he'd bring Jimmy to the drop-in church daycare while he went to work. He was low on diapers, but if Patty didn't show up to take the baby back, he could pick up some more at Walmart. Maybe some of those puffed rice treats Jimmy liked so much. Their baby department was a one-stop shop.

Too bad he could never find what he needed most on a store shelf. Something to bring back the woman who used to be his best friend.

CHAPTER THREE

Matt

Matt's stomach rumbled when he woke up, but he only had time to grab a granola bar before his quick rinse in the shower. He'd set his alarm early and skipped his morning workout, but he had to keep a brisk pace. It would take an extra thirty minutes just to bring Jimmy to daycare before work.

Thank God, Kim, the lady who ran the place, had a soft spot for his mom. Kim's mother had been a patient at the nursing home where Matt's mom worked, and Kim said Mrs. York had gone above and beyond in taking care of her. Finding a good daycare was hard enough; finding a good place willing to take drop-ins was even harder.

He'd lain in the bed the night before, staring blankly at the *Farscape* action figures on top of his dresser, trying to plot out a plan to find some extra money, not only for his custody fight, but to help out his mom. The nursing home had never paid well, and she had let go of her second job a few weeks back. At her age, forty hours a week was hard enough; sixty was out of the question. Only now, without the extra income, she struggled to make ends meet.

His mom had supported him on her own his entire life. Now he needed to step up for her.

Jimmy played with some plastic blocks in his playpen as Matt toweled off, the baby's happy babbling the only sound in the quiet bedroom.

His toes dug into the soft rug next to the bed for a moment before he slipped on his boxer briefs and khakis. He loved his apartment, but maybe it was a luxury to have his own place right now. Maybe he should move back in with his mom for a while and help her with the bills.

He shut down the line of thought as quickly as it came. He'd need this place if he ever wanted a chance for custody. His mom had made it very clear, no matter how much she had his back in everything else, she'd never be a part him trying to "snatch that baby away from his mother." Too many years as a single mom gave her a huge blind spot. Besides, a judge would never take him seriously if it looked like he couldn't support himself on his own.

No. What he needed to do was earn some more money, which meant taking on a second job, maybe even the bartending thing Robby had suggested.

A stack of diapers, wipes, and a change of clothes went into Jimmy's bag. If he hurried, he could get to Little Darlings before they served the kids breakfast. "Wanna go see Miss Kim, Jimbo?"

Jimmy laughed and clapped his hands as Matt

swooped him up into his arms and grabbed his keys by the *Buffy* keychain Patty had given him once upon a time.

Money worries couldn't compete with the kind of joy his son displayed. He laughed along with his boy, all the way to the car, and sang his favorite Wiggles songs on the road to the daycare. They arrived with five minutes to spare before the eight o'clock breakfast time.

The lobby of the daycare had sky-blue walls painted with puffy white clouds and a dozen brightly colored balloons floating among them. Two preschool age children sat together on a white bench below a large window into the newborn area. The director and one of the assistants stood behind the check-in desk on the right.

Kim raised an eyebrow when he and Jimmy stepped toward her. "Is that Jimmy York I see?" Her voice was exaggerated for the toddler's benefit.

Jimmy giggled when he heard his name.

"You want to go have a muffin with Miss Stephanie? Are you hungry, baby?"

Matt gave his boy a quick kiss as the assistant whisked him away to the little cafeteria, the two preschoolers following behind them. He set the diaper bag on the desk. "Thanks for taking him at the last minute."

She shook her head, the tiny beads in her braids clinking gently. "You know I am always here for your family." Her brow wrinkled. "His mama still messing with you?"

He hated talking about Patty and the way she was behaving, but Kim had to understand why he so desperately needed her to be able to take Jimmy with barely a moment's notice. He nodded, jaw tight, as he pushed his credit card toward her. "I just wish she'd agree to a permanent arrangement." Every time he broached the subject, though, she shot him down.

Kim patted his hand before accepting the payment. "He'll be safe with me. And he's welcome anytime." She swiped the card, then handed it back. "Now get on out of here," she drawled. "You're gonna be late for work."

A quick glance at the clock perched near the red painted balloon confirmed she was right.

He double timed it back to the car. His job was too important to dawdle. He cued up his favorite gamer podcast to take his mind off his money troubles, and it worked like a charm. He even found a few new cheat codes to try when he got home.

Score.

Robby's car was the only one there when he arrived.

Climbing out of his Ford, he strapped on his hardhat and approached the home site. The build was coming along nicely. The windows were delivered late yesterday, and they'd install them today. This was one of two houses they were working on this month in the development.

Cooper Construction was sub-contracting for Berringer Homes these days, and while it meant less creativity among the designs, it also meant guaranteed work as long as this subdivision kept growing. Steady construction work during the winter season was nothing to sneeze at, though now, as they moved into spring, it would mean a much more robust market.

Robby stood in the open, unfinished garage, scribbling something onto the paper on his clipboard. Though he had worked with the guy for more than a year, he could probably count on one hand the number of times he'd seen him without the clipboard in his hands or without his ever-present long-sleeved Oxford shirt.

Stepping forward, his foot crushed a soda can someone had left in the dirt in front of the house. Robby looked up, then froze in place.

Matt smiled despite himself. He found it hard to be nervous around someone even more anxious than he was. "Hey, Robby."

The man's eyes widened at the greeting, and it only made Matt's smile surge.

He didn't talk much at work, he knew, but it was kind of funny that a simple hello would prompt such surprise, especially after they'd just hung out last night. It just took him a while to warm up to people, and he needed this job so much, he usually found it safer to keep his head down to avoid any trouble. He had more than enough trouble at home.

"I had a really good time at the party." He tipped his hardhat as he walked past. "Thanks again for the bartending suggestion. I think I'm going to give it a try. Maybe flash a smile or two."

Chuckling, he caught Robby's blush out of the corner of his eye.

Not even a minute later—he wasn't sure, but he thought he heard Robby laugh softly, then start humming under his breath. Shaking his head, Matt pulled the gloves out his back pocket and slipped them on to start his day.

***

Robby

Robby didn't even realize the song in his head was passing his lips until Kane belted out the chorus.

Oh no. He might have been dancing too.

He closed his eyes, clamped his jaw shut, and prayed the ground would swallow him whole.

Not only did the ground refuse to comply, but Kane added insult to injury with a full belly laugh so loud the crews working down the street probably heard him. "Aw, don't stop on my account, kid. I was ready to sing the harmony."

Brick laughed.

Great. Not only one, but two people had witnessed his performance.

The big man tousled his hair. "Keep practicing, and you can give Ed Sheeran a run for his money."

Kane put his hand over his heart and waltzed around the room by himself, humming the melody to one of the singer's older ballads. Then, he fell flat on his backside when Brick subtly stuck his big booted foot in his path.

Watching the former biker wipe out so spectacularly cured Robby of any lingering embarrassment. He held his hand out to Kane. "No offense, but maybe you should stick to dancing with a partner."

Kane laughed as he accepted the help up, and if Robby hadn't planted his feet so firmly, he would have tumbled onto the floor beside him. "I haven't had much practice, but maybe my wife will take pity on me when I tell her about this." He smirked at Brick. "Especially since they weren't my own feet I tripped over."

Brick dismissed the pointed words with a wave of his hand. "No one cares about your big-ass feet. What I want to know is what has Robby here on Cloud Nine?"

"Big night last night, brother?" Kane waggled his eyebrows.

And just like that, the blood came rushing back to Robby's face. With the things he'd seen and done in his lifetime, most people would've lost the ability to blush, but Robby had no such luck. If there had been anything in the garage, he would have been tempted to hide behind it. Unfortunately, the wide-open space mocked him.

"Don't be an asshole." Brick's words may have been harsh, but his tone remained mild. He took a swig from a gas station coffee cup Robby hadn't noticed before. "Seriously, though, did you have a date or something after you left last night, Robby? You know you could tell us if you're seeing someone, right?"

He did. Brick would probably celebrate the idea. The guy had known for months how he felt about Matt but had never once made him feel like a fool for chasing a lost cause. Not that there was any chasing involved. It was more like *staring longingly at a lost cause when no one was looking.*

Or maybe everyone was looking.

Brick had figured it out and so had Kane.

Robby hadn't quite worked out all the nuances of how to be subtle. He shrugged, trying to pull it off anyway. "No date. Nothing's going on. Really."

Of course, Matt picked that moment to stick his head back into the garage. "Did I leave my water bottle in here?"

Trying to ignore Kane's smirk, Robby relaxed his features into a soft smile. "You didn't bring one in."

"Must've left it in the car," Matt murmured and disappeared as quickly as he had shown up.

As the front door closed, Kane snickered. Brick elbowed him in the side.

"Aw, c'mon," Kane groused. "That shit was funny!"

The corner of Brick's mouth quirked up, and Kane huffed in response. "It always comes back to Matt. What happened when you two were out on the porch last night? Did you finally manage to have a conversation with the guy? Is he what all the happy singing was about?"

Robby's smile fell, and it must have been obvious because Kane sighed and looked at the ceiling.

"I'm not trying to hurt your feelings. Trust me, I'm the poster child for holding on to lost causes. Thirteen fucking years after we broke up, I hadn't let go of Mandy."

"And look at you now." He knew he sounded ridiculous, even as the words came out of his mouth. It didn't change the truth of it. Kane and his wife had the kind of relationship he could only dream of. And he'd resolved five years ago to look at life on the bright side whenever he could. At times, optimism was the only thing able to keep memories of his past from eating him whole.

Kane rubbed his cheek, the pressure briefly turning the pink line of his scar white. "Yeah. And God knows, I'm grateful. But the way I was living all those years, that shit wasn't good for me. Not any more than this is good for you."

"What Kane is trying to say is—"

Kane elbowed Brick as he stepped forward. "Don't tell me what I'm trying to say. I can say it just fine. Matt has an old lady and a kid. Maybe he's happy; maybe he's not. Who knows?"

He lifted his shoulders in an exaggerated shrug. "Maybe he likes a little of the D on the down-low. You wanna find out? Be his dirty little secret on the side? Or do you want a chance to be really happy? What I am *trying* to say is to put yourself out there. Find some dude who wants the same shit you do. Find somebody who can love you. Stop wasting time on a fantasy and live your life, kid."

It used to bother him when the guys called him a kid. He used to think it meant they saw him as less than equal. But could he really blame them? It's why they were so protective.

His friends didn't see him as less. They saw him as worthy of their love and protection. It's what he thought he'd had with John. He just hadn't seen the predator hiding underneath.

Unlike his birth family, his friends didn't care if he was gay.

They didn't care if he loved video games or Marvel superheroes or whether he had bad luck at romance. They made sure he had home-cooked meals and laughter and acceptance. And they wanted absolutely nothing in return.

No. It didn't bother him anymore if they thought he was a kid. Not when he'd never shown them anything different.

Not when the alternative was so much worse.

Oblivious to the turn of Robby's thoughts, Kane strapped on his hard hat. "That's all the relationship advice I have in me, brother. But I'm here if you need me." With his closing words, he stepped through the doorway into the house.

Robby couldn't miss the sympathy in Brick's eyes. "Is that what you think too? I'm wasting time on a fantasy?" Fantasies weren't all bad. They could never break your heart.

"I can't tell you if you're wasting your time. And I won't. You have to figure it out, you know? Ask yourself those questions…or don't. Kane's trying to help, but it's your life." He tilted his head. "Are you happy?"

Thankfully, his friend didn't wait for an answer. He simply followed Kane into the shell of the house.

Robby gripped his clipboard tighter, then released the clutch to let it hang at his side.

Was he happy?

He had people who cared about him. A job, an apartment, and a car. More than he thought he could ever have when he left his hometown of Sherman seven years ago or when he left John two years later.

But was he *happy*?

No. He had control of his life, though, which was something he couldn't have said five years ago.

Kane did have one thing right. Matt was a fantasy. A safe haven where he could pin his affections. Maybe it was time to stop hiding behind the safety of yearning for the unattainable. Put an end to the loneliness.

Face his fears. Starting tonight.

***

Matt

Matt couldn't go to his apartment to relax after he picked up Jimmy from daycare, because he'd promised his mom he'd bring the baby to her place for a family dinner tonight. She was making her "famous lasagna," which she thought was his favorite meal. Marinara sauce gave him terrible heartburn, but he didn't have the heart to tell her.

Groaning, he unbuckled his son from the car seat in front of her house and carried him toward his childhood home. All he wanted was a shower and to go to bed, but it would have to wait.

His mother waited on the front porch, her arms open to take the little boy. "My baby! Come see Gi-Gi." She hugged Jimmy close, and he squirmed to get down on the floor. Laughing, she obliged as soon as they stepped inside. "It does my heart good to see my two favorite boys."

Turning to Matt, she patted his cheek. "You look

tired, baby. Why don't you sit down? Dinner will be ready in a few minutes."

He dropped to the sofa with a grunt and watched his son totter around the living room before laying down on his stomach in front of the TV and promptly falling asleep. It was tempting to close his eyes and follow suit.

But it would be rude.

"How was your day, Mama?"

"Fine. Just fine." Her voice had almost a singsong quality when she was in a good mood. She filled up two plates with food and set them on the table. "I spent most of the day with Mrs. Kennedy. The lady loves to talk. It's a shame her kids don't come visit her more often. She gets so lonely."

She talked more about the elderly residents she attended during the day as he settled down with her at the dinette to eat. She waited until the meal had nearly ended before the conversation turned south. "When is the last time you talked to Patty?"

He chewed slowly, considering his words. Ultimately, he was too tired to soften them much. "Last night, when she called me out of the blue to take Jimmy."

His mother tutted. "You need to work things out with her."

"We're not having this conversation again, Mom." Standing, he shook his head to silence her inevitable argument.

"I invited her over here."

He froze, his mouth open slightly. "What?"

"You heard me. Now sit back down." She shook her head as he ignored her command. "Patty Hayes is family. And family helps family. I raised you better than to turn your back on yours the way your father did."

It always came back to this. "It's not the same, and you know it. I am always there for my son, and I always will be."

"And for Patty?" she pressed.

"Patty is not my wife, Mom." He balled his fists. "It's never going to happen."

She slapped her hand on the table. "And that is the problem."

"You don't get a vote." He stepped back, knocking the chair behind him to the ground with a harsh clatter. Forcing a deep breath, he bent over and picked it up.

His mother looked like he'd slapped her.

He laced his fingers, searching for calm. "Mama, Patty and I tried, but we weren't ever really a couple. It's not like you and Dad."

She raised her eyebrow. "So, you just tripped on the way to the comic-book store, and your dick fell inside her?"

"Mama!" He'd never heard her say the word *dick* in his life. Not even during their extremely awkward sex talk in seventh grade.

"Don't *Mama* me, Matthew. If you're old enough to do it, you're old enough to talk about it. I'm perfectly capable of speaking frankly. Are you?"

"With my mother? No." He buried his head in his hands.

"Stop acting like such a prude."

He lifted his head, staring at her, slack-jawed.

"I'm tired of tiptoeing around this for your tender sensibilities, son. This is long overdue. You got her pregnant. You need to marry her. End of story."

Patty chuckled. "I'm afraid I don't meet his base requirements."

Both Matt's and his mother's heads whipped to the side to face her. She looked like a fierce warrior goddess, heeled black leather boots over her jeans, her arms crossed, eyes blazing. She must have let herself in the front door. God only knew what she'd say next.

He spoke through his clenched jaw. "Patty, don't do this."

Her laugh intensified into something dark and mean. "Don't do what? Tell the truth? Come on now, Matty. Denying the truth got us into this mess in the first place."

"I mean it." He stalked toward her. "Don't."

She threw back her shoulders, her posture practically screaming *fuck you*. "What? Don't tell your precious Mama I was your beard for eight goddamn years? Don't tell her you only fucked me because you were drunk and wallowing in guilt after Shawn died? That you could never get it up with me a single time afterward?" She snarled. "Maybe the real reason you were so screwed up about Shawn was because he had the one thing I'll never have. A dick."

His mother made a strangled sound from the table as she processed Patty's words.

It was a low blow bringing up his old roommate. And Patty was wrong. He and Shawn had barely

JEN DAVIS

been friends, much less anything more. But Matt
had felt guilty. He should've seen the signs the guy
had been partying too hard. Should've tried to get
him help.

He'd never been interested in sex with Shawn or
any man. Or any woman. He didn't want to have
sex with anyone. The night he and Patty had
conceived Jimmy was a fluke, fueled by the Fireball
shots and the platonic love he'd convinced himself
might be something more. He'd tried. God, how
he'd tried to hold on to the fragile spark, to hold on
to her, but the zing—the flare—wasn't there. Those
months of trying to pretend it was only made it
worse.

"Stop this." Matt kept his voice calm, even as
embarrassment heated his skin and his mother
backed out of the kitchen, scooping up the sleeping
baby on her way to the bedroom.

"We're just getting started." Patty twirled.
"Don't you like the independent Patty? So much
better than the mopey, pitiful girl who cried over
you. I've given up on the dream. You should be
happy." When he didn't answer, she cocked her hip
against the table and met his eyes with a level stare.

"I never wanted this."

The day after they'd conceived Jimmy, Patty had
left to spend the summer with her grandma in south
Louisiana. He'd spoken with her every day.
FaceTimed. She'd helped him navigate his guilt
after he moved back in with his mom. Comforted
him. Eventually helped him laugh again.

For him, the phone connection allowed things to
feel like they always had been between them. Only,

40

for her, everything had changed. With physical distance from her, it had been easy to talk himself out of his misgivings.

Then, she'd come back. He'd known the first time she kissed him, he didn't feel the spark. For a while, her morning sickness gave him breathing room without any pressure for a repeat performance in the bedroom. And he could manage the kissing when he needed to, even if it made him more and more uncomfortable every time.

This was *Patty*, though. If he couldn't make it work with her, what chance would he have with someone else? He couldn't lose her—not his best friend.

But when the time came to get down to brass tacks…when his excuses about studying or waking up his mom wouldn't work anymore…he'd tried *willing* his body into action. He'd tried and failed. Not once. Not twice.

Three times.

Each failure cracked his beautiful, fierce, best friend a little bit deeper. Until she shut it all down just after Jimmy was born and started dating some jerk who had no interest in her dreams—or the little boy she'd created with another man. She shut Matt out of her life and only shared Jimmy when it suited her schedule.

Patty growled, returning his attention to the here and now. "I stuck by your side! All through high school. I was your date to every dance. Your study partner—"

"My friend," he supplied.

"Friend," she spat. "I defended you. When

everyone said you were queer. I told them to get fucked. I was the reason you didn't get your ass kicked clear across Fulton County. I told you my dreams, my fears, my secrets. And you never said a word!"

Her screech woke Jimmy, who started crying. His Gi Gi comforted him with hushed words through the closed door of the bedroom.

"What did you want me to say?" He rubbed the heels of his hands against his temples. "What do you want me to say *now*? It's not like I'm out there picking up men. There isn't anyone. The only person I have ever been with is you."

She pushed him. "I don't know if that is better or worse. You weren't lying to me? You were lying to yourself."

"I wasn't lying to anyone! My love for you wasn't pretend. What we had all those years was real, and it was important to me. But it wasn't about sex. Not until you—"

"Took advantage of you?" She made a noise in the back of her throat. "For fuck's sake, can you just say what you mean for once?"

"I'm sorry I hurt you. Maybe it's not the truth you're asking for, but it *is* the truth." He reached for the bourbon his mom kept on top of the refrigerator and took a swig right from the bottle. It burned like fire in his throat. Coughing, he set the bottle back on the counter. "Oh, God."

She laughed, and for a moment, she was the Patty who convinced him to wear matching Storm Trooper costumes to a Halloween party where no one else dressed up. The Patty who recorded him throwing up after the first time he got drunk and played it back the next morning. His best friend. God, how he missed her.

As quickly as she appeared, she was gone. Her laugh evaporated, and the smile lighting her face fell into a frown. "Don't do that." She pulled at one of the braids in her hair. "Don't make me forget to hate you."

"You don't have to hate me." He reached out, but she dodged away from his touch. "We were friends for so long. *Best friends*. Why is it so terrible for me to want our friendship back? Why wasn't it enough?"

Her hands shook as she filled a glass with water from the tap. She seemed to grow steadier the more she drank. Wiping her mouth with the back of her arm, she set the glass on the counter. "When I first met you, I thought I was so lucky. Here was this smart, funny, absolutely gorgeous guy, and nobody realized it except for me."

She took in a deep breath, then blew it out. "I fell in love with you before we made it out of freshman year. I knew you didn't feel the same way, but you didn't seem to be interested in anyone else either, so I figured I would bide my time. Some guys are late bloomers and shit. Plus, I had you all to myself. We laughed at the same jokes. We cried at the same movies. We held hands; we danced together. We had everything but that one single thing."

"Sex," he murmured.

"I thought I didn't need it. Then I told myself, I didn't need it with *you*. There were plenty of guys who wanted me. When I had an itch, I scratched it.

But then—" Her breath caught. "Then somehow, some way, I had you."

She slammed her fist into the palm of her other hand. "I had you, and it was *everything*. Everything I ever dreamed about. You kissed me and held me, and when you were inside me, it was real. It was real to me!"

"It was real to me too, Patty." And he'd never been closer to another person. Still, he knew it wasn't right, even after, when he'd tried to force it.

Her eyes filled with tears. "You said you were sorry. There I was, my heart so full it was ready to burst. And you were *sorry*." She swiped at her cheek with an inpatient brush of her hand. "Then, when I found out Jimmy was coming, I managed to convince myself we could make it work anyway. We could be a family. Nothing but a stupid dream. I'm tired of wasting my dreams on you."

"What do you want, then? It can't be just about getting even with me."

She cocked her hip against the counter and tapped her chin. "Don't flatter yourself. My life is no concern of yours."

"Jimmy is my concern. He's my son too. Even if you wish he wasn't. Because of him, we'll always be connected." Just not the way she'd wanted.

"Yeah? Is that why you're trying to get custody?" Her voice went cold. "Because you respect our connection?"

She stalked toward him. "Try to take my boy, and I will destroy you. You haven't got one single friend to help you fight me."

"You're not taking him tonight." He'd barely

had the chance to spend time with him. "Mom just got him back down to sleep."

Patty squinted as she listened to the silence that had replaced Jimmy's crying. "The fuck I'm not." She stomped into the bedroom and returned with the boy asleep on her shoulder. "You might have called the shots in our relationship, but I call the shots when it comes to our son."

CHAPTER FOUR

Robby

The flashing lights and pulsing music inside Nitro made Robby feel like he'd stepped back in time. Few things had changed about the place in the past five years. A line of assorted drinks and cocktail napkins covered the shiny black bar on the right; the familiar hanging silver fixture cast light from above. Bodies pressed against the bar, three or four deep.

It was just as crowded to the left, though harder to make out the details of the men on the dance floor. He knew from experience, though, they would range in age from barely legal to guys old enough to be their fathers. They'd all be dressed to attract, from those in expensive designer clothes, to others in tiny white shorts, suspenders, and nothing else.

The smell of the piped-in smoke mixed with various brands of cologne and the hint of sweat.

Someone's hand squeezed his butt.

Yes, it was just like going back in time. Only now, he was older and not quite as desperate. At least, not in the same way he was before. This was a little higher-end than the bar where he'd met his ex, John, and the men who had come before him. In their heyday, this was where they'd come to party as a couple.

"Holy shit, Robby, is that you?"

He recognized Parker right away, even though, like him, the man was a little older than the version in his memories of this place. Parker had to be about twenty-five now, though he still held on to the twink look that had always attracted older—and wealthier—men. His blond hair was long on top and short in the back. He wore skinny black slacks and a form-fitting V-neck blue shirt, which matched his eyes. His cheeks sparkled with a hint of glitter.

"You look amazing," Parker gushed, sweeping him into a weak hug.

He hated hugs like that. Give him strong arms and a firm squeeze any day. Still, he liked Parker well enough to return the embrace. They had been friends, sort of. "Thanks. You too."

The crowd parted as Parker tugged him toward the bar. "Lemon drops," Parker announced to the bartender. "Keep 'em coming."

In a heartbeat, the shots appeared in front of them, and Parker knocked his back.

Lemon drops had been nearly a tradition when Robby'd been a regular here. He tugged at the neckline of his own too-tight shirt.

"I haven't seen you in forever, dove, and look at those strong shoulders of yours. Where have you

47

been hiding?" Parker pushed a shot his way.

Robby ignored it. With his history, booze was a slippery slope. "I've been working. Saving up. I haven't really been out in a while."

"Not since you broke up with John." Parker nodded, a knowing look in his eyes. "I should probably tell you, he's here."

A bubble of apprehension tickled Robby's chest, but it mingled with a dozen other emotions coming up at the same time: nostalgia, longing, anger. He tried to distance himself from the onslaught. "How is he?"

Parker tilted his head to the side, then bounced it to the other and back again. "He's John. Bossy. In control. Delicious Daddy."

"That's not what I meant." He forced himself to act like it was normal talking about his ex. Like he hadn't spent the last five years trying to forget their time together had ever happened.

The salacious look on Parker's face fell away. "He was a bear for the first few months—and I don't mean in the obvious way. He loved you. It was a shock when you left."

Probably because John kept his boys until they grew too old for his taste. Rarely did one leave of his own choosing. "A shock, yeah. But love? I wouldn't assign emotions to it. You know how those arrangements work. I was his property, not his partner."

Parker shrugged, but the careless effect was strained. "You make it sound like it's all bad. I like feeling like I belong to somebody."

There was belonging to someone and there was

belonging to someone. For more than a year, John had controlled every aspect of his life, from the clothes he wore to the food he ate. John chose his friends and his entertainment. And he called all the shots in the bedroom. If Robby had an opinion on any of it, he kept it to himself or faced the consequences.

"I guess I've changed," he said grimly. He pushed the shot in front of him back toward Parker.

"Maybe you want somebody to belong to you now."

Parker's hand on his sent a chill up his spine. He knew what the man was suggesting. Attractive as Parker was, there wasn't even a temptation to say yes. He eased the man's hand away and took a small step back.

A subtle nod from Parker told him he understood.

"I think I'm just going to dance a bit. Enjoy the music." He took another step back, then spun on his heel. Parker's offer had made him a little sad.

But he wasn't here to wallow. He was here to have a good time. At twenty-three, he was no longer fresh meat. Things could be different this time. He'd been lonely for so long.

For the first time in his life, he had close friends. But watching their domestic bliss reminded him day in and day out what he was still missing…someone of his own. A relationship, in a perfect world, but right now, he'd settle for a square jaw and broad shoulders. Maybe tonight, his self-imposed chastity could finally come to an end.

After just seconds on the dance floor, a set of

strong hands gripped his hips and a solid body pressed at his back. Though he couldn't see the man's face, he gave in to the pleasure of the guy grinding against him. Moments later, another dancer in front of him closed in. The new guy was Hispanic and thick with muscles. Decked out in a mesh white shirt over hairless brown skin, the man smelled of a musky aftershave, which made Robby's libido stand up and take notice.

He closed his eyes and reveled in the feeling of being sandwiched between the two men. The erection of the man behind him ground into his backside as the guy in front of him pushed the evidence of his arousal against his pelvis. The strobe lights flashed bright, even through his eyelids. The driving tempo of the music echoed in his bones.

He nearly drowned in a sea of sensations when warm, wet lips trailed over the skin of his neck. Shuddering, he clasped his hand gently behind his partner's neck. It had been so long, he'd almost forgotten how good it felt to be wanted.

His hips moved restlessly, seeking the friction the other man provided.

Then, suddenly, the Hispanic guy disappeared, and the dancer behind him gasped and scurried back.

He opened his eyes and, for a moment, forgot to breathe. Until a firm grip circled his upper arm and pulled him off the dance floor, toward the bar.

It was no mystery why there was now a five-foot bubble of empty space surrounding him. John Madigan was not a huge man, not particularly tall or muscular, but his presence was undeniable. He exuded a power borne entirely of his will.

Though in his early forties by now, his ex still had his college-professor type of good looks. Robby had always thought he looked a little like Liam Neeson in the movie he made with Jodie Foster.

John's brown hair still parted on the left. Only now, there were a few streaks of gray. He had a few more soft lines around his hazel eyes, but there was nothing else soft about his face. His jaw was hard, and his gaze locked on Robby like a laser beam.

"I thought he was lying." John squeezed his arm tighter.

Robby accepted the pain for a moment, before he realized he could shake off the man's grip.

When he did it, John's eyes widened for a moment, but he didn't try to retake his hold. "Parker told me he saw you, but I didn't believe it. Not until I saw you myself."

"Here I am." He lifted his palms, then gave John his back as he motioned to the bartender for a bottle of water.

Only it was John who spoke first when the server came over. "Two gin and tonics. On my tab."

He ground his teeth, accepted the drinks, and handed one to his former lover. He hated gin and tonic, mostly because the drink reminded him of the man standing in front of him now. Lifting it to his mouth, he pretended to take a sip. The smell alone brought him back to nights that had shamed him months and years later.

John raised his eyebrow. "I'm glad to see you're not guzzling it down. You know how you get when you drink too fast."

If only he still drank so he could down it just for spite. "I can make those decisions for myself, thanks."

The smile John gave him made him shiver. "Of course you can. You're all grown up now. You've got a man's body." His ex stepped closer, his familiar clove scent making Robby's pants grow uncomfortably tight. As many problems as he'd had with John, sexual attraction had never been one of them.

He put his hands against John's chest to push him away, but not before sinewy arms snaked around his waist. Before he could protest, John's mouth was on his, his tongue slipping inside. Moving. Massaging.

John's right hand slid against the front of Robby's pants, cupping his growing erection, then stroking it, a hot secret, hidden from the room in the small space between them.

He groaned, and still kissing him with booze on his breath, John pulled him into one of the dark corners of the room. Despite the crowd, anyone could find a secluded spot in the club, designed for encounters just like this one.

Roughly, John pushed his back against the wall. The man's deft fingers unbuttoned his pants. His hand slid down the front of Robby's boxer-briefs, headed toward his—

"No, John."

It was like he hadn't said a word. John's hand continued its descent into his underwear, wrapping itself confidently around his straining erection.

Then, he stroked.

Temptation sang a siren's song to give into the pleasure. John could play his body like a violin. But there were reasons Robby had walked away. By the end, things between them had become unbearable, and he would be damned if he fell into this tarpit again. Memories, long suppressed, flashed through his head. The games, the humiliation, the piles of cocaine he snorted to make him forget how awful he felt. Almost.

"I said *no!*" he shouted, shoving his former lover away.

John released him as he reeled back, his face slack in shock. It quickly turned thunderous. "What the fuck?"

Adjusting himself back into place, he refastened his button. "I told you to stop."

"You forget yourself. I set the rules here, not you." John raised his hand, but Robby slapped it away.

"I haven't forgotten anything, but maybe you have." He stepped forward, his chest bumping John's. "I left you. I support myself now. Pay my own rent, buy my own food. Which means I get to set my own rules."

For the first time, he realized he'd actually grown bigger than his ex. It wasn't a huge difference, but it gave him an extra shot of confidence. "Now I understand why you like 'em young. No grown man would ever let you walk over him the way you did me."

John scowled. "All grown up now, are you? You think you don't need a daddy anymore?"

He poked his finger at John's chest. "I don't need you."

"As if anyone else would have you." John flicked Robby's hand away, then smoothed his palm down the front of his shirt, putting himself to rights. "If you had a man, you wouldn't be here. Spare me your high and mighty act. You have nothing. And without me you *are* nothing."

Direct hit.

If he had a man, he wouldn't be trolling this meat market.

The bloom of his confidence withered on the vine.

John always could home in on the perfect way to break his spirit. He had the ability to deconstruct Robby's every thought and action and manipulate him with his deepest insecurities and fears. Like abandonment and rejection.

There was nothing more terrifying than the people you love turning their back on you.

Well, he might not have a man to share his bed, but he did have people who loved him now. It wasn't the same, but it was something. Something that mattered.

He smiled. It wasn't easy, but it was real. "You're wrong." The soft words barely carried over the music.

John must've heard the truth in them, though, because his cruel grin slipped, and he blinked slowly. "You kissed me back. You wanted me. Wanted what I can do to you."

Maybe.

It was easier not to answer. Instead, he stepped

around his old lover and beat a path to the front door. He didn't run the way he wanted to. It was a confident walk, one with loose limbs and his head held high.

The mask held all the way to the car, all the way back to his small apartment. Once he got home, he zeroed in on the bathroom, turning the shower on blazing hot. He stripped away his club clothes, then climbed in the tiny stall, scouring away the smell of the booze, the smoke, and John.

The hot water barely registered.

He refused to think; he just went through the motions, lathering the soap and rinsing away every touch and every kiss. What he couldn't wash away was the knowledge of what he'd done—something he swore he'd never do again—which was fall back into John's arms. Even if he'd stopped things before they went too far, he'd let them start in the first place.

As he scrubbed himself raw, he relived every touch of the man's hands, body, and mouth at the club tonight, castigating himself for each one.

Hating himself for enjoying it.

It wasn't until he stepped out—skin tender and red—and put on his PJs that he allowed himself to unpack his feelings over what John had said.

As if anyone else would have you.

Without me, you are nothing.

You have nothing.

He pulled his knees to his chest on his bed, wrapped his arms around them, and rocked gently.

"You're wrong," he whispered. "Wrong."

If he believed it, why was his heart breaking?

And why couldn't he put it back together?

Eyeing the nightstand, he considered the contents inside the drawer. It was only for the worst nights. A last resort.

But this was one of the worst nights, wasn't it? One of the worst in a long, long time.

CHAPTER FIVE

Robby

As Robby walked into the chilly, yellow-lit room, he wrinkled his nose against the burnt scent of coffee sitting on the burner too long. It didn't stop him from pouring himself a cup, but he knew from experience it would taste as bad as it smelled.

It didn't matter. He always needed something to do with his hands when he attended one of these meetings. For some reason, it made him feel a little less exposed.

Clutching his Styrofoam cup, he shuffled to one of the folding metal chairs laid out in a circle at the center of the room. Lots of chairs to choose from. It looked like a lean night for the N.A. group.

He recognized Thomas, the guy who ran the meetings, from his sporadic visits over the years and acknowledged him with a nod. The guy looked the same, though his craggy face was a little more weathered, and his receding hairline had moved back another inch or so. He had to be pushing fifty

57

now.

Thomas offered a sympathetic smile, like he knew what was going on in Robby's head. But, of course, Robby wouldn't be here if life were going well.

Cara, another familiar face, stared down into her lap.

The other three guys were strangers.

Thomas cleared his throat. "Hi, everyone. It's time to get started." He stood. "My name is Thomas, and I'm an addict." He paused. "Heroin. I've been clean for ten years now, but you guys keep me accountable."

He retook his seat and tilted his head at Cara.

She wrapped her arms around herself. "I'm Cara," she mumbled. "Not sharing tonight."

Damn. The way she held herself didn't bode well for the older woman. Last time Robby had seen her, she'd been off the pills for years. She was a mom of two teenagers. If she could fall off the wagon, anyone could.

Robby stood. "My name is Robby, and I'm an addict. I've been clean for almost five years. It's been a while since I needed one of these meetings. But I'm really glad you're still here."

He sipped at the nasty brew in his hand, debating whether to talk about his trip to Nitro. Even at his lowest, sharing the sordid details of his past with John had always been beyond him. It was easier just to talk about the drugs. "I wanted to use tonight. I didn't."

The guys he didn't know went on to introduce themselves, and he relaxed, falling into their stories.

With such a small group, the meeting wrapped quickly, but it gave him the renewed resolve he needed.

Thomas approached him as he tossed his now empty cup in the trash by the door. "I'm glad to see you're still fighting the good fight, my friend. You know, you can call me anytime things get tough."

Robby had never really been into the sponsor thing. He'd never trusted anyone enough, but he had called Thomas to talk him off the ledge a few times in the first year. "I appreciate it. I've still got your number."

They walked out together toward the cars parked down the street.

Two guys stumbled ahead of them, arms linked, into the storefront next door. It was hard to make out many details about the office in the dark, but Robby recognized the pride flag in the window.

He paused, trying to catch a glimpse inside. "You know this place?"

Thomas nodded. "It's a community center for LGBT folks. We've had a couple of the kids sit in on our meetings." He frowned. "Some of them have been through hell, man."

Hell. Robby knew it well. "I'm sure." Shaking his head, he resumed the trek to the car.

"Have you—do you have a good support network, Robby?" Thomas stopped beside a red Mazda pick-up. "I've worried about you."

Robby shrugged. "I've got people. But none of them who…know. I have a new life now. I don't want them to know this side of me. I can't risk losing them."

Even the thought of going back to a life without Brick and Kane made his stomach clench. He loved them, and he knew with his whole heart they loved him back.

"I understand. It can be easier to talk about the hard stuff with strangers. It doesn't matter what they think but hear me out. You can't ignore your recovery or your addiction. The system works if you work it. Whether you use me or someone else in your life, just make yourself accountable. You feel me?" Thomas unlocked the door and swung it open but didn't climb in.

"I feel you." Robby held out his hand and Thomas gave him a firm shake. "I'm not going back to the way things were. No way. No how."

He'd keep it together, no matter what life threw at him next. It couldn't be as bad as what he'd already endured.

***

Note to self: Avoid the club scene at all costs.

Robby scribbled the thought onto the last piece of paper attached to his clipboard, then let the stack of schedules, supply requisitions, and memos drop down to cover it.

He always kept the old wooden board in his hands on a job site. It helped him stay organized, an essential skill for his role as the foreman's assistant. But just as importantly, he needed access to those loose-leaf pages of his journal where he could unload the thousand and one feelings sitting on his chest at any given point of a regular day.

It was vitally important to keep them to himself. The last thing he needed was for his co-workers to know what a giant dumpster fire he was on the inside.

"Where did I put those plans?" Usually, he was so meticulous with his papers. Misplacing them was like a sign flashing how far off his game he was after his disastrous night at Nitro. Seeing John had thrown him into a real tailspin. He hadn't wanted to use so much in he didn't know how long.

The idea of going back to the club had seemed so liberating at first. Reclaiming his past or some garbage. Though in truth, loneliness had prompted it more than any big ideal. Now, he felt worse than ever. Scratch that.

He'd felt worse than ever last night. Today was a little better. The meeting had helped some.

Hugging the clipboard to his chest, shame over his lapse in judgment warred with pride over the new life he'd built. He had a best friend now, one who would do anything for him. Brick was the perfect example of someone who could have it all, and he exuded a contentment Robby wanted more than his next breath. Jealousy could be an insidious emotion, even though he knew Brick had dealt with his own demons before he found his happy ever after.

Robby lifted yesterday's pizza box and looked underneath it. Maybe he could find what he needed if he cleaned up some of this mess. The plans weren't hiding under the remnants of their Papa Johns.

"Crap." Everything felt so scattered. He was

supposed to hand those plans over to Brick first thing when his friend arrived.

Not that Brick would give him a hard time about losing track of them. In the past few months, Brick went from a growly bear with a thorn in his paw to someone who would offer friendship and family to the nobody assistant who everyone thought of as a kid.

Ha. He was hardly the person they thought he was. Though it would've been nice if it were true. He'd lived through things the men on the crew couldn't even imagine. And he hoped they never did.

Brick stuck his head into the unfinished kitchen Robby had slipped into and ran a hand over his close-cropped dark hair. A year ago, a big guy like him would make Robby turn in the other direction. On the street, size had been a weapon easily wielded against the weak. Brick was easily six-foot-four and stacked with thick muscles from his years as an underground fighter.

"Come over to the house for dinner tonight. Kane and Amanda will be there too."

Robby shoved the pizza box into the industrial-sized trash bag in the corner, his attention split between Brick's offer and his search for the plans.

"We're having spaghetti," Brick offered. "C'mon, you know you're family to us."

Family. The ultimate enticement. The kind of high he never got with powder or pills. Love. Belonging. Acceptance.

But he had a different plan for tonight.

Robby grinned as he threw away some old water

bottles on the concrete floor. "I was kind of hoping to hook up with Matt and play PlayStation online."

"I'm glad to hear it." Brick folded his beefy arms in front of his chest. "It's about time you got up the nerve to get to know him better. But if you change your mind, our door's always open to you."

Brick had no idea what a gift he offered. Or maybe he did. Brick had said he had no other family either. Maybe his friend needed him as much as he needed Brick.

Robby held his clipboard close. "I know."

He might have said more, but his eye caught on the man passing through the room, several two-by-four's hoisted on one shoulder and a roll of paper in his hands. His breathing hitched, as it did every time he laid eyes on Matt.

"Found these in the garage," Matt murmured, slipping the plans into Robby's hand, then drifting out of the room as quickly as he'd drifted in.

What a view.

Brick interrupted before he could sink into a fantasy. "I don't know how I ever missed the fact you're in love with that guy."

Love? More like a king-sized crush, but Robby wouldn't trifle over semantics. He held out the plans. "And, uh, these are for you."

Brick took the papers. "You better catch up with him if you're gonna invite him to play your game."

***

Matt

Matt didn't expect to feel so disappointed when Robby had forgotten his offer to bring those headsets to work yesterday. He'd built it up too much inside his head. It had probably been one of those offhanded comments people made when they hung out together.

He wouldn't say anything. Bringing it up would only embarrass them both. Besides, he'd had his hands full last night anyway.

Bending at the knee, he deposited the two-by-fours in the master bedroom. He turned to go grab another load and almost walked right into Robby, who now stood at the threshold to the hallway.

"Sorry we didn't have a chance to catch up yesterday. I'm about to take a supply run for Xander but…here." Robby held out a plastic grocery bag and grinned.

Matt peered inside and found a pair of black headsets with an attached microphone. "You didn't have to do this," he murmured. Though he was glad Robby had.

"Are you kidding? This is as much for me as it is for you. I should've brought them yesterday. Believe me, I would have had more fun playing with you than the night I ended up having."

Tempting as it was to ask, something in Robby's tone told him it was better to leave it alone.

"I put a note in there with some instructions." Robby swayed a little on his feet, color rising in his cheeks. "Okay, I, uh, I'm gonna go. Hope to see you tonight." He hightailed it out before Matt could say another word.

He wanted to read the note now, way more than it made sense. Which was why he tucked the folded paper into his wallet and stowed the headsets in his glove box. He could wait.

The note burned a hole in his pocket as he nailed up the wood in the master closet, throughout the workday, and the entire way home.

Still, when he let himself in his apartment, he didn't read it right away. He didn't want to be too eager, even if the only person who would know would be himself. So, he warmed up the leftover Walmart rotisserie chicken he had in the fridge and stacked the meat inside two halved pistolettes.

He ate in silence, by himself, at his small kitchen table. The meat was juicy, and the drippings mingled sumptuously with the thin sheen of mayo he'd smeared on the bread. He ate slowly, savoring each bite, proving to himself he had no reason to hurry.

No reason at all.

Rinsing his plate and silverware, he busied his mind with thoughts of Jimmy. He already missed his son. He didn't have a problem with the idea of sharing with Patty. But he only got time with Jimmy on her terms, and last night, she'd only taken the baby to prove she could.

Tomorrow, he would find himself a second job. Half the money would go to his mom; the other half could go back to the lawyer. His mother might refuse to testify on his behalf, but he would make the best possible home for the baby, which had to count for something. The only way to do right by his boy was to make it happen.

Resolved, he sat down on the soft, tan, second-hand loveseat and unfolded the note Robby had written.

I had a great time hanging out with you the other night. I'm psyched to play with a friend I have IRL.

Sorry it's a day late, but I brought the headsets as promised. I know you probably don't have a PS+ account, but they offer a free 30-day trial, and I hope you'll give it a try. My username is RobHulkSmash. I'll be online tonight.

—R

He'd looked into getting a Plus account a year before, but he just couldn't justify the sixty bucks when it could be spent on diapers or food. But a free trial wouldn't hurt. Worst case scenario, he'd lurk online, hate it, and never come back.

It only took a few minutes to fire up the PlayStation and get the trial set up. Scratches and dings covered the console—he'd bought it used at GameStop—but it worked fine. A quick search later, he'd found Robby and sent out an invitation to connect.

Thankfully, he was playing one of the only two games Matt owned.

The headphones sprang to life with a cacophony of voices. He teetered on the verge of pulling the device right back off when he heard Robby speak.

"Matt! You made it." He sounded downright happy about it.

He forced himself to answer. "Hey, Rob." It was the best he could do. Too many strangers in the conversation.

Playing with real people didn't change the dynamics of the game much. He still killed his targets, only now he focused his kills on the other team. Robby tried to engage with him a few times, but he only managed a few grunts.

About thirty minutes in, his phone chimed with a text.

Robby: Wanna break off to a private party? We can stay on the team and just have the two of us on the headset.

Matt shot back a thumbs-up emoji and set up the two-way connection. It was a relief not to have so many voices in his ears.

"Shoulda realized the noise might be too much, man. Sorry."

"Nah." Matt shook his head, even though no one could see him. "It's fine. Thanks for the invite."

They fell into the game, and at first, only Robby spoke, but as Matt's discomfort fell away, he found himself answering more and more.

The conversation centered entirely on the gameplay, which helped. Like, "Look out for the sniper," or an occasional, "Bull...I totally hit the target."

Before he realized it, the clock had ticked past midnight, and he found himself downright yelling at the screen when their team won by the skin of their teeth.

"Great job, man." Robby's words were a little slower than usual. "I've got to sign off, though. I've been up since five."

He glanced at the clock. Normally, he would have gone to bed hours ago. "Sure. It's cool." He winced. Hopefully, Robby hadn't heard the disappointment in his voice.

Robby hummed. "Hit me up if you want to play tomorrow. I'll be on around four."

"Later." He'd barely said the word before Robby disconnected.

Climbing in his bed, he considered his plans for the next day. He'd bring diapers to Patty's in the morning, a perfect chance to check on his son. Job hunting in the afternoon. PlayStation with Robby when he was done.

A total break from his regular monotony. His skin tingled with excitement.

He fell asleep, dreaming of a real-life military mission, Robby at his side, taking down the enemy with a partner who had his back.

CHAPTER SIX

Matt

The visit to Patty's place could get the day off to a great start or a terrible one, depending on the state she was in. The complex was a little sketchy, but neither he nor she could do anything about it.

Time and age had warped the gray siding on the front of the building. It was relatively small, with two units upstairs and two units beneath. Cracked, old, green paint and rust marred the metal railing along the second story. Patty had one of the downstairs apartments.

Dread pooled in his stomach when he knocked. Who would answer the door—normal Patty or the fire-breathing one? His poor mama was still scandalized over the poison Patty spewed at the house the other night.

He didn't have to wait long. The door opened to reveal his old friend, freshly showered, her braids pulled back in a low ponytail. She wore jeans and a Gorillaz T-shirt.

She cocked her hip and smirked when she saw him standing there. "Couldn't stay away, huh?"

He held up the pack of Pampers. "Thought you could use these."

Grunting, she stepped aside to let him in.

He could smell a trace of cleaning products, which tracked with the absence of dust and grime in the small living space. Whatever her mystery job was, it obviously didn't pay much, but at least Patty did her best with the place she had.

Jimmy sat in the playpen Matt had purchased for him, just below the light fixture designed to hang over the kitchen table Patty had pushed to the side. He babbled to himself while stacking several colorful plastic blocks.

"You can put them on the kitchen counter." She gestured to a clear spot next to the sink.

He did as she asked, then unzipped the diaper bag on his shoulder. "I brought some milk and a few things I thought he might like." He put the half gallon in the fridge, which was mostly empty, except for a McDonald's bag, rolled at the top, and a few slices of cheese.

The pantry didn't look much better, though there were a few cans of SpaghettiOs, some dry rice, and a box of off-brand cereal. He added three bags of instant mashed potatoes—Jimmy's favorite—along with cans of green beans, chicken, and tuna. The cabinet still looked a little bare when he was done, but it was an improvement.

"You don't have to do all that, you know?" Patty rubbed at the back of her neck. "I've got a job. I just haven't been to the store yet."

"I know, Pat." He almost reached out to her but pulled his hand back at the last minute. "Any word on a permanent schedule? I can help out with childcare if you need it."

She waved him off. "My shifts are mostly at night. It makes more sense for Jimmy to stay with my mom."

He swallowed his disappointment over the fact she didn't offer to let Jimmy stay with him. He didn't have time to fight again. At least the job seemed to be making her happy. Not only was it good for Jimmy, but Patty had been his best friend for years. He wanted it for her too.

"Antoine and I broke up." She folded her arms, almost daring him to call it a good thing.

No way he'd step onto a landmine like her love life. But it *was* a good thing. And it explained why she'd been in such a foul mood last night. She was better off without him, though. He didn't treat her right, but she took it. Maybe she thought she had to, to keep him. But the Patty he'd grown up with had always been tough and independent. Matt liked her better that way—at least when she wasn't trying to bust his balls.

"I'm sorry if you're sad about it, but I'm glad you've got a job that makes you happy." He poured as much encouragement as he could into his smile. "I'm really proud of you."

Patty held up her hand, and years of habit had him shutting his mouth so fast his back teeth clacked together. "It's just not the life I thought I was going to have, but it's getting better. It's going to keep getting better."

"Good," he murmured. Patty had dreamed of becoming an illustrator for graphic novels. She'd had amazing talent too. He couldn't remember the last time he'd seen her with her pencils. And he wasn't touching the subject with a twenty-foot pole. "Thanks for giving me time with Jimmy next weekend."

"Whatever," she grumbled. "Give him a kiss and go. I've got shit to do."

She didn't have to tell him twice. He swept up his son and swung him around, his chubby little legs flying behind him.

"Da! Da-dee!" Jimmy's unabashed happiness to be in his arms always took his breath away.

He stopped spinning and hugged his boy to his chest. "Are you having a good morning with Mommy?"

Jimmy bounced enthusiastically in his arms. "Bami. Bami. Bami."

That was new one. Matt raised his eyebrows at Patty.

She sighed. "He's talking about *Bambi*. We've watched it like ten times this week, including once this morning. It's his new favorite."

"Hey," he ventured. "I heard they might be releasing a new *Serenity* mini-series."

She shook her head. "It's just a rumor. They're done with the comic. It was never as good as the show."

Firefly had always been a favorite of hers.

"But it's canon. You know if there's more to the story you can't turn it down." He grinned.

"Stop trying to butter me up with nerd-talk."

Patty smirked. "Now, go."

Though his heart wanted him to stay longer, he released his son back into his playpen and gave Patty a small salute. "You need anything, just call."

"I will. And, hey, I'm sorry for saying all that shit in front of your mom. I'll apologize to her the next time I see her."

His mom would forgive her. She loved Patty like a daughter.

From Patty's place, he set out for the first of three bartending jobs he'd found online before he left home. His search terms had actually come back with four hundred seventy-six hits, but he'd spent an hour paring them down, first ruling out any requiring previous experience, then those which specified hours he would be on the construction site. Even if none of the places on his list worked out, he still had plenty other choices.

He wasn't in the market for a dance club or anywhere the music would be too loud or the place too packed. Big crowds could mean more money, for sure, but he had too much to learn, and he knew this would already be a trial by fire. If it got too hot, he'd burn alive.

He picked places with names he equated to a bar guys might go to chill: Frank's Place, The Spot, and Closing Time.

The Spot was closest and from the outside appeared just as he'd expected. A small standalone building, almost like a shack with two tinted windows, both with turned off neon signs boasting beer brands. One car sat in the modest parking lot, and as Matt approached the door, he caught the muted sound of music seeping out. He didn't realize it was R&B until he walked inside. An old Luther Vandross song.

Inside, a single elderly guy in a worn overcoat sat on a barstool, sipping a drink from a highball glass. His eyes never looked up from the scarred wood of the bar; the dark skin of the hand he had wrapped around his drink peeked out from fingerless gloves. Only the slight tightening of his jaw betrayed his awareness of Matt standing behind him.

"Can I help you?"

He started at the woman's voice. Intent on the man, he hadn't even noticed her on the opposite side of the wraparound structure.

As she stepped out of the shadows, he could see she was a heavyset white woman in her forties, her dark hair pulled back in a ponytail. She wore black jeans, a red tank-top, and a suspicious expression. "Sir?"

"Yeah," Matt mumbled, his eyes making a quick survey of the room. He caught sight of two empty tables on the far side of the room, but the dim light kept him from making out too many details. "I'm here about the bartending job."

She raised her eyebrows, two hand-drawn black arcs above her eyes, and swept a critical gaze from his head to his feet. "Pay's five dollars an hour, plus tips. Weekend days only."

His eyes returned to the old guy on the stool. If this was the average daytime clientele, he doubted he'd get too many tips. He could make more money working at McDonald's. But how to get out of here without being rude?

The discomfort must have shown on his face because the bartender waved him off. "Didn't think so. Get on out of here."

Okay. Next stop.

Closing Time turned out to be nestled between a Mexican restaurant and a sporting goods store at a strip mall. The parking lot only had a few open spaces toward the back, but there was no telling how many of those people were eating, shopping, or day drinking. Steeling his shoulders back, he covered the distance to the door in long strides.

Though some kind of coating on the window kept him from seeing in, when he crossed the threshold, he realized the effect only went one way. He could see clearly back out into the parking lot, and, more importantly, sunshine mingled with the overhead lighting, illuminating every corner of the room.

Like The Spot, the bar was shaped like an oval so it faced both sides of the room, but the similarities ended there. The space was bright and clean, the dark wood of the bar, unmarked. Red pleather covered the barstools, and booths lining the left side of the room had matching upholstery. The right side featured four tall, round tables and four dart boards, two of which were currently in use. Two old-style arcade games stood in one corner and two women shot pool all the way in the back.

He counted about twenty people, most on the right side, but one couple shared a basket of fries at a booth. The room smelled like chicken fingers.

Everyone looked to be around his age, except for

the man behind the bar who greeted him with an easy smile. The crinkles around his eyes and the gray in his hair made him look close to fifty. "What can I get you? Longnecks are two for one right now."

He returned the man's smile, though he doubted he projected the same ease. "I'm here about the job." He held out his hand and the guy shook it. "Name's Matt York."

"It's a pleasure, Matt. I'm Tom, and I sure am glad to meet you."

Turned out, Tom owned the place and served as both bartender and short-order cook for the time being, since two of his employees ran off together, leaving both of their significant others behind.

Tom rubbed at his clean-shaven jaw. "Tell me you're not interested in any relationship drama."

He most definitely was not. He had enough drama to last him a lifetime. "No, sir. I'm just trying to earn some extra cash to help take care of my mom and my son."

Tom's friendly smile somehow grew even warmer. "A family man? Oh, I like to find guys like you. How old is your boy?"

Matt pulled his phone out of his back pocket and lit up the home screen photo of Jimmy. "He turned one in November."

"Looks like my grandson." Tom beamed at Jimmy's photo and thumbed Matt's attention to a picture posted on one of the beams.

Tom didn't look black, but the child in the picture was. And sure enough, he did remind Matt of his own little boy. "Yes, sir."

"I appreciate what you're trying to do. Shows me you're responsible, which is what I am looking for. I only ask for you to be on time, to treat my customers well, and not to make trouble." He pulled out a clipboard from under the bar, and it made Robby's face flash behind Matt's eyes. "Just fill out this application, and if it all checks out, you can start tomorrow. It's just weekend days for now. Okay with you?"

It was perfect. He found himself mouthing along to the Beyoncé song playing from the overhead speakers as he worked on the form. He even chuckled as he handed in the paper and caught sight of three guys reenacting the dance moves from the video.

He left with a promise to return the next morning at eleven for his first shift.

The next two hours disappeared with a hastily prepared turkey sandwich and a crash course on a website Tom recommended, learning some basic drink recipes. He was studying so intently, he nearly jumped out of his skin when his phone alarm went off.

Four-fifteen. Robby had told him four o'clock. Fifteen minutes was not rude, but not desperate—or so he told himself as he fired up his PlayStation. He'd barely put on his headset before a message popped up on his screen from Robby inviting him to play.

When he accepted, Robby's familiar voice welcomed him back. "I'm so glad you're here. My team is getting its butt kicked."

"Let me get into position." He quickly got his

character into place to provide cover fire. And just like the night before, he fell into an easy rhythm with his co-worker, and their team came out on top when the time ran out.

"Eat dirt!" Robby crowed as the scores popped up on the screen. "You rock at this, Matt. How long have you been gaming?"

"Always. Long as I can remember. But we all grew up on PlayStation, right?"

Robby didn't answer.

He tried again. "What about you? Were you playing *Final Fantasy* when you were a kid or were you always into shooters?"

"I didn't play until I was older. My family—the town where I grew up was kind of cut off. Nobody had a PlayStation. Most people didn't even have internet. It was too rural."

Matt wanted to ask what he did to entertain himself without gaming or the internet, but something in Robby's voice made him suspect the questions would be unwelcome. Like he'd done so easily all of his life, he was tempted to let the silence prevail.

No. Not this time. "You'll never believe it, but I took your advice."

"Huh?"

That's right. Reengage. "About bartending. I picked up a side-job. I start tomorrow."

"Awesome!" The pride in the way Robby said it was almost palpable. The stumble in their conversation was forgotten.

"I've been studying some of the basic drink recipes, but if anyone asks for something I can't find on the website, I'm screwed."

Robby made a noise of disagreement. "You can Google anything. It's going to be great. Don't worry."

"I hope so." He exhaled. "I really need the money. People are depending on me."

"Like your son."

"Yeah. Jimmy. And my mom. I've got to do right by them."

"If anyone can, it's you."

An ember of pride burned in his chest at Robby's encouraging words. For the first time, he thought maybe he could.

***

Robby

Robby cursed himself silently for gushing, but the way Matt talked about being there for his son, well, the kid was lucky. He braced to get shut down, but instead, Matt chuckled.

"Thanks, Rob. It's nice to have someone believe in me. I'm really glad we're hanging out."

It was a good thing Matt couldn't see the blush burning his cheeks. No way he'd be able to hide his swelling crush face-to-face. They played another hour or so before the timer beeped on his phone. As much as he'd been feeling better, he'd promised himself he'd attend another meeting tonight.

"I've got to sign off, but I can't wait to hear all about the new gig on Monday."

"I won't leave out a single detail. I promise."

The plan, small though it was, made him feel ten feet tall as he drove downtown. The feeling convinced him he really didn't even need the meeting, but he went. Other than Thomas, there were all new faces. Only two of the folding chairs were open tonight.

The dragon always did ride hard on a Saturday.

Robby didn't have much to share tonight, but he introduced himself, then settled back to listen to others offer their truths.

One guy who started taking Oxy after a car accident and couldn't stop.

A nurse who lost her license swiping pills from a locked cabinet.

A kid who stole from his parents to buy heroin.

Then a small, dark-skinned, androgynous person stood, clad in jeans and a gray sweatshirt. A twisted scarf covered their hair. But what struck him most were the big brown eyes, fringed with dark lashes. Those eyes looked older than time. "My name is Sara, and I'm an addict. The first time I took pills from a stranger was after my first night sleeping on the street."

Robby's heart sped up, knowing how the rest of the story would unfold.

Only, it didn't. Sara clamped her mouth closed and retook her seat so quickly, the front legs of the chair lifted briefly from the floor.

He had to talk to her. Let her know he understood.

It took all of his patience to wait out the rest of the meeting, but as soon as Thomas called it a night, Robby made a beeline to her at the table with the stale coffee. Her eyes hardened instantly when she realized he'd sought her out.

"See something you like, doll?" The sharp edge in her gravelly voice reminded him of dozens just like it he'd heard over the years. The kind that said a good offense was the best defense.

He held up his hands. "I just wanted to introduce myself. See if you could use someone to talk to."

She scoffed. "Talk, huh?"

"Yeah. And to make sure you had somewhere to sleep tonight." How many nights had he wondered where he'd find a safe place to rest?

"You're precious, but yeah. I stay at the Q-Center next door." She cocked her head. "And no, I'm not inviting you to join me."

"Q-Center?" She had to be talking about the place with the pride flag in the window he'd seen the other night.

Sara sighed. "Yes. Q. Like queer. It's a community center—and a place to sleep sometimes for people who need it. A safe place."

His gaze skittered across the room before focusing back on her. "A safe place might've made a real difference for me a few years back. I'd love to see it."

The heroin-kid swiped a couple of cookies off the table before stalking off.

Sara watched him for a moment before glaring into her coffee cup. "I told you it wasn't an invitation."

"I don't mean tonight. Tomorrow maybe? I'm not looking to make you feel unsafe in your home." But something inside him practically shouted he needed to see it firsthand.

"Nothing is driving me out of there. Not you. Not anyone. They won't let me stay in the women's shelter anymore. Not since some asshole outed me as trans." She gulped down more of the burnt brew. "It's not safe at the men's shelter. And the streets—"

"I know. Nobody is safe there."

She gave him a skeptical once-over. "You know firsthand?"

He grimaced, and she didn't wait for further confirmation. "Yeah. I see it now. You hide it really good, though. The hustle."

The hustle. It had been years since he'd hustled anyone. "I guess you could call it that. Don't like to think about it much." Draining the dregs of his own coffee, he set the cup on the table beside him and immediately regretted it. He needed something to do with his hands.

"Can't say I blame you." She gestured for him to follow her to a sofa on the perimeter of the room. The blue upholstery was worn, but the comfortable cushions welcomed him.

Sara's frank gaze bore into him. "You're pretty. I'll bet it was a blessing and a curse."

No way he would go there. "It got me out of the cold but nowhere I wanted to stay. I got out, though. Found my place. You can too, you know. I'd like to help you if I can." He rubbed his toe over the long fibers of the patchwork rug in front of him. "Or maybe just be a friend."

"And you want what, exactly, in return?" She lifted her chin.

How many times had he sat on the other side of a conversation like this one, waiting for the other shoe to drop? How many of those offers to help had come without strings?

None.

"I don't want anything from you." He slid an inch or two away from her, his left hip hitting the arm of the sofa. It didn't make a big difference in the space between them, but the movement made more of a statement than his words ever could.

She shook her head, blinking rapidly, then shrunk into herself. "Yeah," she murmured. "Guess I'm not exactly your type."

He fought the urge to scoot back toward her, to offer her comfort. Touch was far too easy to misunderstand, though. And besides, if Sara's experience had been anything like his own, she'd had enough uninvited contact to last a lifetime.

Instead, he clasped his hands together on his lap. "I didn't come here to get laid." He wasn't mean about it, but he said it as firmly as he could. "I've got everything I need at home. I don't want your money or your shoes or your body. Do you understand?"

"Everyone wants something." The way she said it tugged on memories he scrambled to shove down.

"I want to see the center. Learn what they do there. Maybe I can help people…like me." He released his grip on his own fingers and held out his hands in front of him, palms up.

In his heart, he knew there was only one way to convince her. He had to show her they were the same. Even trying to speak the words felt like

83

fingers squiggling around inside him.

Sara snarled. "Spare me the Dudley-Do-Right routine. I don't even know what I'm doing here talking to you." She gripped the arm of the sofa and pulled to her feet.

"I get why you don't believe me. Everyone wanted something from me too. I only had a place to sleep if I earned it. On my back, on my knees, or on my belly."

Finally, Sara's frigid stare softened, and he felt flayed open.

The words caught in his throat, but he pushed them out. "I did things that still turn my stomach. There's some stuff I don't even remember, and I don't try because it's better left dead and buried. You get me? But I made it to the other side. You can too."

She grunted. "To where? My own mama didn't want me. Who out there is going to...unless I give 'em a reason?"

His heart surged. God put him in this place for this purpose. "You *are* the reason." She needed to hear that friends could be real...not everyone wanted to use or abuse. "My family didn't want me either, but I've made a new one. Let me tell you about my best friend, Brick."

CHAPTER SEVEN

Robby

Robby always arrived first at the construction site each morning, at least the one where Kane and Brick were working. He probably shouldn't fashion his day around seeing his friends, but he spent time at the other build with Cy, Evan, and Will too, just not as much.

And today he'd see Matt. He grinned. They could be gaming together again tonight.

Brick wandered in, his hardhat already strapped on. "Looks like somebody is having a good morning."

Robby motioned to the box of donuts he'd set out on the makeshift counter when he'd first arrived. "Krispy Kreme has that effect on me."

"Bullshit," Brick mumbled, one of the sugary treats already crammed in his mouth. "Only one thing makes you all goofy-looking." He swallowed. "One person."

Kane shoved his phone in his back pocket and

85

swiped a donut for himself. "No kidding. It looks like you took my advice and made friends with the guy. Is he living up to all your hopes and dreams?"

"He's nice. We have fun together." And maybe if he and Matt could be friends, it would help him get over his hopeless infatuation.

"You need to get out more, brother." Kane leaned against the island. "Seriously, meet some new people. Broaden your horizons."

Robby thought back to his night at the club and shuddered. That was a bust, but Kane probably had a point. "How? Where? You make it sound so easy. But a meat market is not the answer."

Brick made a strangled noise against the back of his hand. "Meat market?"

"Don't pretend like you're a prude," Kane scoffed. "Or do you think Robby's one? It's you who is always saying he's not a kid, brother."

The telltale reddening of Brick's neck meant Kane had hit the nail on the head.

Robby stared at him in disbelief. "You think I'm a *virgin*?" He laughed at the absurdity of the idea, but there was no joy in it. "Do you have any idea the kind of stuff I had to do just to survive when my parents kicked me out?"

Brick's face paled, and Robby could've kicked himself.

"I'm sorry." He forced a smile. "Forget I said anything."

"I understand better than you think." A haunted look reflected in Brick's eyes.

He couldn't imagine his badass friend ever feeling as trapped and desperate as he'd once been, but he recognized the truth when he saw it. He nodded his understanding, then looked away.

"So, the club scene is out." Kane broke the tension as if the other men hadn't just nearly bared their souls. "What do you like to do for fun?"

"I play PlayStation."

Kane frowned. "You meet people playing games?"

Matt entered the room quietly and pulled a water bottle from the cooler on the floor.

As he turned to walk away, Robby reached out, his hand touching Matt's arm for a split second. "Hey, wait. How was your first day at the new job?"

Matt paused, then glanced from Brick to Kane before ducking his gaze. "It was fine."

Brick waved his hand at nothing in particular. "We'll let you get back to it, Robby." He turned to Kane. "Come give me a hand upstairs." The big men made their way out of the room with the subtlety of two drag queens at a burlesque show.

Or maybe it was only obvious to him, because Matt didn't give them a second look. Instead, he let out a breath, and his shoulders relaxed. He ventured deeper into the kitchen and cocked his hip against the counter. "It was so much easier than I thought it would be. Most people ordered beer, really, or simple drinks like Jack and Coke. I only had to Google three times."

"Awesome!"

Matt grinned. "I didn't have to talk to anyone, except to say thanks. And the best part? I walked out of there with a hundred and fifty bucks in tips, which isn't even counting what I'll get on my paycheck. You know how much this is going to make a difference to my family? One weekend in tips will pay my mama's light bill."

He'd never seen Matt so animated, so…happy.

"I owe this all to you, Rob. I would have never thought of bartending on my own." Matt reached out for Robby's left hand with his right one and pulled him closer before wrapping his other arm around for a brief hug.

It ended in a second, but the contact lasted long enough for him to learn the feel of Matt's body against his own. Almost exactly the same height. Maybe a little more muscle mass, but not too big and not too small. And the smell of him, fresh cotton and man.

He gripped the island to still his shaking hands.

Matt's grin froze into place, seconds after he stepped back. "I—I mean, uh, sorry." He held his hands up in front of him. "I didn't mean to—"

His heart fell, and something hard and angry rose in its place. "What? Touch me?" He did *mean* to enjoy it. Dammit! The hug had been…amazing, and he'd ruined it. Or Matt had ruined it. Either way, the other man's reaction practically screamed *hands off.*

Robby scoffed. "Don't worry. I get the message loud and clear." He gestured to the area around him. "This is my dancing space. That is yours."

Matt's forehead wrinkled, the mangled *Dirty Dancing* reference obviously lost on him, and it only drove up Robby's embarrassment…his anger…at himself—and at Matt, who was a much more convenient target.

"I *can* control myself around you, Matt," he

seethed. "Gay people do it all the time. And you won't catch it. Your manly man-ness is safe." With the words still hanging in the air, he hugged his clipboard to his chest and walked out without looking back.

Not even an hour later, Robby wished he could take it all back. Still, he hid out in the trailer like a chicken all day—even skipping lunch—until Matt left to go home. Then, he rushed to catch Brick before the big man climbed inside his blue Chevy pick-up.

His friend narrowed his eyes at Robby's fast approach. "What's wrong?"

"I, uh, think I outed myself to Matt. I think I might have also accused him of being a homophobe." The more he thought back on the entire interaction, the more he was sure he'd overreacted.

Brick leaned against the cab and laced his hands over his stomach. "Did he deserve it?"

"Probably not. He gave me a hug and kind of froze up afterward."

"And?"

He covered his eyes with his palms. "There's no *and*...just me always waiting for the other shoe to drop."

"So, apologize."

Robby uncovered his peepers to see Brick looking at him blandly. "How am I supposed to face him? I quoted *Dirty Dancing*." He banged the heel of his hand against his head.

"I—I've never seen that movie, but I'm sure it can't be as bad as you think. All I'm saying is if you fucked up, own it. Apologize. If he's really your friend, it will be enough."

Apologize. He could say he was sorry. It would suck, but it was the kind of thing his mama always called a natural consequence. Those were the times she didn't have to punish him, because the way something worked out would be punishment enough.

Like the time he climbed Mrs. Peterson's tree without permission, then fell out and landed on his backside. He couldn't walk right for days.

Or the time he tried his father's bourbon and ended up with his head in the toilet, begging God to make the misery end.

He'd earned his lumps back then, and he earned them now. He could only hope he hadn't poisoned their seed of friendship before it ever really had the chance to bloom.

***

Matt

If he didn't need the money so damn much, Matt would have called out sick from work, just so he wouldn't have to face the almost-friend he had so deeply offended. Of course, it would have only delayed the inevitable, but at this point, he would take any reprieve he could get. With things messed up with Robby, the world had turned upside down. Unfortunately, being able to afford food for his mother trumped his urge to hide under his covers, which was how he came to be here, casing his work site from the car.

No sign of Robby yet, which was unusual, but Brick's pick-up was parked along the curb.

He opened his car door. Closed it. Sunk down in his seat.

What were the chances the big guy knew what happened?

Hell, *he* barely knew what happened. The most important part, though, he'd hurt Robby with his bumbling, self-conscious bullshit.

He'd been so excited about his job, and Robby had been happy for him. Then he made the colossal mistake of putting his hands on the other man.

But the touching wasn't really the mistake, was it?

It all went bad when he had realized how the touch had affected him. When his body responded against Robby's lean strength, and the man's damn wavy hair brushed against his cheek.

He'd frozen. God only knew what kind of look he'd had on his face. Did Robby see how horrified he'd been?

Obviously, but for all the wrong reasons.

Fuck.

Robby was gay.

And now he thinks I'm judging him for it.

Finally, for the first time in—forever, really—he had made friends with another guy, and he fucked it up because he was getting a boner.

He'd be excited it had finally happened if he weren't so damn embarrassed.

Why did he have to be so bad at…people?

Peeling away the fingers he had clenched on the

steering wheel, he opened the door again, this time forcing himself to relinquish the safety of his sedan. This was just like any other day. He'd say he was sorry and retreat back into the quiet solitude the job had always given him.

It didn't matter if he wanted to tell someone about the drunk guy who serenaded his girlfriend on top of a table at the bar. Or how he couldn't wait to try the new free download from PlayStation, which would be available tonight.

Keeping to himself wouldn't be the end of the world. He was good at it. It came easy. Or at least, it always had before.

Simple. He'd just keep his mind on his work. The seams in the ceiling sheet rock where he'd spread joint compound yesterday needed sanding, and if he wanted it to look smooth, he'd have to do it by hand. Too much pressure would gut the mud into valleys, not enough and the whole thing would look lumpy.

He abandoned the car and tackled the master bedroom first. Situated out of the way, no one would cross his path unless they made a point to do it.

Setting up the extra-tall ladder, he alternated sanding with double checking his work with a flashlight. Earbuds piped his favorite Otis Redding and Sam Cooke playlist directly into his brain. "I've Been Loving You" never failed to transport him to another place entirely.

A tug on the left leg of his khakis brought him back to earth. Popping the bud out of one ear, he glanced down…and almost lost his footing when he met Robby's gaze. He disentangled from the music entirely and carefully descended the ladder.

"I was an idiot." Robby spoke before Matt's feet hit the floor.

Definitely not what he was expecting.

"You've never said or done anything to make me believe you would judge me for—being gay. I let my hang-ups take something small and turn it into something big." Robby wrapped his arms around his waist, his ever-present clipboard conspicuously absent. "I probably imagined the whole thing."

It would have been so easy to let Robby think their awkward moment had only been in his imagination, but it would make him a really shit friend, and this was his chance to make things right. "You didn't imagine it."

Robby reared back, and Matt held up his hands in supplication.

"Wait, please. Just hear me out." He dragged his hand over his head. "I'm not great with people. Obviously."

Robby stilled, watching him carefully.

"I only had one friend growing up, and she was a girl. Is a girl." This wasn't going well. "What I'm trying to say is—I froze. Not because you're gay. How would I know if you're gay? I froze because I hugged you without thinking about it, and then I was afraid I'd done the wrong thing. I overthink stuff. And you—you're the first guy friend I've ever had. I didn't want to mess it up, and, well, I went ahead and messed it up."

"What you're saying is," Robby drawled, "you're even more socially awkward than I am."

His face lit up. "That's the coolest thing I have ever heard in my entire life."

Matt scowled. "You're not making your life sound very exciting."

"Ha!" Robby laughed. "You have no idea. Maybe I'll tell you the story someday. And maybe you could tell me about the girl with enough game to manage to keep you all to herself."

"Eh. Maybe one day." Or, hopefully, never. "Are we good, Rob? 'Cause I'm really sorry I kind of freaked out on you."

"Yeah. We're good. Especially if you can overlook an occasional, irrational, emotional outburst, fueled by intermittent low self-esteem." Robby punctuated the statement with an exaggerated smirk, and it was like a fifty-pound weight lifted from Matt's shoulders.

"You need to work a little on selling yourself, Rob. Seriously." He had never thought of his friend that way. He hoped Robby didn't either. "I have a class tonight, but you want to game with me afterward? I think I'm going through withdrawals."

Robby's eyes crinkled at the corners, and he bounced on the balls of his feet. "You see the new download? I'm so stoked to jump in."

And just like that, the world was right-side up again.

CHAPTER EIGHT

Robby

Robby ran a dust-cloth over the TV for what was likely the fourth or fifth time in as many minutes, though calling it a dust-cloth was probably—no, definitely—an insult to dust-cloths everywhere. In reality, he dusted with an old tube sock which he'd worn a hole through the toe of months ago. It worked just as well.

The past few nights had been awesome, staying up late, taking out targets on the PlayStation with Matt. They'd gotten into a groove, logging on just after dinner and setting up a private chat on the headsets. Every night, the conversation started off about the game, but in bits and pieces, they evolved into more.

One night, he shared with Matt his love of all things Marvel. How he still couldn't re-watch the *Avengers: Infinity War* movie and how it never stopped bothering him when Rhodey had been recast after the first *Iron Man* movie. Matt liked

95

Don Cheadle better in the role, but, heck, it just proved the man wasn't perfect.

And it wasn't like he hated all recasting. The Incredible Hulk was hands-down his favorite character, and he loved Mark Ruffalo. It might have been a good segue into how he always thought of Brick like the Hulk, but he kept that little nugget to himself.

He admitted his soft spot for a good romance too. Not the tearjerker kind, but the ones where the guy inevitably screwed up and had to make a grand romantic gesture and a promise to love the woman until the end of time.

Another night, Matt told him about the time he'd shared an elevator with Stan Lee at DragonCon, and he was so star-struck, he hadn't said a word. The convention was a sci-fi fantasy lover's haven, and Matt was freaking adorable in his full-on geek mode.

He also told Robby about his dreams of becoming an architect and how he was taking night classes to knock out his last few electives.

At one point, they'd talked about their favorite games, and Robby gushed over his VR headset. Yeah, the set-up had set him back a few hundred dollars, but he had bought all the gear used at GameStop, and it had been worth every penny. Matt had never so much as stuck his toe into the virtual reality pool, and of course, Robby had to remedy the injustice with an invitation to come check it out.

Which was how he now found himself obsessively cleaning his already spotless apartment, waiting for Matt to arrive. Everything had to be perfect, or at least as close to perfect as his low-rent one-bedroom could be. The carpet was vacuumed, the sofa cushions fluffed. A bowl of potato chips graced the coffee table, and drinks were chilling in the fridge.

The pizza was due to arrive in about half an hour. He'd gone back and forth about whether to have it here when Matt arrived but decided they would enjoy it more if it was hot. Plus, if things got awkward, they could focus on the food.

Please don't let things get awkward.

His heartbeat picked up at the soft knock on the door. The place was as clean as it was going to get. Shoving the dust-cloth under one of the cushions, he advanced to the door.

Please go well. Please. Please. Please.

His cheeks strained at the too-big smile on his face as he opened the door; his back teeth clenched so tightly, they threatened to splinter in his mouth. But one glimpse of Matt fidgeting with a grocery bag and shuffling his feet on the porch made the tension melt away in an instant.

"You need a hand?" He reached out to snag the brown paper bag.

Matt had been holding it horizontally because it had a vegetable tray inside. "I wasn't sure if I was supposed to bring anything." As he stepped over the threshold, his gaze flitted from one end of the room to the other, looking everywhere except at Robby.

It was impossible to stay nervous around someone even twitchier than he was. "This is perfect. Thanks." He pulled off the clear plastic protecting the food and placed the platter next to the chips. "Snack food 'till the pizza gets here." He dipped a broccoli floret in the reservoir of ranch dressing, then popped it in his mouth.

"You had me at pizza." Matt swiped a handful of chips from the bowl and crunched them with a grin.

"Wait. You haven't even heard the best part yet." He cleared a path to the kitchenette in five long strides. He pulled the glass pitcher from the fridge and held it up triumphantly.

Matt followed him over. "Tell me I'm not looking at the famous Rum Punch." He lifted one of the two tall glasses on the counter and tipped it forward for a fill-up.

"I didn't taste it," Robby admitted, pouring for Matt. "But I've made this recipe so many times, I'm practically a pro." He filled his own glass with sweet tea and clinked it against Matt's. "Cheers." Closing his eyes, he tipped his head back and indulged in the sugary goodness. Not quite as exciting as a cocktail, but smarter.

Matt groaned. "Oh yeah. I'll take this over a beer any day of the week. What's in it?"

The recipe rolled off his tongue, the ingredients long memorized from years of tinkering with the perfect proportions. He'd played bartender countless times for John and his friends.

The pizza arrived a little ahead of schedule, but the savory sauce was the perfect complement to the sweet drinks. The quiet prayers he had sent up not to bungle the evening quickly faded until they were forgotten. Over pizza slices, they laughed about Kane's hatred of all fictional motorcycle clubs. They speculated about how much Cooper

98

Construction was making from its deal to subcontract for Berringer Homes. And they dished over their favorite celebrities, almost all with roots in sci-fi or fantasy.

Matt tried out a few of the virtual reality games, but they all made him sick to his stomach. *Resident Evil*, in particular, prompted him to pull off the headset and declare the experiment an unmitigated failure.

Thankfully, the nausea seemed to vanish the minute Matt took the visor off, and Robby spent the next five minutes forcing him to watch the videos he'd made on his phone of Matt screaming at imaginary monsters.

He couldn't remember the last time he laughed so hard. "You want me to make another pitcher of punch?" He rubbed his hands together. "Oh! Or you can make this one. Show me your new bartending skills."

Matt shot him a dubious look. "My bartending career has spanned one shift. You really want to take a chance with my hands in your favorite recipe?"

He took Matt's hand and pulled him toward the kitchen. "The best thing about this drink is how hard it is to mess up. There are only degrees of how good you can make it. And I don't mind sharing my secret, which is to use orange and pineapple juice from concentrate instead of fresh and then use club soda instead of water to dilute it."

He probably should have released Matt's hand as he broke the recipe down, but it felt so good being skin to skin. Matt's palm was cool—his fingers long and strong. The best part? He showed no signs of discomfort. He didn't try to disentangle himself or step back. If anything, he moved closer as Robby used his other hand to pull the various rum bottles forward for inspection.

"Most people will tell you to use half light and half dark rum." He lowered his voice, as though he were sharing a secret. "The dark gives it a depth of flavor, but you need to split the other half between the light rum and coconut rum."

"Coconut." Matt was so close, his breath fanned over Robby's jaw as he spoke. "Not spiced rum?"

He sucked in air through his mouth and imagined he tasted the breath that had left Matt's body. He took a moment to savor the idea. Just a few inches and he could taste Matt's mouth for real. He pulled back.

A dangerous line of thought. He'd made so much progress with Matt, he would *not* obliterate it with an overture guaranteed to embarrass them both.

"No. Ah, if you're looking for a good fit for Captain Morgan, I'd suggest it as a substitution for tequila in your margaritas. It's especially good for those of us who have a rocky history with Jose Cuervo."

Either Matt didn't notice his retreat, or he didn't react to it. Instead, he asked more questions about drink recipes and created a single-serving version of the Rum Punch under Robby's tutelage.

Matt smacked his lips together in approval with his first taste. "Almost like a real bartender made it!" Drink in hand, he settled himself back on the sofa. "I may need to crash on your sofa tonight, man."

"It's all yours." He sat on the sofa's far end. "Don't you have a shift at the bar tomorrow?"

"Sure do. Ten AM. I've got my boy too. He's going to stay with my mom while I finish my shift." Matt released a yawn into the crook of his arm.

Robby perked up. Matt never brought up his son. "What's his name?"

"Jimmy. He's one. Smart as hell, my kid. Best thing I ever did. I just wish I could have him with me all the time."

"Your ex getting in the way?"

"My—oh, Patty. Yeah, you could say that. Things with her are complicated."

"Tell me about her." Robby wanted to know everything.

Matt's pinched expression eased. "We met at DragonCon. I'd never been, but I saved all the money I earned from cutting grass and washing cars to pay for the ticket, and it was worth every cent, just to watch from the sidelines. Heck, it would've been worth it for *The Walking Dead* panel alone."

He swallowed more punch. "Patty recognized me from school, even though I didn't recognize her. To be fair, though, she was covered in body paint and dressed in some kind of sexy alien costume from the Shatner-era *Star Trek*."

His gaze went distant. "We read the same comic books, loved the same sci-fi shows. She embraced my inner geek. We were like two peas in a pod all through the rest of high school and college. Until we slept together, and it all turned to shit." He shook his head. "I ruined our friendship by letting it go somewhere I knew it shouldn't go. I hurt her, and she hates me."

Wow. Hate seemed like big leap from embarrassed or disappointed. How could anyone hate Matt? "I doubt she hates you, she—"

"Trust me. She tells me every chance she gets how much I hurt her. How I took advantage of her friendship." Matt scowled into his drink before taking a big gulp. "She thinks I'm gay. That I'm lying to myself and when we were together, I was lying to her."

Robby gaped. "Wh—why would she think that?"

He buried his head in his hands. "Because I never dated anyone in high school. Never had any crushes or hook-ups. The only person in my life was Patty, and we were just friends. After a while, though, I knew she wanted more. I thought, what the hell? You know? I *did* love her. I do."

Robby's breath caught when Matt's hand rested on his leg. When had they gotten so close? He looked up to see a new awareness in the man's eyes. It made his dick wake up and take notice.

"But you don't love her the way she loves you." Robby licked his lower lip.

Matt's eyes were wide, the brown rings of his iris shrinking against the blackness of his pupils. He shook his head slowly.

Robby inched closer. Just a fraction, but he felt the heat of Matt on his skin.

"Is it possible she may be right?" Robby's voice barely rose above a whisper. "Have you ever—have you ever kissed another man?" His heart banged against his chest.

"I've never kissed anyone except Patty. I never wanted to."

The grip on his leg tightened, and his dick was so hard, it almost hurt. But he found it a pleasurable kind of pain. He fought the urge to wrap his fingers around it while Matt's eyes were locked on him. "Do you want to now?"

Robby's left leg rested firmly against Matt's and his entire body strained for more.

He didn't wait for an answer. Ignoring the warning sirens blaring in his head, he leaned forward and finally, finally took what he wanted. His lips met Matt's, and he groaned with the rightness of it.

Matt held still at first. A second. Two. Then, he yielded, and the surrender tasted so damn sweet. They kissed softly, breathlessly, as if neither had ever kissed another person before. As if they both knew this moment could change everything.

Robby slid his tongue over Matt's bottom lip, tasting the bite of rum, and for a heartbeat, Matt's tongue peeked out to brush against him.

But all too soon, Matt pulled away and rested his forehead against Robby's.

"We can't. I can't."

Robby's heart thudded against his chest. Had he read everything wrong?

"I ruined one friendship this way before." Matt shook his head. "You mean too much to me to risk it."

"But you did…want to kiss me." He might die of embarrassment if Matt said no.

"Yeah. Which is the crazy thing. I don't really

understand what's happening with me. *Am I* gay? Now? All of a sudden? I never thought so, and now, here you are, and I want—I'm…really confused." Matt rubbed his hand over his heart. "I don't want to screw things up between us. Not like I did with Patty."

A hundred arguments sprang to Robby's lips, like how the deepest love could come from friendship or how love was better with someone you really knew and trusted, but Matt had to come to those conclusions on his own.

"Okay." He shrugged with a nonchalance he didn't feel. "We'll stay friends, but in the meantime, those questions you have? About who you are and what you want? You owe yourself the answers."

He stood, then turned off the TV and the overhead bulb. Only a thin beam from the light below the microwave illuminated the rough planes of Matt's face. "It's late. Get some rest. You've got a big day ahead of you."

CHAPTER NINE

Matt

Matt woke up with a fuzzy head, and it took a minute to figure out the source of the obnoxious beeping somewhere nearby. He traced it to a small digital clock on the coffee table. Eight o'clock. A handwritten note rested beside it.

Had to step out for some errands. I hope the alarm worked okay. Didn't want you to be late for your shift. Hit me up later if you feel like playing.

—R

Late for—oh, shit. His heart raced. He couldn't lose this job. What time was it again?

Eight-oh-one.

Oh yeah. He had a couple of hours to run home, shower, and change. Sending a silent thanks to his friend, he lurched off the sofa and foraged for his shoes.

Hopefully, he hadn't made too much of a fool of himself last night. The kiss he'd shared with Robby had been a shock to his senses. He wanted to take out the memory and examine it from every angle, but there was no time for it now. If he was going to make it to work to open up, he needed to hustle.

A hasty shower at his apartment and two microwaved scrambled eggs later, he was unlocking the front door of the bar with ten minutes to spare. He made quick work of setting up the cash register and prepping the bar.

Customers arrived in a slow trickle. A couple with matching blond hair and dark jeans around eleven. Three or four frat guys just before noon. By two o'clock, though, a dozen twenty-somethings were kicking back with their beers. Matt stayed poised—on the ready to serve their refills and collect his tips as each bottle ran dry.

He was so intent on anticipating their needs, he didn't see Patty until she parked herself on the stool directly in front of where he stood at the bar.

She looked happier, more relaxed than he'd seen her in a long time. The braids gone from her hair, a headband pulled her short twists away from her face. A hint of makeup gave a slight blush to her cheeks. And best of all, her eyes twinkled with her small smile.

"When I dropped off Jimmy with your mama, she told me you were tending bar, but I thought she was pulling my leg." She looked him up and down. "Never in a million years did I think I'd see the day

Matt York worked in a bar."

"What are you doing here, Patty?" He kept his voice mild. The last thing he needed was to cause a scene and drive away his paying customers.

Delving her hand in her purse, Patty dug out a five-dollar bill and slid it across the bar. "Bud Light. And keep the change."

He stifled the urge to point out she should be saving her money to get a better apartment. It wouldn't do any good. Instead, he reached under the bar for her drink and popped open the top before swapping the bottle for the fiver.

She took a long pull from her beer, her shoulders swaying slightly to the Rhianna song piping from the overhead speakers. "You look like you sucked on a lemon. Buck up, Matty. You're always worried about when you'll get to see Jimmy. At least you know you can pick him up from your mom when you get off."

True. Even if he did have to fit play time around shifts at the bar.

"I miss you." She sighed. "Can't we just be in the same place for a little while?"

Matt glanced around the room. No one was looking for a drink. "I'm working, but if you can respect that, you can stay."

She surprised him by nodding and ordering a hamburger. He watched the room using the high mounted mirrors while he stepped into the back and dropped a pre-made burger on the griddle. The patty was thin, and by the time he had the bun and chips in the basket, it was done all the way through.

Stuffing the bottles of ketchup and mustard

under his arm, he grabbed the food and placed it in front of her. She ate as he filled a few drink orders.

He leaned against the bar in front of her when he was done.

She'd made it about halfway through her meal. "So not only are you tending bar, you cook now too? It's even edible."

With anyone else, Matt may have played it down, but Patty knew better than anyone how underdeveloped his culinary skills were. She'd been there when he'd set off the smoke detector making a grilled cheese sandwich. He'd tried to wave the smoke away with a hand towel, which caught on the flame of the gas burner. Suffice it to say, the exercise had ended with a spent fire extinguisher, flakes of black ash floating around the kitchen, and a thoroughly petrified, blackened parody of a briquette sandwich.

"I've been practicing. I may never be a master chef, but I can handle the basics. Haven't set anything on fire in at least nine months."

Patty grinned into her food. "Maybe you can give me some tips. Unless it's pre-cooked with a clear film on top so I can stick it in the microwave, I'm probably going for a bowl of Lucky Charms."

Matt wrinkled his nose. "I'll never understand how you think those hard, little fake marshmallows qualify as food." It was an argument they'd had more times than he could count over the years. Sliding back into the debate was like slipping on an old comfortable pair of shoes.

"Funny how a man who can't melt cheese on two pieces of bread can be such a food snob."

His heart squeezed painfully. It had been so long since he and Patty had hung out this way. For all the awful shit volleyed between them in the past year, there were a thousand happy memories built around nearly a decade of friendship. Late night study sessions over cheap Little Caesar's takeout pizza. Binge watching old episodes of the *Battlestar Galactica* reboot. Sitting side by side while he played *Final Fantasy* and she sketched out the characters into fanfic comics.

It struck him how deeply he loved her. Other than his son and mom, there was no person on this earth who he'd felt more connected to than Patty. Only their bone deep bond prompted him to make love with her that night. A mistake, yes, but it was the wrong thing done for the very best reason.

"You're thinking too hard." Patty tapped her temple. "You're gonna pop a blood vessel up there."

Matt nearly jumped out of his skin when a hand landed on his left shoulder.

"Sorry I didn't check in sooner," Tom said, an easy smile on his face. "Why don't you grab a few minutes break, and I'll keep an eye on the bar?"

He'd been so involved in his conversation with Patty, Matt had completely forgotten his boss had promised to drop in this afternoon. "Yes, sir. I appreciate it."

Grabbing his bottled water from the ice from the cooler where he'd stashed it at the beginning of his shift, Matt peeked at his watch. How the heck was it after three o'clock already? Only three more hours until he was done for the night.

He took the empty barstool beside Patty.

She crunched a potato chip, then pushed the empty basket away before facing him. "You seem comfortable here. All these people don't bother you?"

"Nah. I don't really have to talk much. I just get them what they ask for. Take their money." He shrugged. "I'm just an extension of the bar, no different than a piece of furniture."

"Just the way you like it." Patty covered his hand with hers. It was soft and cool, and he didn't pull away. Her presence next to him soothed his aching loneliness.

Why couldn't she be like this all the time? His life would be so different. "You always did understand me."

Her hand twitched. "I thought I did. I thought we'd be together forever. Now it's like we're strangers or, even worse, enemies."

"You act like I cut you out of my life. That's not what happened." God knows, he'd never intentionally give up his best friend. He would have done anything to keep her.

Well, he would have done *almost* anything.

"No." She released his hand to take a sip of her beer. "But it hurt too much being around you. After."

"I never meant to hurt you. You've got to believe me." Though he couldn't regret their night together. Not when it brought Jimmy into his life.

"Why *did* you do it? It's not like I pushed you. I never even *tried* to take it there." Her stare, normally so accusing these days, instead looked sincere and haunted as it searched his solemnly. "I would have never risked us."

Tough as it was to deal with a drunk or angry Patty hurling insults his way, a conversation with a thoughtful, mournful Patty was so much harder. This Patty deserved an answer. Unfortunately, he didn't really have one.

What she'd said was one hundred percent true. He had initiated something sexual between them—not her—and blaming the alcohol could only carry him so far. It gave him courage, for sure, but he knew what he was doing. He'd needed so much to feel normal again after finding Shawn dead, and Patty was like a salve on the open wounds of his heart.

"I did it because I loved you."

She scoffed.

"You asked me, and I'm trying to answer you." He raked fingernails over the thighs of his khakis. "I never wanted to be with anyone that way. But after a while, I wanted to want it. You were safe and beautiful, and I knew you loved me too. I thought if there was anyone in this world who it would be right with, it would be you." The very idea of sharing something so intensely personal with someone he didn't love and trust completely—it didn't just leave him cold; it made his stomach churn.

Except with Robby.

"But you hated it," she murmured.

"No!" Matt took her left hand in both of his. Some of her warmth had already disappeared. "I didn't hate it." But he'd known it was wrong.

Known it from the moment her tongue brushed against his. He'd tried to tell himself it was because he was nervous, because it was his first time or because he was doing it wrong. He'd lied to himself.

His love for Patty might have been enough for a single spark, but it never ignited the fire he knew he should feel.

Meanwhile, with Robby, sparks were starting to shoot all over the place.

Patty groaned. "For future reference, *I didn't hate it* isn't exactly a glowing endorsement. Why won't you just come out and admit you're gay? Stop lying to yourself."

Was that what he was doing?

It's not like he spent his nights jerking off to gay porn or exchanging pictures of his privates with strangers online. Yes, he'd had a passing attraction to guys here or there, but the same was true with women. It just never held up to deeper scrutiny.

He closed his eyes, and Robby's face wove itself into the darkness. His kiss echoed in his bones.

Almost never.

His tingle of attraction for Robby Jordan showed no signs of blinking out yet. In fact, the more they hung out, the harder it got to ignore. And after last night, he doubted he ever could.

His lips parted in an unbidden smile...and froze as Patty's breath fanned across his cheek.

CHAPTER TEN

Robby

Robby squinted at the GPS on his phone as Siri's version of a British man told him to turn right. A little warning would have been nice. He had no way of turning from the center lane.

He fumed. Something vaguely familiar about the neighborhood nagged at him, but he was too wired to give it much thought. Besides, directions had never been his strong suit.

"Please proceed to the route." How could an automated voice sound sexy and judgmental at the same time?

Technically, it was possible Siri did warn him about the turn half a mile back. It usually did. His mind had been elsewhere, though.

Bailing on Matt this morning had been a mistake. He'd made up the thing about having errands to run, afraid to face the aftermath of their kiss. He'd only felt the overriding need *not* to be there when the guy woke up.

113

He'd driven to the animal shelter and spent the morning playing with dogs. The joy and unfettered love those pups gave settled him like nothing else could. No one wanted them; chances were, at least for some of them, his was the only attention or affection they would have in a day. It was humbling, heartbreaking, and affirming all at once. And it left absolutely zero time to wallow in his own insecurities.

But all good things had to come to an end. When the shelter closed for lunch, he had to go home and face the music.

The sofa had still held a trace of Matt's cologne, but it had been the only sign the man had spent the night. He'd sat on the center cushion and hugged the throw-pillow to his chest, reliving each glorious minute of the night before.

Why had he bailed this morning?

Not because he didn't want to see Matt, but because he didn't want to see the look on his face when he regretted their kiss. Gracious, their kiss. He couldn't get it out of his head, no matter how he tried to occupy his thoughts with other things. Because now he knew the texture of the man's lips. The feeling of Matt's surrender against him.

He craved more.

His lapse in self-control could have ruined their friendship. He didn't have it in him to wish it undone, but what if Matt did? What if they couldn't go back and they couldn't go forward?

Two hours of unproductive panicking later, he drove to face his fears. If Matt wanted to blow him off, the hit would be better coming outside of work.

He would have time to process it alone, if he had to. It would be better than having to paste on a pretend smile to hide the disappointment in front of his friends.

Brick would burn the world if he thought someone had hurt him. It warmed his heart, but he didn't want Matt to face his buddy's wrath over a little awkward regret.

"Please proceed to the route." Siri's inflection didn't change, but it sure felt like the phone was fussing at him.

"I'm *going*." Gripping the wheel, he turned into a gas station parking lot to reorient himself and get back on track. The bar was just two more minutes away.

Without any other navigational drama, he found the place and parked. Cars packed the parking lot, but with Closing Time in a strip mall, there was no telling which business had the lion's share of the customers. Hopefully, Matt wouldn't be too busy.

Robby dropped the visor and gave himself a once-over in the mirror. He needed a haircut; his mom would be aghast at how his bangs kept falling into his eyes. Brushing his long locks back with his hands, he checked one side of his face, then the other—for what, he didn't know. He looked like himself. It wasn't like Matt would care anyway.

He closed the visor with a snap.

This was ridiculous.

The idea didn't stop him from practicing his smile as he climbed out. Not too big; he didn't want to look like a shark. Maybe a smirk. No—a lopsided grin. Everyone loved a lopsided grin.

Now, what to say?

"Hey, buddy, long time no see."

Lame.

"Fancy meeting you here."

Lamer.

"I heard you were the guy to see about some Rum Punch."

Eh.

He paused outside of the door and almost hightailed it back to the car. But Kane's voice echoed in his head, telling him to nut up or shut up, and it gave him the push he needed to grab the handle and venture inside.

Only to stop in his tracks at the scene in front of him. Matt—on a barstool with his eyes closed—with a woman sitting beside him. She was black, her skin just a shade lighter than Matt's. Her hair was natural: with little twists pulled away from her face with a cloth headband.

Not beautiful but striking. Her eyebrows were lined and perfectly arched. And the way she stared at Matt—her brown eyes were liquid and reflected a longing so deep, it made Robby's stomach clench.

Slowly, she leaned forward, and a smile blossomed on Matt's face.

Robby turned on his heel before he had to see their lips meet. His mouth dried up like a desert, and his heart dropped to his stomach.

It didn't matter how many times he'd reminded himself Matt was unattainable. That he was grateful to have just their friendship. He'd only lied to himself. Well-intended lies, perhaps, but still patently untrue.

If anything, the time he'd spent with Matt only added fuel to the fire, and their kiss leveled it up to an inferno. Now reality smacked him square in the face.

His body went on auto-pilot, his mind checking out while his heart screamed for comfort. He blinked as he found himself standing in front of Nitro. Somehow, he'd missed how close Matt's bar was to his old haunt. Just a half a block away and across the street. Obviously, some part of him had taken note, because here he was.

It wasn't hard at all to walk in—mostly because he'd broken the ice with his recent return and, even more importantly, because John never hit the bar scene this early in the day.

The music thumped across the walls and from the floor up through the soles of his feet, pushing a constant, reverberating tingle into his legs. The familiar sensation comforted him, born of a hundred nights experiencing the same thing.

He settled at the bar and lifted a finger at the bearded bartender serving a couple a few feet away. Even in the early afternoon, most of the bar seats were filled and more than a dozen men were grinding against each other on the dance floor.

"What can I get you, sugar?" The bartender hooked a thumb in the suspenders he wore over his bare chest, drawing Robby's eyes to his smooth pecs and pierced nipple.

"Hook us up with some lemon drops, Lucas." Parker put a hand on his shoulder before perching on the stool beside him. "Leave the bottle and just put it on my tab."

The bartender winked, then turned to the wall of liquor bottles displayed behind him. He pulled down a bottle of Absolute Citron and set it on the bar before pushing forward a box of lemon wedges and a shaker, presumably filled with sugar. "Can I get you anything else?" Lucas leaned toward Parker, covering the man's hand with his own.

Parker smiled, but it didn't reach his eyes. "Just some shot glasses. We'll call you if we need you."

Nodding, Lucas pulled the glasses from under the bar. His eyes moved from Parker to Robby, then back again. He blew Parker a kiss as he backed away toward the men gathered a few feet down.

Robby tugged the glasses toward himself. He could have a drink, dammit. It wasn't the same as using. "I always associate these with you, you know." The vodka made a satisfying splash as he poured it.

Parker licked the top of his hand and sprinkled the sugar on his damp skin. "Remember when we killed the whole bottle? The last time the gang was all here." He reached into the box for a lemon wedge. "Five years ago, maybe? I think it was my birthday."

As he'd done so many times in the past, he mirrored Parker's actions, smattering his hand with sugar and grabbing a lemon. He didn't wait to play out the ritual, licking the sweetness before tipping back his shot. The citrus flavor played across his tongue for a moment before he followed it up with the tart lemon.

A shiver rolled down his spine, but he shook it off impatiently and poured another shot. "I can't believe you still come here."

Parker lifted his brows, his eyes mocking. "I saw *you* here not so long ago. It's not like I'm drinking by myself today, Lambchop."

Jerk. He hated the nickname, and Parker knew it.

As the second shot warmed his chest, he shook off the irritation. He'd come here to feel better, and dammit, he would.

Parker put a hand on his arm. "Grab the bottle. Come with me. There's a private room in the back."

Why the hell not? He clutched the bottle to his chest while Parker grabbed the shot glasses and lemon wedges, then led him to a roped-off back door. The security guy standing there didn't so much as blink as they passed.

His thoughts drifted back to Matt and the woman at Closing Time. What were they doing now? Did Matt leave with her? Did he take her home?

Parker snapped his fingers three times. "Are you high right now, dude?"

Robby swatted the guy's hand out of his face and joined him in a shiny leather booth. "Cut it out. I don't do drugs anymore. Just give me my shot glass."

Parker slid it across the table, then reached out and rested a hand on his arm. "It's still kind of unreal seeing you again. When you stopped coming around, I thought maybe you'd found a new Daddy or you moved back to where you came from."

His skin itched beneath Parker's touch. He pulled his arm away. "I don't need a Daddy. And I'm never going back to where I came from. You know better."

Not many people knew the whole of his story, but Parker had been one of the only friends he'd been able to talk to during his early years in Atlanta. When Robby had been with John, Parker's boyfriend had been older as well, though markedly different from John in other ways. They'd gone to all the same parties, the same clubs. They had the same hardships, the same…restraints, though in many ways, Parker'd had it worse. At times, it seemed like no one could understand what his life had become more than the man sitting with him now.

It had felt natural to share secrets back then. Dreams. Hurts, both past and present, of the body and the heart.

Parker knocked back a shot, not bothering with the sugar. They'd left it in the main part of the bar anyway. He stared at the glass as he set it back on the table. "Never say never, my friend. Sometimes, new problems can make the old ones seem a lot simpler by comparison. Your old man might've thought you were property, but he never tied you to the—"

"Don't." He barely recognized the low timbre of his own voice. It brooked no room for argument. He ground his teeth against the vicious words rising in his throat.

His old friend held up his hands in surrender. "Okay," he agreed as he poured them both another shot. "You didn't stick around here. You didn't go home. Where did you go?"

Robby downed his drink, then sucked a lemon wedge. Going through the motions gave him the chance to calm his pounding pulse. He dropped the rind on top of the small pile growing in front of him. "I didn't go anywhere."

Parker raised a skeptical eyebrow.

"I didn't," he repeated. "When I left John, I didn't have any money. I didn't have much more than when I left my parents' house." But there was one major difference.

He turned to face Parker fully. "Only it was *my* choice to leave John. I didn't even recognize myself anymore. I couldn't live that way for another second."

"I get it. You weren't happy, but when you left, John was really hurt."

Robby laughed darkly. "*John* was hurt." He shook his head. "Do you have amnesia or something? They treated us like toys. To be played with and traded off."

Parker rolled his eyes. "Maybe it got worse in the end, but you've got to admit, it was a sweet ride in the beginning."

Heh. Not sweet. Livable, but not sweet. "The first time I walked into his apartment, I thought I had it made. It was the nicest place I'd ever been in. Big TV mounted on the wall and everything cream colored and perfect. But he let me know from the very beginning, I was there to cater to him. His hands were gentle, but don't fool yourself. The first night, he had me naked and crawling just for the honor to suck him off. And the worst part—I was so grateful, I thought it was a gift. Because I could have a hot shower and a soft bed. I didn't think I deserved anything better."

A shudder went down his spine. "John cared more about his knock-off Rolex than he did about me. God knows, he took better care of it."

Another shot slid down his throat before Parker clutched his fingers around the bottle.

"Please." Parker sneered. "You don't even know how good you had it." His hand shook as he tipped more vodka into his glass, and a few drops spilled. "John has a reputation for taking care of his own. You always had food to eat, new clothes to wear."

Heat climbed the back of Robby's neck. "But at what cost?"

Parker slammed a fist against the table. "Not the kind of cost I had to pay with Harry, that's for damn sure!"

"Then, it's a good thing Harry's dead." His own time with Parker's ex had changed him in ways no one knew about to this day. They never would.

Parker sighed in agreement. "Yeah. Best thing that ever happened to me. But John never got off on hurting you. Even when you started acting out. He loved you."

"He *owned* me!" Robby roared, jumping to his feet. The abrupt motion paired with the lemon drops made his head spin, but he forced himself to stay upright. "Maybe nobody has ever loved me. Maybe nobody ever will. But I will not be desperate enough again to accept some sick, selfish imitation. Not again."

Pulling the vodka bottle from Parker's hand, Robby gulped back the booze. The bottle thunked against the wood when he released it on the table. "Stop selling yourself short. You deserve better too.

122

Why are you defending him anyway?"

"Maybe I wanted him for myself. After you left, he wouldn't even look at me, said I reminded him too much of you. Do you know how much better my life could've been with him?"

Disgusted, Robby stumbled away from his old comrade, intent on escaping the demons of his past. He made it two steps before he realized just how deep he'd fallen down the rabbit hole. This back room hadn't existed five years ago, but he'd been in plenty of places just like it.

Older men on leather chairs or sofas, their pretty young pets at their feet. Teenagers, he'd bet, in barely there briefs or tiny shorts and nothing else. Nothing but the occasional collar and leash.

He spied at least one guy crouched beneath a table, his head buried in some other man's crotch. Another sat on his partner's lap, their table doing nothing to hide the swivel in his hips or the glazed look in his eyes.

The boy could've been him—was him at his lowest point—same curly brown longish hair. Same pale skin and long lashes.

He froze as the dead-eyed boy's gaze trained on his face. They locked stares for a minute before the teenager looked submissively to the floor. How many times had submission saved him? Saved any of them? Hell, he still defaulted to the compliant, wide-eyed innocence most men had left long behind by his age. Because the strong protected the weak.

Unless they preyed on them. A lesson from a stranger in the shelter he never forgot.

If he asked any one of these young guys if they

wanted to be here, he doubted he'd find a single one who said no. After all, they'd all have a place to sleep tonight. And even without seeing them, he knew the drugs would be plentiful.

Hell, some actually did like it. Or let themselves believe they did.

John had loved to show him off at parties like this. Made him—

Covering his mouth with his hand, he stumbled toward the door. He'd almost reached it when he heard Parker call out.

"You think you're out, Lamp Chop. But you just don't get it. You might leave this place...but it never leaves you."

CHAPTER ELEVEN

Matt

Matt rolled his head from side to side, stretching the tight muscles in his neck. The clock ticked at a maddeningly slow pace as the end of his shift drew closer. The nightshift guys were due to relieve him any minute, which would be a blessing because he could barely think straight after his encounter with Patty.

The way they'd hung out and just talked reminded him of the years they'd spent as best friends. They could tell each other anything. With her, he could just be himself.

If only he understood who the hell he was.

Patty acted like she found the answer obvious. Like he could just rip off some cosmic Band-Aid and proclaim himself gay once and for all. It wasn't as simple as speaking it into reality, though.

True, he didn't sit around at night fantasizing about women, but he didn't sit around fantasizing about guys either. One particular guy, maybe, but it was more about the man himself than whatever hung between his legs.

His breath caught at the direction of his thoughts, and an unfamiliar stirring forced him to subtly adjust himself in his khakis.

Wouldn't Patty just love that?

He'd been downright positive she was going to kiss him earlier, and the relief he'd felt when she winked and pulled away damn near overwhelmed him. He could still hear the low chuckle she made as she sauntered out the door.

Nothing like he'd felt with the anticipation of Robby's kiss. With her, he'd wanted the world to swallow him whole. With Robby, his body sang with the rightness of it all. Remembering it now, he practically vibrated with pleasure.

And confusion.

Why Robby? Why now?

And, most importantly, would it last?

So far, the attraction seemed to grow stronger the closer they became.

He almost jumped out of his skin when a finger tapped him on the shoulder. His tight muscles relaxed as Jessica's tinkling laughter sounded behind him.

"Sorry I startled you."

When he glanced over, she'd tied a short, white apron around her waist.

"Why don't you hit the road? Tom's a good guy, but he won't pay for extra time on the clock unless he approves it first." She flashed him a grin and pulled her straight brown hair into a ponytail.

Thank goodness.

Matt returned her smile and gave her a small salute before he stepped out from behind the bar.

Maybe he could swing by Robby's place before he picked up Jimmy. No doubt, his mom would love the extra time with her grandson.

Just an hour or so. It didn't have to mean anything. After all, he'd promised to introduce Robby to *The Expanse* before the whole kissing thing went down. What better way to convince them both things were totally normal between them?

Satisfied with his justifications, he walked out the front door and nearly tripped over the man sitting in front of him on the sidewalk.

He recognized the unruly brown hair and Oxford shirt instantly. "Robby?"

He looked up at his name and gave a wavering smile when he recognized Matt. "Fancy meeting you here." Robby blinked twice before accepting the hand Matt offered to pull him up.

Instantly, he knew Robby was wasted. Even without the telltale smell of alcohol, the soft focus of his eyes and his unsure footing gave him away.

Matt felt a pang of worry. Had he pushed Robby into this drunken state? Was it their kiss? Their decision to stay friends? The questions barely had time to register before his awareness focused on something earthier and more consuming.

Robby slung an arm around his neck and leaned against him, his body languid and loose. "I'm sorry to crash your party, but I'm in no shape to drive."

The man's body clung so close, he could smell a hint of the CK cologne on his skin. The urge to bury his face into the crook of Robby's neck nearly overwhelmed him.

He locked his body into a rigid line to resist the compulsion, but Robby seemed oblivious, boneless against him.

"Can you give me a ride?" Robby murmured.

No way he meant the words as dirty as they sounded. He swallowed. "Sure," he croaked. "Let's get you home."

The drive back to the apartment seemed to last forever. Robby's head lolled against the passenger seat and stared at him with slow-blinking eyes and an unreadable expression. The air weighed heavy in the confined space, prompting him to crack open a window to breathe.

Something had changed, whether they would acknowledge it or not. He hadn't felt this awareness last night before their kiss. Maybe not ever.

He stuffed it down as he helped Robby to his front door and eased him down to the sofa where he'd slept the night before. "What's going on, Rob? I thought you didn't drink."

Robby didn't look at him. "I didn't plan on it. Just sort of happened. 'Course, that wouldn't fly with Thomas."

"Thomas?" Jealousy might be unfamiliar, but Matt recognized it right away.

"The guy who leads my N.A. group. Apparently, booze is a gateway or whatever." Robby shrugged. "I wasn't looking to use, though. Just…to take my mind off things."

He bit the tip of his thumb gently and glanced at Matt from the corner of his eye. "I came to see you first."

Matt shook his head, trying to dislodge his immediate thoughts of Shawn. His addiction. His death. Robby had given him too much information—and not enough. He took the easiest route. "You came to my bar? I never saw you." Closing Time had a steady stream of people all day, but it never got so crowded he could've missed his friend.

Robby dropped his hands to his lap, lacing his fingers together. He scowled as he spoke. "You were probably too busy with your lady friend." Blinking, he relaxed his features and smiled, but it didn't look like it happened naturally. "But, hey, it's cool. It's not like you knew I was coming, and, uh, you're trying to figure things out, right?" Even with the corners of his mouth turned up, his eyes were hard. It was very un-Robby-like.

Obviously, his friend had caught part of his heart-to-heart with Patty. "I guess we must have looked pretty intense. I was talking with Jimmy's mom. We have a…complicated relationship. I think I mentioned it last night."

"You said she hated you." Robby's eyes narrowed. "That was not hate I saw. The woman looked like she wanted to have you for dinner."

"Yeah." He shifted in his seat. "Well, I'm not on the menu. At least not for her, which is the problem we keep coming back to."

"But you—" The lilt of a question lingered in the air. "Never mind."

"It's cool. We're friends, Rob. You can ask me anything."

Robby's flinch at the word *friends* was almost

imperceptible. Almost. He pasted on a smile neither one of them could even pretend was genuine. "Thanks for the ride home, man. I'm obviously not myself. I think I need to grab some sleep."

Matt wanted to ask about the drugs. About whether Robby would be okay here alone. But in the end, he did neither. "Sure. My mom's watching Jimmy for me, so I'd better get going. But call me if you need me, okay?"

Robby turned to face the back of the sofa and curled his body around the pillow.

He didn't even say goodbye.

***

Robby

Robby kept his eyes squeezed shut until the quiet snick of the door announced Matt's departure. What was wrong with him? Matt didn't owe him any answers or explanations. They were friends, the kiss notwithstanding.

Whatever. His awkward exchange with Matt wasn't even the worst part of this crapfest of a night.

He dragged himself off the couch and stumbled into the kitchen. A bottle of vodka lay on its side in the freezer. It was always there, just in case. He guzzled it without bothering to pour it in a glass first.

Shards of ice shot through his brain, but he drank until he emptied the bottle. Oblivion was the goal, but he'd take pain over the thoughts crowding his head, a thousand times over.

The scene at Nitro had thrown him into a tailspin even worse than the last time he went there. Why the hell had he gone back?

Because when someone hurts you, you always hurt yourself more. Cancel out one pain by introducing another. And numb yourself as much as you can.

He certainly wasn't thinking about Matt and what's-her-name while he was kicking back lemon drops. Then, in the back room—

His heart kicked into high gear, fluttering like the frenzied wings of a hummingbird, as the image of the dead-eyed boy strong-armed into his brain. The memory of his own past drenched over it like hot tar.

A hand at his throat, blocking his air.

Pressure on his collarbone so heavy he thought it would crack.

The sea of faces. The laughter. The cheering.

Makeitstopmakeitstopmakeitstop.

He stumbled into his bedroom, tearing open the nightstand drawer. The razorblade gleamed, a promise to release him from the grip of his memories, to replace the pain in his heart with the cold sting of a clean, swift swipe.

But he'd promised himself—he'd sworn—he wouldn't go back. He could lie to the world, but he'd be damned if he lied to himself.

Clenching his teeth, he slammed the drawer closed. The past would stay in the past.

He'd come too far in the five years since he'd left his old life behind to turn back now. Living through that nightmare didn't break him then, and the memories would *not* break him now.

CHAPTER TWELVE

Robby

The next morning, Robby sipped his McDonald's mocha, trying to ignore his nerves as he looked up at the Q-Center. He needed to get his mind off of what happened the night before, and he'd meant what he'd said to Sara about wanting to see inside the place. Maybe help some of the young people struggling with their identity or in need of acceptance.

Hell.

What was he thinking coming here? He was hardly someone who could hold himself up as an example to other people. Especially any younger than himself. Only a hypocrite of epic proportions could put himself out there with a past like his.

Tightening his hand on the cup, he gritted his teeth and turned back toward the car. He made it three steps before a familiar voice called out his name.

"Robby," Sara called out, "you gonna come in,

doll, or just stand there, prettying up the sidewalk?"

Busted. Shrugging, with an aw-shucks grin, he followed her inside. A handful of sofas, a TV, and a large throw rug dominated the right side of the room, while three office-style cubicles lined the left. Two tower-style computers with monitors were set up in open stations beside them.

A few steps further in, he stopped beside a scuffed and scarred wooden rectangular table, surrounded by about a dozen mismatched chairs. "Where is everyone?"

"It's early yet. Most kids don't start trickling in until the late afternoon." Sara gestured to the two closed doors along the furthest wall. "Those are the overnight rooms."

"This is a shelter?" A place like this could have transformed his life.

"No. Not officially. And minors don't stay here. As much as I wish we could take them in, it could shut us down." An older man with white hair and a Santa Claus beard stepped out from one of the cubicles. "But from time to time, we do offer an alternative for someone who would otherwise have to sleep on the street."

He offered his hand. "Paul Foster. I'm a pastor at the Episcopal church a few streets over. My husband Chris and I run this place."

Robby accepted the handshake. "Robby Jordan. You're doing important work."

The reverend nodded. "Where are you from, son?"

Just thinking about Sherman made Robby break out in a cold sweat. "Um, a small town a few hours from here. You've never heard of it."

"I might. Try me."

Robby swallowed, his eyes already scanning for the exit. "I don't like to talk about it."

"Stop giving him the third degree, Paul." Sara's chiding was gentle but effective. "I think Robby might be willing to help out as a volunteer, maybe mentor some of the street kids."

"Really?" Paul raised his eyebrows. "Excellent. We're always looking for volunteers. Sara will get you started." With a wave, he went back to the cubicle where he'd been working.

Robby bit back a sigh of relief. "The guy's really a pastor?" he asked under his breath. "Old Reverend Green would have an aneurism over a man of God married to another man."

His childhood preacher had been all hellfire and brimstone. Old Testament through and through. All of his sermons felt like a warning about what would happen to anyone who strayed from just the right path. It was a miracle Robby managed to hold on to his faith all these years, despite the damage his old church had done to his heart.

"Paul's the real deal." Sara pulled out one of the heavy wooden chairs and sat down. "So is this place. I think you could make a difference here."

"Me? I barely made it out of my teens alive. All the stuff I did? What I lived through? I'd make a terrible role model."

She tilted her head. "You said it yourself. You lived through it. The same things they're trying to live through right now. *You* made it to the other side. And you made an impression on me, which isn't easy to do. Just think about it." Grabbing his hand, she pulled him toward the cubicle where Paul had stepped in. "In the meantime, there are plenty of other things you can do to help. How are you with paperwork? I'll introduce you to Chandler, our outreach organizer. He can always use some help."

Now she was speaking his language. "I'm a pro. Just hand me a clipboard and point me in the right direction." Sara could kill two birds with one stone. Pawn off her paperwork and help him avoid thinking about a rocky past both distant and far too recent for comfort.

***

Thanks to a head-clearing day of distraction at the Q-Center, by Monday morning, Robby had almost convinced himself he could ignore everything that had happened between him and Matt both Friday and Saturday nights. They'd been friends before, and they would keep being friends now. And friends didn't judge. Not for ill-advised kisses or drunken jealousy. Or even admitting a drug problem.

What the hell had he been thinking, sharing some of his shame?

He should've gone to a meeting last night.

Taking a deep breath, he relished the last few moments of solitude before the rest of the team arrived at the work site. Flipping to the back page on his clipboard, he scribbled one of his favorite affirmations.

God forgives my wrongdoings and never remembers my sins.

It was from Hebrews. He'd always been more partial to the New Testament.

Maybe it wasn't fair to expect Matt to take the high road to the same degree as his Heavenly Father, but one could always hope.

Hope is a many splendored thing.

He squinted at what he wrote.

"It's love," Kane thundered as he read over his shoulder.

Instinct pulled the clipboard to his chest, but Kane had already walked over to the corner of the unfinished garage and set his cooler on the floor. He winked as he popped open a can of Red Bull. "*Love Is a Many Splendored Thing*. It was a movie in the fifties."

Oh yeah. William Holden.

He tried to imagine Kane watching the classic romance and failed. The confusion must have been obvious because Kane chuckled. "Mandy watches all kind of weird shit these days. I blame the pregnancy hormones. Besides, if it gives me an excuse to cuddle up next to her on the sofa, I'm not gonna turn it down."

"Yeah, well. You shouldn't read someone's personal papers," Robby huffed. "It's rude."

"Rude? Sounds like Kane's up to his old tricks." Brick ruffled Robby's hair as he moved to stand by the cooler. "You fucking with Robby, man?"

Kane downed the small can of caffeine and tossed it into the trash barrel beside him. "Nothing worth getting anybody's panties in a wad."

Brick gave him an appraising look but said nothing before he turned his attention to Robby. "Everything else okay?"

Nope.

"Sure," Robby said brightly. "Everything's fine."

Brick raised his eyebrow. "Fine, huh?"

The room fell silent as Matt walked in.

The man flashed him a tentative smile, then nodded to the other guys as he moved into the house.

Kane whistled. "What's going on there? I think I just saw the closest thing to an expression that dude's had on his face in the past year."

Brick elbowed him in the ribs. "Stop teasing."

Some of the tension eased from his stiff shoulders. It was hard to be uptight around these two. "It's okay. We've been hanging out. He's a friend." As much as he'd like it to be more, friendship was no small thing.

"Does he talk and shit?"

A poet, Kane was not.

"Yes." Robby narrowed his eyes. "We talk. We play PlayStation. He even came over to hang out at my apartment the other night."

Kane waggled his eyebrows, and Brick elbowed him again. "Fuck, brother, that shit hurts."

Robby laughed. "You'd better stop talking and get working in the attic before you end up with bruises you have to explain to your wife."

***

Matt

Memories of his old roommate had plagued Matt ever since Robby's drunken revelation. Honestly, with their kiss, the new job, his civil conversation with Patty, and Robby's admission, Matt's head was reeling. It was hard to focus on just one thing.

But how many times had he blown off the warning signs with Shawn? Put his homework first? Or plans with Patty? Or dinner at his mom's?

How many times did he promise himself he would ask if Shawn was okay when the guy came home wasted or passed out? They'd only lived together a few months, but Matt had known something was wrong. The guy was like two different people when he was high versus when he wasn't. In the last few weeks of his life, he'd lost so much weight, a stiff wind would've knocked him over.

Still, Matt put off a conversation about it. He didn't ask any questions. And he found Shawn one Sunday morning, dead on the living room floor, a needle still hanging from his arm.

He wouldn't make the same mistake again. This time, he'd be there for his friend even if it was uncomfortable. Even if he didn't think of him entirely as a friend at all.

Resolved, he tracked Robby down in the trailer outside of the house. "You got a minute, Rob?"

Robby looked up from the papers on his desk. A blush stained his cheeks and a wooden smile flashed across his face. "Sure. Did you have a good day at the bar yesterday? You had your boy this weekend, right?"

"Yes. To both questions." Matt closed the door behind him and took a seat across from Robby. He swallowed down his nerves. "I want to talk about you, if it's okay."

Robby's gaze swept down, and he began rearranging the plans and office supplies around him. "I'm cool. I just overdid things a little. It happens. No big deal."

The temptation to accept the brush-off rose like a tidal wave, but the memory of Shawn's slack face tamped it down. "I'm kind of new to having friends, so I'm probably doing this all wrong. But I'm going to get up in your business for a minute."

The only sound in the room was the quiet hum of the air conditioning. Robby sat frozen, silent. Like ignoring Matt's words would make him unsay them.

"I want you to know I am here for you. If you're struggling with drugs or booze or…anything. You can call me anytime. We can talk or play games or hang out. You don't have to go through this alone."

Robby looked up, his expression neutral. "I haven't done drugs in a long time. Years." He exhaled. "I don't really drink anymore either. Saturday, obviously, was an exception."

"Did you—did I have anything to do with your slip? Was it the kiss or Patty or—"

"No." Robby clenched his jaw and tugged against his collar.

His answer was emphatic, but Matt couldn't tell if it was truthful.

Robby's gaze flicked to the door, back to Matt, then the door again. Clearly, he wanted out.

"Listen, man, I don't want to make you uncomfortable." Matt leaned forward. "Just promise me, you'll reach out if you need me. Please."

Robby stopped looking the door and met Matt's stare. "I will. I promise."

CHAPTER THIRTEEN

Robby

Matt leaned back in his chair with Robby's assurance. His attempt to reach out was both awkward and sweet. And mortifying.

Flexing his fingers, Matt bobbed his head a little, like there was music in the room only he could hear. "I—I heard some of the *Battlefield* maps were on sale today."

They'd been on sale almost twenty-four hours, but it didn't take a genius to see Matt was trying. The games were a safe topic and easy way to an extend an olive branch.

Matt tapped his foot in a patter against the floor, his entire leg shaking with the staccato movement.

His nerves eased some of Robby's own. "Really? We can check 'em out tonight if you're not too busy with the baby."

The bouncing stopped. "Nah. He's back with his mom. I'd like to hang out a lot." Matt glanced down at the plans. "Hey, are these the proposals for the custom build on Maple?"

"Yeah." Robby frowned. "I think they're still trying to figure out how to work in something weird the client wanted to do with the second floor. Some kind of rooftop deck? I dunno."

Matt rubbed his chin. "I've actually got an idea about the proposal. There are a couple of sketches in my car if you think they might help."

"Awesome." This time, Robby's grin was real.

It didn't waver as he followed Matt down the steps, but it fell away as he came face to face with the very last person he expected to find at work.

John Porter stood with his polished loafers in the center of the muddy construction site. He'd folded the sleeves of his button-down shirt to his elbows. The shirt was tucked neatly into his pressed black slacks. He crossed his arms and gave off a cool expression as he surveyed the build. "Not a bad little set-up you have here."

Robby took the last step down and faced his ex, head-on. "What are you doing here?"

"Just visiting an old friend." His face was all innocence.

Robby didn't buy it for a second. "We were never friends, John."

Like a viper, John's hand shot out and gripped the back of Robby's neck. "That's not how I remember it at all. We were the best of friends." He tugged Robby toward him and gripped his hip with his other hand. "God, you feel just like I remember. The other night only whetted my appetite for another taste."

Robby strained against John's hold on him. "Let

me go. I don't want you here."

"You heard him," Matt growled. "Get lost."

John purred into Robby's ear as if Matt had never spoken. "Then where? I heard you were back at our old haunt Saturday. Maybe looking for me? Let's go back into your trailer, and I'll give you what you've been missing the past few years."

Wedging his hands against John's chest, Robby tried to push him away. "I was not looking for you. We broke up for a reason, and I have no interest in going there again."

Releasing his neck, John cupped him over the fly of his nice jeans. "Your mouth says one thing, but your body is saying something else."

Matt shoved between them and John stumbled back. And before Robby could even breathe, John's overwhelming presence vanished altogether. His body jerked away like a puppet on a string.

Brick stood beside Robby, his chest heaving, with veins bulging from the side of his neck. He had John's collar gripped in his thick fist. "What is my body telling you right now, motherfucker?"

The color drained from John's face as Brick's second hand wrapped around his throat.

"You think consent is a joke?" Brick shook him like a rag doll.

Matt crowded closer to Robby, his nearness an unexpected comfort.

"We got a problem out here?" Kane's long strides covered the yard in the blink of an eye.

John thrashed in Brick's grip. "No," he gasped. "Wasn't. Hurting. Him."

"The fuck you weren't." Brick let go, and John

crumpled to the ground in a heap. "I heard every bit of your bullshit no-means-yes game." He growled.

Brick actually freaking growled.

Gingerly, John sat upright. "We have a history," he rasped. It looked painful when he swallowed, and he rubbed his throat. "I'm not some random guy. I took care of him."

Robby stepped forward. Having his friends surrounding him gave him an extra shot of confidence. "I don't know how I can make it any clearer. I have moved on with my life." He squatted in front of the man who was the center of his world for more than a year and looked him dead in the eye. "I want you to leave, John, and don't come back. There's nothing for you here."

The seconds passed as John held his gaze. It was a message, one of dominance no doubt. That kind of thing had always been important to him. Eventually, he huffed and staggered to his feet. "You talk a pretty big game in front of your thug friends," he hissed.

Brick started forward, but Matt grabbed his arm and murmured something too quietly for Robby to make out.

Either John didn't notice or he was too worked up to care. "I remember what you looked like on your knees. I *will* see you there again." With as much dignity as he could muster, he brushed the construction dust from his slacks.

Then, Matt moved like lightning, knocking him to the ground again. "If you see him again, you'd better turn and run in the other direction."

Brick delivered a powerful kick. "You should

probably get the fuck right out of town. It's been a while since I broke any bones, but not so long I forgot how."

John whimpered—a sound Robby had never heard from him in all the time they'd been together—and stumbled to his car. The site remained silent until his flashy red Camaro disappeared down the street. Only then did chaos erupt.

***

Matt

Brick ripped off his yellow hardhat and threw it in the dirt. His chest heaved with unspent aggression as he stomped over to Robby. "If that rancid cunt steps foot on this work site again, I will take his head off his motherfucking body."

Kane crossed his tattooed arms over his chest. "And I know how to make a body disappear. He's fucking with the wrong family."

As awful as the whole display had been, Matt's chest filled with pride over the loyalty Robby had in these two men. He'd had the same kind of bond for a while with Patty, but for more than a year, life had become an uphill climb he'd been traversing alone.

But he wasn't alone now, was he? He had Robby, unless he managed to screw it up.

He kept quiet as the big guys continued to rant and rave about Robby's ex and the various ways they could dispose of a body. From anyone else, he probably would have blown it off as posturing, but

146

with these two, he couldn't be sure. They argued for a while over the merits of sulfuric acid versus wild hogs before agreeing Robby didn't need to know the details.

It was like Matt wasn't even there, which was fine, because he didn't know what to do with the leftover adrenaline from the whole confrontation. He'd knocked a man *on the ground*. He'd never wanted to hurt anyone so much—ever—in his entire life.

Robby didn't say much, but he did nod at Brick's order to come find him if he needed anything.

Brick and Kane still debated, albeit in hushed tones, as they went back into the house.

"I wish you hadn't seen that," Robby muttered. He eased himself down to sit on one of the steps leading to the trailer.

"Only *you* would worry about *my* feelings after going through such a thing." Matt rubbed at the legs of his pants, willing his racing heart to slow down.

Robby smiled. "If I'm worrying about you, I don't have to worry about me, now do I?"

Matt settled on the step beside him. It was a tight fit, but not an uncomfortable one. "You used to go out with that guy?"

"John," Robby acknowledged. "Yeah. We lived together for about a year and a half, not long after I first came to Atlanta."

"How long ago?"

Robby rested his head against the railing. "Seven years or so."

Seven years? "I thought you were my age." Seven years ago, he was still a junior in high school.

"I'm twenty-three. You're doing the math, aren't you?"

He'd been sixteen. God. "How old is he?"

Robby shrugged. "Forty-one? Forty-two? He kept his age kind of close to the vest. I think he was in his mid-thirties when we were together...and seemed kind of prickly about it." He furrowed his eyebrows. "Well, I guess, on one hand, he didn't like to be reminded of his age, but in some ways, he played up the whole Daddy dynamic."

"Daddy dynamic?" Matt echoed.

"He likes 'em young. What can I say? I had nowhere to go. My parents kicked me out with nothing but the clothes on my back. I slept on the street. In the shelters." A shudder wracked his frame. "I may have been a kid when I left home, but in the few months it took me to find John, there was nothing left innocent about me."

The longer Robby spoke, the deader his voice sounded. It made Matt's chest tighten. He had so many questions. Why would Robby choose a man like John? What had happened in his early months in Atlanta? The look on Robby's face stopped him from asking.

Obviously, the answers were nothing good. Still, this was *Robby*. "You don't act like—I mean, you're *you*. You're sweet, and maybe you're not innocent, but you definitely don't seem jaded."

"I don't? Good." Robby huffed out a breath through his nose. "I've been through some stuff. I've done whatever I had to do to get by. Some of it I haven't thought about since. You want to know how I stay me? That's how. I dig a hole and I bury things there when I can't bear to face them. They're not entirely gone, but they're far enough away I can focus on having a different kind of life. I can believe I deserve friends and family, someone to love me."

Could Robby not face his past—or was he just not ready to share it?

"I was the person I needed to be back then." Robby gestured to himself. "This is the person I need to be now. Both of them are real. They just live in different places. I adapt. It's survival."

Something about those words made Matt uneasy, but if he were being honest with himself, the last half hour had pushed him entirely outside of his comfort zone. "Well, whoever you are, I'm here for you. I might not be able to get rid of a body, but I'm great at providing a distraction, and I'm an even better listener."

"Thanks. It means a lot to have people who can accept me for who I am. Whoever that is." He gripped the railing and pulled himself to his feet. "You deserve the same thing."

Matt turned over those words as Robby returned to the trailer. He appreciated the sentiment. The only problem? Maybe like Robby, he wasn't sure who he was.

And there was no one he could talk about it with. Not Patty, for obvious reasons. Not his mom. Gross.

So how did he figure it out? If he knew who he was for sure, maybe he could safely explore whatever he felt toward Robby.

There was a definite attraction there. Patty was so sure he was gay, but it felt more complicated.

Why did he only feel this way about one man? He'd never really spent enough time around any other gay guys to see if there could be a spark there. Maybe the first step was in changing what he was exposed to.

He looked over his shoulder, then pulled out his phone. A quick Google search provided the names of about two dozen places listed as gay bars. And one was right down the street from Closing Time.

Briefly, he wondered if the club was where Robby had been drinking before he asked for a ride home Saturday night. He brushed it off. Even if it was, it seemed unlikely Robby would be going out again tonight.

Resolved, he stuck his phone into his shirt pocket. He'd keep his PlayStation plans with Robby, but afterward, he'd try the bar. No one would have to know. And maybe it would give him the answers he'd asked about himself for as long as he could remember.

CHAPTER FOURTEEN

Matt

Matt glanced uneasily at the sea of men packed tightly into the bar. He couldn't really get a good look at any one of them, with the lights dim and pulsing.

Running a hand over his khakis, a painful awareness reared its head, reminding him he had no idea what he was supposed to be wearing to a place like this. Though from what he could see, the attire ran the gamut from dressy to casual to shorts so short they should be illegal to wear in public.

Ignoring his nerves, he stepped up to the bar and motioned for the bartender's attention. The bearded man didn't even ask for his order; he just pushed two shots in his direction and walked away.

Jell-O shots. How bad could they be?

He squeezed the contents of one paper wrapper into his mouth and followed with the other.

Pretty good, actually. He could barely taste the alcohol at all. Just cherry flavoring. He raised his hand and ordered more, this time placing a twenty-dollar bill on the bar.

After he swallowed two more, a handsome blond man sidled up next to him. "Willing to share one of those with a new friend?"

"Help yourself." He handed one over, hoping his bravado didn't come off as forced as it was.

The blond took his time, sweeping his tongue over the shot and curling the Jell-O into his mouth. "First time here, darlin'?"

He nodded, watching with fascination as the man's tongue slid another shot into his mouth.

The guy chuckled. "Take the last one and come dance." He slid his hand over Matt's arm. "Don't look so scared. I won't bite. Not on the first date."

He came for this, right?

He downed the last shot and followed his new friend to the dance floor. It only took a few seconds to remember he didn't know how to dance.

But, it seemed, he didn't have to.

The blond took hold of him by the hip and the opposite shoulder and moved his body to the pulsing beat of the music. Soon, Matt could pick up the rhythm on his own, and his partner moved even closer.

Having a stranger's body crushed against him was awkward, but it got a little easier when he closed his eyes. He tried to parcel out the sensations and couldn't deny the physical pleasure of moving with the music and the closeness of another person.

He let himself imagine for a moment he was dancing with Robby, which worked almost too well. Because when he opened his eyes and saw a stranger, it was worse than feeling nothing. It was kind of gross.

No more pretending. From that moment on, he concentrated wholly on his partner, who, by the way, looked a bit like an actor on one of his mom's soap operas. The fit man filled out his skinny jeans in all the right places. He had high and well-defined cheekbones. The man probably could have done a little modeling.

So, when the guy leaned toward him, seeking a kiss, he let it happen.

And it left him positively cold.

The stranger's lips mashed all against him, his tongue making an insistent play to get inside Matt's mouth. It was awful. Nothing like what he'd shared with Robby.

He stepped back and shook his head in an unspoken apology, but he couldn't think of any explanation where he wouldn't insult the guy.

"It's okay." The man blew a kiss into the air. "Plenty of fish in the sea."

Grateful for an easy exit, he scurried back to the bar. More Jell-O shots followed. And more men approached. Tall men. Short men. Black. White. Asian. Skinny. Muscular. Fat.

He danced once or twice more, but he couldn't bring himself to try anything else.

His experiment ended as an abysmal failure.

At least he learned he liked Jell-O shots.

It was almost midnight when his Lyft driver dropped him back home. He fell into bed and dreamed of being back on the dance floor. Only this time, Robby snuggled in his arms, and the kiss was one that rocked his world.

***

Robby

Robby had just settled in for his standard frozen dinner in front of the TV Tuesday night when a knock on the door forced his attention away from an old rerun of *Big Bang Theory*. He scowled as he set the plastic tray on the coffee table. Probably someone trying to sell him something. As it was, he already had more Girl Scout cookies than he'd ever know what to do with.

Still, he couldn't ignore whoever it was, no matter how gross his pot pie would be when it got cold. Maybe he could politely send the kid packing by pretending to be sick.

He coughed as he swung open the door. "I'm sorry. I—Parker?"

His old friend shot him a Cheshire grin and breezed past him into the apartment as if he'd been invited. "I couldn't stop thinking about you after you left the club. I just had to track you down and see your amazing new life for myself."

Closing the door, Robby felt acutely aware of the small, spartan space where he lived. Compared to the apartment he'd shared with John, it looked more like a hovel than something his old friend would consider amazing. "How did you find me?"

Parker wrinkled his nose for a split second before settling in on the sofa. With his perfectly styled hair and designer royal blue silky shirt, he would have been far better suited someplace higher end. He waved off the question. "A friend of a friend has a LexisNexis account and helped me track you down. We made a drinking game out of it."

Robby perched on the edge of the sofa cushion beside him. He couldn't think of a thing to say.

Parker didn't suffer from the same problem. "Hanging out together again felt a little like old times."

"It wasn't."

"You mean because you're not with John anymore? The two of you always seemed meant for each other. The way he always fawned over you and bought you things. Like your PlayStation and all those nice clothes." Parker leaned forward like he was sharing some juicy gossip. "I saw you smiling with him the other night. And I saw the two of you slip off to a dark corner."

Robby gritted his teeth. "Are you kidding me? When have you ever not seen me smiling? It's what I do. It's what we all do."

Parker's salacious grin dissolved.

"It was one of the first lessons I learned. Well, the *first* lesson was to look for a guy in a button-down shirt and slacks, right?"

"And a blazer," Parker murmured.

"Yeah. It took me one night on the streets and three in the shelter before the guy on the bunk next to me clued me in on the way things work."

Smile. No matter what happens. No matter what they ask you to do. Do it and smile.

The advice had served him well.

"He told me, 'Just flash those puppy dog eyes and roll over when they tell you to.' He was right." Going home that night with the guy who called himself Tex may have meant a few unpleasant minutes in the bedroom, but it had given Robby a safe place to sleep for the first time since his dad had thrown him out.

"Of course he was right." Parker settled back in his seat. "Mother Nature made babies look so innocent and cute for a reason."

Robby nodded. "People want to take care of them. It's a biological imperative. Even ugly animals are cute when they're babies."

"Yeah, well, your buddy should've warned you to watch out for the predators." Parker smirked. "In the wild, they eat the babies first."

Robby rubbed at the tension building in his neck. The lesson had come a little too late. "Why are you really here, Parker? Did John tell you he tracked me down at work?"

"He did?" Parker's eyes narrowed. "What happened?"

"I told him to get lost." Which part of him wanted to do with Parker now. "Now I'll ask you again. Why are you here?"

His old friend shrugged. "Guess I wanted to see how the other half lives. What my life might've been like if I'd left the way you did." Parker looked around, barely trying to hide his disdain. "I've got to be honest. I don't see the appeal."

No. He wouldn't. But Parker didn't know the small part of Robby's soul he'd sacrificed to get here. Holding the dark memories at bay, Robby stood and walked back to the front door. "It was nice of you to drop by."

He smiled and they both knew the familiar expression for the lie it was. "Maybe we'll catch up some more later."

Parker swept a kiss over his cheek on the way out.

Robby spent the next hour trying to shove old memories back into the box where he kept them locked tight, but for some reason, they wouldn't fit. John had found him at work. Parker had come to his apartment. The old life he'd worked so hard to escape was too close for comfort.

He paced the floor. Twice, he almost poured himself a drink.

Then he picked up the phone. Stared at it. And made the call.

Matt answered on the first ring.

Robby gathered his courage. "Can you come over?" He hated how small his voice sounded.

"I just got out of class. I'm on my way." No questions. No delays.

He was there in ten minutes. "Tell me what you need."

Robby growled. His own weakness made him want to put a fist through the wall. Instead, he sank into the sofa and dropped his head into his hands. "I need to be someone else. Anyone else."

The cushion beside him sagged under Matt's weight. "No. No way. I like who you are."

It was only true because Matt didn't really know who he was. Robby looked up. "My own family didn't like who I was."

At least not once they learned the truth about him.

"I grew up in a very religious household. Small town. Almost a relic from the past. It was all I knew, though. My parents, my brothers and sister. We were all close, you know? But they didn't know I was gay."

Matt scratched the back of his head. "They never suspected?"

Robby hugged a pillow to his chest. "Who knows? My dad sure seemed shocked enough to find me kissing Luke Potter in the barn when I was sixteen. He threw me out on the spot. I had nothing but the clothes on my back and twenty-three dollars in my wallet."

"Which is how you ended up alone in Atlanta." Matt nodded like something had clicked in his head.

He didn't even know the worst of it. None of his friends did.

They only saw the Robby he wanted them to see.

The sweet people pleaser was second nature. Seven years ago, in fact, it was the only way he knew to be. Loving, innocent, and earnest. That kid was the best version of himself. But unlike his sixteen-year-old self, the adult version had experienced every emotion on the flip side of the coin. He knew what hate felt like. Desolation. He'd been jaded before he turned eighteen.

The things he'd done—just to survive—would shock and horrify the people who knew him now, the people who loved him.

Those sides of Robby: the whore, the thief, the chameleon, the addict…and worse…those facets of him still lingered beneath the surface. But if he shoved them down hard enough, he could pretend like they weren't there. Like they'd never had been.

Like he'd never committed the ultimate sin.

His father would have never been right about him.

"Things were hard. I don't want to go into it all, but in the end, drugs helped me get through the worst of it." Looking back, he hated himself for it. For the drugs and for so much more.

"Do you want to talk about what happened?"

"No. I want to forget it all. I would, but all of a sudden, my past is right here, and it's like it wants me back. I don't want to go." He wanted to grab onto Matt with both hands and hold on until everything else went away.

"Your ex seems like a bastard."

Yeah, well, Robby's threshold for bastards was pretty high. "I've known worse. I don't want to talk about John. I don't want to think about John or the person I was when we were together. I want to be better and stronger and to be able to deal with stress without wanting to drown in oblivion."

Matt grabbed his hand. "You are better and stronger, because whether you wanted to or not, you didn't choose oblivion. You chose me."

If you were mine, I'd always choose you.

Robby looked down at their linked hands, squeezed, and pulled away. Matt wasn't his, at least not in the way he wanted. He was here, though, which counted for a lot. "You want to check out those new map downloads?"

Matt swiped the controller from the coffee table.

"Your account or mine?"

CHAPTER FIFTEEN

Robby

Shuffling from one foot to the other, Robby stood outside Brick's door waiting for someone to answer his knock. Liv had texted him to come by after work, but she didn't say why. If he was lucky, a plate of pasta waited for him in the kitchen.

Liv opened the door, grabbed him by the wrist, and pulled him inside.

He caught a whiff of a light, floral perfume.

"We," she declared, "are all going out tonight."

"We are?" On a random Wednesday?

She pursed her lips, drawing his attention to the shiny pink gloss there. Liv wasn't usually one to wear makeup. She also had on a cute dress with a flared skirt and strappy shoes. Not her normal teacher attire.

"What's the occasion?" And why was he here?

"Jonathan came home in a terrible mood Monday night and hasn't come out of his funk since. He wouldn't talk about it." She smoothed her hair.

161

"When I was talking to Amanda this afternoon, she told me the same thing was going on with Kane. I don't suppose you know any reason why the two of them were set off?"

He stared at his shoes. Brick and Kane had seemed okay at work, but if he was being honest, they had kind of been walking on eggshells yesterday. He didn't want to lie about what happened with John, but he had no intention of reliving the experience.

She hummed. "Well, whatever happened, I figured it would be nice for us all to go out and have a good time. Jonathan said you were working at another site today, so you didn't see him, but he's still wound up a little tight." She ruffled his hair. "He loves you. If anyone can help me get him out of this funk, it's you."

How could he say no?

"Kane and Amanda are at the restaurant. Matt is meeting us there too."

He perked up at the mention of Matt's name. "Yeah?"

Brick scowled as he emerged from the bedroom. He tugged at the collar of the polo shirt straining across his broad chest. "You have anything to do with this, Robby?"

"Oh, hush," Liv tutted. "Just get in the car. We haven't been to Moe's in ages."

Moe's was a small bar and grill just a few blocks away. He had only been there once before, when Brick and Liv first met. They had pool tables in the back. Unfortunately, pool was not his forte.

Still, if Liv thought it would make Brick happy,

he considered it no hardship to go back. Especially if they still had cheese sticks on the menu.

Kane and Amanda were already seated at a table when they arrived.

Brick grumbled at his wife. "How come Kane gets to wear a T-shirt?"

Liv whispered something into his ear, and his cheeks turned a dusky pink. "I'm gonna hold you to that, Livie-mine."

They joined their friends at the table and ordered an appetizer sampler to share. Normally, Kane and Brick would be cracking jokes or flirting with their wives like crazy by now. Instead, Kane picked at the label on his longneck, and Brick tugged on his collar again.

Robby sighed. "I'm sorry about what happened at the site the other day."

"Don't," Brick growled. "Your brain is taking you places you don't need to go." He slashed his hand through the air before Robby could even argue. "You are not responsible for the shit other people do. I know you don't think so much of yourself. I've been there. You've got to hear me, though. You're better than that. Better than your fucktard ex thinks you are. Better than *you* think you are. And I'll just have to keep telling you so as long as it takes for you to believe it. You did the same thing for me."

"I did?"

"Damn right you did. You were the first person who ever wanted to be my friend. Not because I could do something for you or because you were scared of me. Just because...hell, I still don't know why. You did, though, and it meant something to me. It still does. You feel me?"

Robby rubbed his chest. "Yeah. I'll let it go if you will. I know you're mad about what happened. I know you've got my back. What I need right now, though, is to have some fun with my friends. Besides, if the two of you stay like this, your wives are going to disown me."

The waitress set the tray of food on the table, and Brick swiped a Buffalo chicken wing. "Nobody is going to disown you."

Robby frowned as Kane, Amanda, and Liv each grabbed a cheese stick, leaving none left on the platter. "I know. The disowning part was a joke, but I meant the rest. Seriously, though, can you try, please, to let it go?"

"Whatever," Kane grumbled, swiping one of the popcorn shrimps.

The women exchanged curious looks, but neither pressed the issue. Slowly, as the couples made their way through another round of drinks, laughter joined into the conversation, and by the third beer, Kane was extolling the virtues of how pregnancy enhanced his wife's cup size.

Robby stuck with iced tea.

Matt arrived just as they finished eating and surprised the table by ordering two dozen Jell-O shots, a move met with great enthusiasm by Brick and Kane, since their wives had volunteered to be designated drivers. Halfway through, the party moved to the pool tables, where Brick and Liv faced off against Kane and Amanda.

Robby and Matt opted for a dart game on the

other side of the room.

"Are you sure it doesn't bother you for us to drink around you?" Matt asked, pulling the darts from the board on the wall.

"I told you when you asked me last night, it doesn't tempt me to see people drink. Sometimes, things just trigger me." Robby took one of the darts from Matt's hand and tossed it right into the bullseye. "Don't worry. The more you drink, the worse you'll play. Then, I'm practically guaranteed to win."

"Robby? That you?" Chandler, the guy who did outreach for the Q-Center, approached him with a broad smile.

Robby grinned back as the man greeted him with an enthusiastic hug.

Chandler had sapphire blue eyes, all the more gorgeous when paired with his thick, black hair. The man could stop traffic, and he knew it. "Thanks again for all your help this weekend. I've been hoping you'd come back."

Matt cleared his throat.

Crap. Robby didn't mean to be rude. "I'm sorry. Matt, this is Chandler. Chandler, this is Matt. He's, uh, a friend from work. Matt, Chandler's—"

"It's no problem." Matt held up his hands and stepped back. "You guys catch up. I'm going to go order another round of shots."

Robby fought back a smile. If he didn't know better, he'd think Matt was jealous. Though he had no reason to be. Chandler might be hot, but he was happily married. To a woman.

"It looks like the green-eyed monster is making

an appearance tonight." Chandler took a swig of the beer in his hand. "You sure that guy's just a friend?"

Robby snuck a peek at the bar where Matt was holding up a twenty-dollar bill. Maybe his finances were finally turning around.

"Robby?"

"Oh. Sorry. Yeah, he put me square in the friend zone. Believe me, I wish it were otherwise."

Chandler chuckled. "Give it time. I have a feeling you won't have to wait too long and Mr. Tall, Dark, and Handsome will surprise you. In the meantime, I want to pick your brain about the trick you showed me with that Excel file."

***

Matt

Matt stalked back to the table where they'd started the night, then sucked back five Jell-O shots in quick succession. Who the heck was Chandler anyway? Stupid name. Stupid muscles and tight jeans.

He wanted to wipe the smug smile off the man's face. To plant a flag in the ground in front of Robby and proclaim him off limits to the rest of the world. To declare Robby *his*. Not Chandler's or John's.

Not even Brick's or Kane's.

Scowling, he swiped another filled, flimsy paper shot glass from the dwindling supply. The unfamiliar jealousy made him feel petty, but he couldn't shake it off.

He swallowed more chilled gelatin without tasting it.

The scrape of the chair beside him drew his eye to Brick's thick frame settling down at the table. He blinked slowly at his co-worker. "You're too big to move so quietly."

Brick snorted. "In my line of work—" He paused. "In my *old* line of work, sometimes a little stealth could save me a whole lot of problems."

He knew Brick used to be associated with a drug kingpin, but Matt had never been tempted to ask for details. Apparently, not until now. He needed a distraction in the worst way. "What *was* your old line of work anyway?" Elbow propped on the table, he rested his chin in his hands.

The Budweiser longneck in Brick's hand paused an inch from his lips. "You really want to know?"

Lifting another Jell-O shot, he tapped it against Brick's beer in a silent toast.

The big guy took a long pull of his Bud and set the glass bottle on the table. "Let's just say I broke things." His hand clenched around the longneck. "I'm not proud of it, but it's a skill you never forget. I'd do it again in a heartbeat to protect one of my own."

Even with the hard buzz clanging around in his head, Matt understood Brick didn't break *things* so much as *people*. The knowledge should've scared him, but instinctively, he knew Brick's threat would extend to anyone who threatened Robby. "Good," he murmured. "I'm glad Robby has people like you and Kane looking out for him." When he wasn't being a shallow, jealous twat. "Rob always sees the good in people."

Nodding sagely, Brick released his tight hold on the beer and took a shallow sip. "Yeah, well, I always look for the worst. Keeps me from getting disappointed. It's also kept me from getting dead."

Matt absently lined up the crushed, empty paper cups on the table in front of him. "I don't really think about all that too much, I guess. I kind of live in a bubble. It's all about doing what's necessary for my kid. Being the kind of dad I wish I would've had."

Brick leaned back in his chair. "I think all of us have the same thing in common. No dad. Deadbeat dad. Asshole dad." He circled the air with his finger to include Robby and Kane in his assessment. "We've all got different stories, but we're all gonna have to figure out how to be decent parents without any firsthand exposure."

"Yeah. My dad bailed when I was a kid, but I've got a good mom."

"Then you're better off than a lot of people." Draining the rest of his beer, Brick set the bottle on the now-empty shot tray. "I'd better get back to my girl but let me know if you need a ride home, man. I think the booze is going to your head." He grinned. "You'd never reveal actual facts about yourself sober."

Was he drunk?

He chewed on his lower lip. For sure, he'd had more shots than he'd had at Nitro Monday night. How many exactly was anybody's guess. How many had he ordered? Did Brick's wife put more on the tray? This week, he'd probably swallowed more shots than in the rest of his life put together.

He stood, and all the blood rushed to his head. Or from his head. Or whatever the hell made it feel like gravity was playing a special kind of joke on him tonight.

Stumbling back, he might have landed on his rear end, but a warm, lean body blocked his fall.

"Whoa, there," Robby breathed, just behind his ear.

He lingered an extra moment before staggering fully upright. "Sorry. I guess I may have gone a little overboard with the Jell-O shots." He twisted his mouth to the side. "Guess I qualify as a lightweight."

Robby wrapped his arm around his waist. "Trust me. It beats the alternative."

Matt scowled. "What happened to your friend?" He made air quotes around the word. Petty? Probably.

If it fazed Robby, he didn't let it show. "C'mon. I left my car at Brick's. Give me your keys, and I'll get you home."

Leaning heavily against Robby's side, he fished the keys out of his pocket, and he must have rattled off the address, because somehow, in no time at all, Robby was tugging him out of the passenger seat of the car and leading him into the apartment.

Robby closed the front door with the back of his foot as he supported Matt's weight. "Sofa or bed?"

Turning his body deeper into Robby's hold, he caught a whiff of cologne, the same one the man was wearing when he'd stumbled into Closing Time. Then, he had fought the urge to lean into the scent. This time, though, he felt no such compunction to hold back.

He buried his face into Robby's neck and breathed deeply. "God, you smell so good."

Robby stiffened beneath him, and Matt lifted his head.

"Was I not supposed to say so?" He knew he ought to be fighting this, but for the life of him, he couldn't remember why.

The line of Robby's rigid shoulders relaxed. "It's okay. I'm just not used to seeing you this way. So, uh, bold."

Robby's arm still curved around his side. It felt both foreign and familiar.

He rested his left hand on Robby's bicep. "I'm not used to being seen." He lifted one shoulder and let it drop. "This way or any way. At least, not until I met you."

"Maybe you just didn't know where to look." Robby smiled. "You're not alone, you know. You've got people who care about you. Kane, Brick—"

"You?" He tilted his face a little closer to Robby's, the intoxicating scent tickling his nose again.

Robby's throat bobbed as he swallowed. "Yeah. Of course."

Matt edged closer still, and from his new vantage point, could make out each of Robby's individual eyelashes. The man's brown eyes were deep pools of melted chocolate being swallowed by his pupils. "The guy at the bar tonight. I wanted to kick his ass." The admission came out before he could stop it.

Robby grinned. "Really?"

"Stupid Chandler." Matt put his right hand on the curve where Robby's neck met his shoulder. "You're not his. You're mine."

Robby gasped, and it was like someone had finally flipped on a light after he'd been sitting in the dark his whole life.

He leaned forward.

So close.

He could finally have what everyone else did. Passion. Desire. With someone he cared about. Robby wouldn't just be his friend anymore.

Never in his life had he ever so desperately wanted to kiss someone. His heart pounded in his chest. His mouth watered, begging for a taste of Robby's full lips, the pink tongue now sweeping over what he knew was pillowy softness.

Would it be as good as before? Could he finally have what everyone else took for granted? For the first time, he thought maybe he could. Maybe, with this growing ache could be the satisfaction always hovering just out of reach.

Closing the small remaining distance between them, he crushed his lips to Robby's. It wasn't a gentle or tentative kiss. It was fire and passion. A claiming. A goddamn revelation.

Robby's mouth stayed frozen beneath his for a fraction of a second, but the fire was catching. Almost immediately, Robby was devouring him with the same intensity. Their tongues dueled against each other, sliding, twining, almost punishing.

As his dick hardened, he released Robby's arm to clench his back and pull their bodies taut against each other.

This! This was how it was supposed to feel to have a hard body against you.

Because Robby's body *was* hard.

Not just the surprising strength of his embrace, the grip of his hands, but the firmness of his torso pinned against Matt's and the answering erection pushing relentlessly against his own.

Matt pulled away from Robby's mouth to trail kisses down his neck. He could eat him alive. "Want," he breathed against Robby's skin, his hand sliding down the other man's arm, only coming to a stop at his hip.

Even as tightly pressed together as their bodies were, he couldn't get close enough. He surged forward.

And stumbled, almost taking Robby down to the laminate floor.

The frenzy came to an abrupt halt.

Robby's chest heaved in panting breaths, and his arousal stood proud, tenting his pants. But he shook his head and stepped back, his arms in front of him creating an effective barricade. "Stop!"

Matt didn't want to stop. Finally, he understood what he'd been missing all this time. How he should've felt when he had sex with Patty. How she must have felt about him.

"Matt!" Robby barked.

It took the sharp sound of his name for him to realize he was still moving toward the other man, his body seeking to recapture the feeling Robby had snatched away.

He froze. "I don't understand."

"You're drunk."

"So?" He trusted Robby. He *wanted* Robby.

"So?" Robby repeated, frustration leaking into his voice. "You told me you weren't ready for this, and now when you're three sheets to the wind, it seems like a good time to give it a go?"

Yeah.

Robby flexed his jaw.

Had he answered the question out loud?

"I would never be with someone who I'm not sure wants to be with me."

"But I—"

"You are too wasted to know what you want right now." Robby dropped his arms, suddenly looking very tired, his Oxford shirt uncharacteristically rumpled. "You told me yourself, you ruined your only other friendship by letting it go somewhere you knew it shouldn't. What if you wake up in the morning and regret this? What if you can't look me in the eye because I was too selfish to stop you?"

"I wouldn't—"

"I will *not* take you without consent!" Robby roared. A vein bulged at his neck against the skin still slightly red from his kisses.

Matt had never seen Robby angry before. This went even beyond anger. It was outrage…and as effective in killing his libido as a bucket of ice water. "I'm sorry," he whispered. "Please don't be mad."

The contorted expression on Robby's face fell

away, leaving something somber behind. "I'm not…mad. This is important, though. I won't compromise our friendship over something you might regret. And even more importantly, I would never risk making you feel used or violated." Robby raked back his hair as it fell into his eyes. "You matter to me. If this is something you still want tomorrow, we'll have a different kind of conversation. If not, well, I hope you can forgive me for not stopping you sooner."

Robby pulled his shoulders back and walked ramrod straight out of the apartment.

Matt stared at the door as it closed with a snick.

His lips still tingled from Robby's kiss; his galloping heart gave no sign of slowing down. Lust—real, actual lust—coursed through his veins, and it occurred to him he might experience blue balls tonight for the very first time.

Though his thoughts threatened to scatter on the wind, he tried to make sense of what just happened. The need and desire screaming for satisfaction, Robby had felt it too. He was sure of it. The intensity of their kiss left no room for doubt.

It was getting harder to stay on his feet with the world spinning so hard. He leaned against the arm of the sofa, only to tip over the side, his butt in the air and his face smooshed between two cushions. The position was crazy-uncomfortable, but he couldn't find the energy to move, beyond turning his head to face the open air of the living room.

He'd take all this apart tomorrow and examine it. For now, he just needed to sleep.

He closed his eyes just as his stomach roiled then

violently rejected everything he'd eaten—or drunk—in the past twenty-four hours. The only small mercy was that most of it went on the floor.

CHAPTER SIXTEEN

Robby

Robby's eyes burned as he stared at the text Xander sent him a minute ago.

Xander: Matt out sick today.

There was no chance he would cry. He wasn't sure he even could these days. The burning in his eyes just meant he'd gone too long without blinking.

Sending back a thumbs up emoji acknowledgement, he shoved the phone back into his pocket. Anxiety latched its cold fingers into his chest, and he rubbed at his sternum as if it might help release the icy hold.

Matt had never called out sick. Not once in more than a year. He knew for a fact the man had come to work with bronchitis and even the flu once. Xander told him he'd tried to send Matt home those days, but it always came down to money. Matt insisted he needed it to take care of his kid.

But today? The day after he had slipped a tongue in the guy's mouth? The day after he'd pressed his erection against Matt's own? *Today* things were bad enough to risk losing eight hours' pay.

He tapped his clipboard against his forehead.

Stupid. Stupid. Stupid!

Why had he let himself indulge in their kiss?

Matt had made it crystal clear he wanted to be friends. He needed time to figure out his feelings. Even worse, he'd crossed a line with his baby's mama once, and it had destroyed a friendship he'd had for years. Any bond Robby had with him was in its infancy. No way it could survive the same kind of regret.

He paced the confines of the small construction trailer.

What had happened last night wasn't nearly as catastrophic as what went down with Matt's old BFF. After all, those two had gone fully horizontal. Still, he'd agreed to honor Matt's boundaries, then crashed right through them.

What should he do? How could he know whether to trust the attraction he felt burning between them?

***

Matt

Robby wasn't at the work site when Matt arrived Friday, and there was no sign of him at lunch or in the hours afterward. Even though Matt wasn't sure what he'd say when they came face-to-face. He just knew they needed to talk.

When it got close to quitting time, he finally worked up the nerve to ask the guys where he was.

Brick wiped his forehead with the bandana he kept in his back pocket. "Some meeting with Xander at the main office, but he said he'd drop by before the end of the day." He checked his phone. "Soon, I'd guess. You've got his number, right?"

"Yeah, thanks." This wasn't the kind of conversation you handled with a phone call.

Maybe it was a mixed blessing. He'd tried all day to figure out what he should say. How he should feel. Though some of the details from Wednesday night were hazy, the high points had branded in his brain.

Like the kiss. The way his body reacted. The way Robby had shut him down so completely.

But it wasn't from lack of desire. He remembered the thick, insistent ridge of Robby's arousal pressing against him. The naked lust. Every time he thought about it, his body stirred all over again.

How did he put it all into words? Expressing himself had never been his strong suit.

You said if this is something I still want, we would have a conversation. Well, I still want—

What? What did he want?

I've been thinking a lot about what happened between us the other night. And I want you to know I still feel—

Turned on? Hard?

The truth, yes, but Robby deserved better. No way the guy was the love 'em and leave 'em type.

178

But what kind of promises could he make? He knew squat about being a boyfriend...to a man or a woman. And while he knew the idea of kissing Robby revved his engine, he couldn't quite wrap his head around the sex part.

What if Robby wanted to—

Of course, he'd want to.

Following the thread to its logical conclusion made his stomach clench. Objectively, he knew anal sex didn't have to be painful. If it wasn't possible for it to feel good, no one would do it.

He'd tried porn of all kinds over the years, hoping he could jump start his non-existent libido. Soft core. Hard core. Girl on guy. Girl on girl. Guy on guy. Some of the stuff in the videos looked like it hurt no matter what the doctored audio sounded like. And none of it turned him on.

But Robby did, and the thought brought him back full circle.

"Matt?"

Speak of the devil. Robby stood in the doorway to the unfinished garage, hugging his clipboard to his chest. Shadow covered part of his face, thanks to the approaching dusk. His tousled brown hair spilled over his left eye, but he made no move to push it away.

"I'm glad you're here." Matt regretted the words as soon as he said them, not because he didn't mean it, but because he so very much did. Clearing his throat, he tried again. "I was afraid—Brick said you were in a meeting with Xander."

Robby stepped farther into the room and leaned against the counter. "You were afraid?"

"That's not what I meant to say."

"Oh." There was a world of disappointment in the one syllable.

"I was, though. Afraid, I mean. Afraid you were avoiding me." He reached down for the water bottle at his feet. His mouth hadn't been this dry a minute ago. Not only did the lukewarm water wet his tongue, it gave him a welcome distraction, if only for a moment.

"Avoiding you?" Robby laughed, but it was a hollow sound. "You weren't even here yesterday. The guy who works through walking pneumonia, and you don't come in the day after we…"

Crap. Matt hadn't even thought about how his absence would look. "I'm sorry. I should have realized." A text message pinged his phone, but he ignored it. "The only time I could lift my head for hours was to throw my guts up. I've never been so sick in my entire life, man. Guess I found my limit with alcohol."

"Do you remember everything that happened?"

Ugh. Why did this have to be so awkward? He stared at his feet.

"You can say what's on your mind. No one will hear you." Robby sighed. "The rest of the guys were leaving when I pulled up."

"I'm not worried about the guys." Damn if he wasn't making a mess of this. "I remember kissing you." The phone pinged again, and the corners around Robby's eyes tightened. "I remember you were worried about whether I did it because I was drunk."

"And?"

180

"Would I have done it sober? Probably not."

Robby put one hand over his mouth and wrapped his opposite arm around his waist. Wounded.

"I don't mean that the way it sounded. This is why I don't like talking. I always screw it up." He flexed his fingers in frustration. "What I meant was the shots gave me the courage to take what I really wanted."

Dropping the hand from his face, Robby moved his right arm to hug himself entirely. "But you said you didn't know what you wanted. The other night—"

"You mean, the first time we kissed…at your apartment? I *didn't* know. I needed time to think, to figure things out." He stepped closer. "And things have changed since then." His phone pinged again. And again. And again.

"Just answer it," Robby growled.

With so many texts, it could only be Patty. He pulled the phone out of his back pocket, and sure enough, a half dozen messages from her lit the screen. "She needs me to watch Jimmy. They called her in to work tonight." He quickly typed back an answer. "I've got to go. But listen, I want to talk this through. Tonight? Please? I'll take him to my mom's. You can come by my place, maybe seven o'clock?"

Robby released his arms and let them hang at his sides. "Sure. I'll be there."

He needed to hustle if Patty was going to make the start of her shift. He got halfway to the door before he looked back over his shoulder. "Hey, Rob? Don't give up on me yet."

181

***

A smart man would have used the time before seven to figure out exactly how to put his feelings into words, but as the doorbell rang, Matt knew no one could ever accuse him of being smart. To be fair, Jimmy was cutting some new teeth, and it had made him super-cranky when he dropped him off. All of his regular methods to comfort and entertain him had come up short.

He barely had time for a shower and change of clothes before Robby arrived. At least he'd be clean when he made a hash of things tonight.

Thank God he'd scrubbed the living room down last night. He'd had to mop the floor twice and spray Lysol to get rid of the puke smell.

He opened the door to solid evidence Robby had run home to shower as well. His wavy brown hair was still damp and combed out of his face. He wore soft pale blue jeans and a lightweight long-sleeve green sweater which set off those gorgeous brown eyes to perfection. Gorgeous, but definitely anxious as well. "Come in."

Robby shoved his hands deep into his pockets as he slipped into the room and stood next to the arm of the sofa. "You wanted to talk."

"Can we sit?"

Wordlessly, Robby slid onto the couch and folded his arms in front of him.

"You aren't the only guy I've ever kissed."

"But you said—"

"What I told you before was true at the time." Matt sat beside Robby, who promptly shot to his feet.

"You mean you made out with some guy *after* we kissed each other?" No more Subdued Robby now. The man's eyes blazed with—anger? Jealousy?

Not fair. Matt stood to face him. "Hey, hey. Don't look at me like that. You seemed to have some connection with Chandler."

"I did *not*," Robby sputtered.

"But you were with him Sunday."

"Only because I couldn't be with *you*!" The words hung in the air, sucking up all of the oxygen in the room. Two dull red spots darkened Robby's cheeks, and the longer the silence held, the bigger they got. "Besides. The guy is married."

"I didn't know." Matt groaned, rubbing his eyes. "Can we please sit down?" He waited until Robby returned to the sofa before he retook his seat. "I've never—felt attracted to women. I couldn't even fake it. I never tried. Which made me kind of a target in high school. I didn't ever fit with anyone until Patty became my friend. She was my lifeline; sometimes she felt like my only connection to the human race."

He ran his damp palms over his khaki-covered thighs. "I knew I was missing something. The way other guys always talked about girls...I could look at someone and find them attractive, but I never wanted to do anything about it. I looked at dirty magazines, internet porn. Nothing. The night Patty and I—there was something. It was a little something, but I grabbed onto it with both hands. I thought maybe I could fake it 'til I made it."

Heat rushed into his face. "Obviously, I was able

183

to see it through, but when I thought about it, it just felt wrong. I kept trying, but it was a bust. When Patty realized we could never—I could never—she just lost it, you know?"

"You told me."

"She swore up and down afterward I was gay. Told me I made her my beard." He'd had to Google the term afterward. "I didn't think I was, but man, I was so confused by then, I went to a male strip show and gave some gay porn a go. But it didn't do it for me either."

Robby dipped his chin. "You're saying you're asexual."

It was a term he'd come across in his exhaustive internet search. "I used to think so. Until I started spending time with you." He bit at the nail on his thumb. "At first, it was like I found the first guy friend I ever had, but somewhere along the way—maybe when I went to your place the night we first kissed—I started feeling something else."

"So, you went out and kissed another guy." The edge was back in Robby's voice.

"Don't you get it? I didn't want it to be you."

Robby's head reared back. "What's wrong with me?"

"Nothing. You are the first person I have ever wanted to touch me. But what if I messed it up? I ruin a chance to be a normal person *and* destroy the only real friendship I have."

"You're already a normal person. Cishet doesn't mean *normal*."

"You know what I mean."

"I do. You don't think you're normal."

"You want to psychoanalyze me, or you want to talk about what's going on between us?" The words came out way harsher than he intended. "Sorry. This is already hard for me. Can you please let me get through it?"

Robby nodded.

"I went to a bar. Danced with a few guys. One of them kissed me. I wanted to want it, but it felt nothing like when I kissed you. Drunk or sober, with you I want it. I think maybe I started drinking to give myself an excuse to do what I'd been fantasizing about without considering the consequences. But I wanted it. I wanted you. Both times. All the time."

"I've been crazy about you since the day we met," Robby admitted.

Holy cow. How could he have missed it? "I didn't know."

Robby rolled his eyes. "Yeah, well, I think you were the only one who didn't. Brick figured it out almost right away. Kane too."

His heart sped up. "Do they know about—?"

"Our kisses? No. Would it be a problem if they did?"

Part of him wanted to keep it quiet; the other part wanted to shout it to the world. "I'd like us to figure out what this is first, if it's okay with you. I'm not ashamed of you, if that's what you're worried about. I think you're amazing, but I'm a private person. I spend a lot of time in my own head."

"Okay." Though there was obviously some hesitation there. "What do you want to do about us?"

Matt shrugged. "I don't know anything about how to be in a relationship, and I don't know how I feel about getting physical beyond kissing. It's all kind of—intimidating to me. I would like to see where it goes, though, if you're willing. If you don't think it will ruin our friendship, and if you don't mind going slowly with me."

Robby nibbled on his bottom lip as he considered his answer. "I never let myself believe anything could ever really happen between us. With your son in the picture, I figured you were straight, and I had no shot in a million years. I *want* a shot, though, if you're offering me one. I can be patient if you can be honest."

"There's nothing left to tell, I swear, but I won't hold anything back if you won't." He reached out and folded Robby's hand in his. The returning squeeze echoed through him.

Robby looked at their joined hands, then back up to his eyes. "What now?"

"More kissing?" Matt lifted his eyebrows.

"There are worse places to start." Robby slid closer and wound his free hand around the back of Matt's neck.

Matt closed the distance between them before Robby had a chance to lean forward. A gentle brush of the lips, and he could taste a hint of mint. Another gentle sweep, this time lingering a bit longer.

Long enough for Robby to take control of the action. No longer holding himself back, he revved up the contact and released Matt's hand to pull him flush against his chest.

It was even better than it was the other night, because now, no alcohol dulled the sensations. Even better, Robby wasn't fighting it anymore. The man was all in.

Every inch of his skin felt hypersensitive beneath the touch of Robby's hands. Strong hands. Gripping his biceps. Squeezing as they moved down. Clutching his hips.

He groaned as Robby's kisses moved down the column of his neck. The hot, wet swipe of the man's tongue made him forget how to breathe. All of his life, this was what he was missing. This consuming fire, this fierce connection.

Panting, he tunneled his fingers through Robby's thick, dark, glorious hair. He could barely remember a time where he hadn't wanted to touch it, slide it away from covering his beauty, see if it felt as soft as it looked. Teeth grazed the cords of his neck, and his fingers tightened, tugging gently—

And before he could blink, Robby was breathing heavy, hunched over, several feet away, near the front door. It happened so fast, he barely registered the man scrambling out of his arms and across the room.

"What?" Matt couldn't even form a coherent question.

Robby's arms curled around his waist, but he said nothing. His eyes were squeezed tightly shut.

Ignoring the ache in his cock, he replayed the last thirty seconds in his mind. He came up with nothing. At least his brain was starting to work. "Robby?" he asked slowly. "Did I do something wrong?"

Robby's throat bobbed as he swallowed. "No." Opening his eyes, he blinked rapidly. "You didn't know. *I* didn't even know."

"You're not making a lot of sense right now."

Robby leaned against the wall and slid down to sit on the floor. "I'm sorry."

Screw sorry. The guy had nothing to be sorry for. Something spooked him. "It was something I did." Moving slowly, Matt slid down from the sofa and crab walked a few feet closer. "My hands were in your hair. Did it freak you out?"

"You pulled it."

Did he? Maybe a little, but he didn't think it was very hard. "I hurt you?"

"No. No, of course not." Robby rubbed at his eyes. "It just brings up some bad memories, I guess."

They must be some *very* bad memories. "Do you want to talk about it?"

"Not even a little. What I want is to forget it." Robby's voice was soft but implacable. He was holding back, but Matt wouldn't strong arm him into sharing if he wasn't ready.

"I won't do it again." He'd be damned if he put a haunted expression on Robby's face ever again. "The hair thing, I mean. Because the kissing thing, I would definitely be down to repeat."

Some of the clouds moved away from Robby's eyes…but not all of them. "Really?"

"It was better than anything." Matt chewed on his bottom lip. "I don't really have a lot to compare it to, though. I'm way behind the curve on this one."

Warmth burned in his cheeks. "The truth is, I

188

don't even know how to go forward from here. I know the mechanics, obviously, but for all intents and purposes, I'm a virgin. And the sex thing, I've got to tell you, it freaks me out."

Robby scooted closer and tentatively took his hand. "You never have to do anything you feel uncomfortable with." He rubbed his thumb along the skin just above Matt's wrist. "I'm not going to lie. I want everything with you. But only when you're ready."

"What if I never am?" Matt held his breath.

"Then I'll be happy with whatever you have to give." Robby kissed his temple, and he could breathe again. "As much I want to stay here with you, I need to get going."

Already? It felt like the night just started. He pulled back, searching Robby's eyes for a sign he'd made a mistake.

But the man smiled as he climbed to his feet. "I'm volunteering tomorrow morning at an LGBT center. I haven't had the chance to meet too many of the kids yet, and I want to make a good impression."

He accepted the hand Robby offered to help him up. "We're good, then? You sure?"

Robby pulled him into a hug, then kissed his cheek. "Better than good." He walked to the door, turning with hand on the knob. "Thanks for taking a chance on me."

Taking a chance? If anyone was taking a chance, it was Robby. But Matt wouldn't look this gift horse in the mouth. He wouldn't mess things up—not like he did with Patty. His screw-up had cost him years of friendship.

Somehow, he knew, losing what he had with Robby would be something he'd never get over. And something he'd never find again.

CHAPTER SEVENTEEN

Robby

Robby tugged at his shirtsleeves on the sidewalk outside of the Q-Center. Between what happened with Matt and what he had planned for today, he shifted from euphoria to anxiety and back again.

Those kisses. Goodness gracious.

Matt's inexperience may have been obvious, but what he lacked in technique, he more than made up for in enthusiasm. The man kissed with abandon, like he'd just discovered the secrets of the universe and he thought he could unleash them with his tongue.

He might have been right.

You'd think months of fantasizing about kissing Matt combined with the two kisses they'd shared before would have prepared him for a no-holds-barred make-out session. And maybe they did, a little. But it was different when he knew it was what

191

they both wanted. His body certainly knew where it wanted to go and how to get there. No hesitation, just a descent into a haze of lust fueled by taste and touch.

Matt was into it too. His body had responded beautifully and instantly, arching against him, seeking more contact.

The entire encounter was the stuff his dreams were made of...until Matt's questing fingers in his hair doused the flames like a bucket of water on a campfire. Memories had assailed him, some hazy, some painfully sharp. All from his handful of nights with Harry. None he wanted to examine too closely. He'd left his old life behind a long time ago, and it was better left dead and buried. Hopefully, Matt would never know how low he'd sunk.

He pushed the feelings down.

Paul greeted him with an enthusiastic wave as he crossed the threshold. The man leaned over the big wooden table, surrounded by four guys hunched over, examining something on the surface in front of them.

"Robby. I'm glad you made it. Take a look at the design Brady made for our parade T-shirts." The reverend swept his hand over the colorful rainbow and dove artwork splashed across poster-boards on the table.

He lifted the one closest to him and examined it. Art had never been his strong suit, but even his untrained eye could see the talent and passion in the bold strokes. "Awesome. Wait...there's a parade?"

"Not for another six months." The reverend held up the other two designs, peering closely at one, then the other before setting them back down. "We want to get all of our ducks in a row. Try out the designs on some fundraising sites and fliers. We're lucky to have such a talented artist in house."

Even without an introduction, Robby knew who Brady must be when he turned in his direction. The deep flush in the guy's cheeks gave him away. But it wasn't until the young man pulled his gaze up to somewhere around Robby's chest when a zing of recognition hit.

The dead-eyed boy from Nitro. Sucking in a breath, Robby stumbled back a step.

Brady looked up at his face for a split second, but it was enough. His tremulous smile dropped away, and a sound just shy of a whimper escaped his throat. The guys around him zeroed in on Robby, anger and suspicion in their narrowed eyes.

"What's your deal, man?" The demand sprang from an older teen with blue chin-length hair and two dumbbell piercings in his right eyebrow. The young man stepped toward him and poked him hard in the shoulder. "You here to cause trouble for Brady?"

Robby held up his hands in the universal sign of surrender and canted his voice low. "I'm not here to hurt anybody."

A second guy, this one with dark brown skin and cornrows, angled himself in front of Brady. "This is a safe space."

The first guy bared his teeth. "Go back to wherever you came from."

Robby dropped his hands to his sides. "I came from a nowhere little town that threw me out on my ass when I was sixteen."

"Boo-fucking-hoo." No sympathy from the guy with the braids.

"I saw him with one of the regulars at Nitro," Brady murmured.

"Get. The fuck. Out." The pierced guy surged forward, pushing him back with both hands, just as the reverend tried to stop him.

"Marshall—" Too late.

The force almost knocked Robby on his rear. "It was the only time I've ever been back there." He modulated his voice and kept going before Marshall could call him a liar. "But I've been to plenty of places like it. You do what you have to when your only other choice is the street."

Marshall grunted. "So, what's your story?"

How much could he share? Could he, finally, force some of his old darkness into the light of day? One look at Brady's bleak expression pushed him to try.

Here goes nothing.

"When I was homeless, for months, I'd use the horny guys I found at the clubs to give me a place to sleep. At least, I could choose my partner when I picked a guy up. I didn't always have the same luxury at the shelter."

The guys surrounding Brady loosened their aggressive stances. They must've heard the truth in his story.

He forged on. "I met my ex at a place called The Edge. He liked younger guys, and I liked his apartment. And, honestly, for a long time, he treated me better than anyone else ever had. As long as he could run the show. But he broke me down a hundred ways over the years. For a long time, I only existed as someone who belonged to him."

"But you got out." Marshall now leaned against the table. The others, even Brady, had dropped into the chairs.

"He—after a while it took more and more to…rev him up." What Robby wouldn't give for a bottle of water right now. His mouth had dried up so much, his tongue felt heavy and thick. "We'd double up with another couple. Sometimes, he'd trade me off. Other times, well, I guess the last thing was finally too much. I took the little bit of fun-money I'd managed to save and used every cent to rent a dirt-cheap studio apartment. Slept on the floor. Took cold showers because I couldn't afford electricity and I ate at the soup kitchen. Then I found a job."

And he still thanked God for it every day. For the job and for Xander Karras, who took a chance on a broken kid with no experience, no high school diploma, and no idea how to take care of himself. "It took a long time to build something for myself. To buy myself a bed. A pot to cook in. A towel. I went to N.A. Eventually, I got my GED. I got raises here and there. One day I made a friend. Then I made another one. Then I met Sara, who led me here."

"How did you end up at Nitro? The night I saw you there." The first words from Brady, spoken in a soft, breathy voice.

Heat creeped up the back of his neck. "When I was younger, Nitro was just a club. It didn't have a

VIP room. I went there the night you saw me because...I was lonely. Looking for someone—anyone—who might want me for a little while."

Marshall nodded in understanding.

"Anyway, I saw a friend from the old days. He brought me to the back, and I swear it wasn't what I was looking for." He leveled his gaze at Brady. "You didn't see me hook up with anyone because all I did was drink, which I really shouldn't have been doing either. When I looked around and saw what was going on there, I got the hell out."

Robby felt lightheaded, and the cotton of his shirt stuck to his back. He'd never shared so much about himself in front of people in his life.

"Don't let this lot drive you away. It takes us all a while to warm up to new people." Sara sauntered over barefoot in an African-print sarong-style dress. No telling how much of his sob story she'd heard.

"You think I'd miss the chance to see you again?" Robby caught sight of a mini-fridge against the wall. "There wouldn't be any water in there by any chance?"

Instead of answering, Paul ambled over and supplied one. The first gulp helped a little, but it took almost the whole bottle to quench the thirst his storytelling inspired.

Thomas had been right in a way; it was easier to talk about the hard stuff with strangers. Especially other people who might have lived through similar experiences. It wasn't completely unlike sharing the low points people talked about in N.A. People with the same struggles were less likely to judge you for yours. And even if they did, it would hurt less than it would from someone you loved.

Easier. But still not easy.

When he set the bottle down, the anger and fear from the guys around him had dialed down to a quiet curiosity. The best he could hope for today was a fragile acceptance, and if he could achieve that, it would be a victory.

"I'll leave if you still want me to go, guys. But I'd like to stay. Support you. Help if I can. Be your friend if you want. I can't do much with art." He waved at Brady's work still splashed across the table. "But I can march with you. I can listen to you. Help you get your GED or get a job. I don't want anyone to feel as trapped and alone as I was."

No one rushed to answer, which didn't surprise him. In the end, Brady tipped his head, brown bangs sliding over his eyes. "You can stay."

Relief and triumph zinged through his veins. It had been one thing when the center had just been a vague idea he'd latched onto, something to give him purpose. But now he'd seen their faces. Felt the bravado and mistrust curated by who knew what kind of treatment by other people. Now, his acceptance here mattered on an entirely new level.

He already had an idea on how he could help. "Hey, Paul. How much do you know about the empty space for rent next door?"

CHAPTER EIGHTEEN

Matt

Patty seemed to thaw a little more every time Matt saw her these days. Today, she was dressed in a simple pair of jeans and a plain white T-shirt. Her skin was clear of makeup and so healthy, it almost glowed.

And she hummed as she packed Jimmy's diaper bag.

His eyes widened and he almost choked when her hum turned into full-fledged singing.

Or it did for a moment or two…until she set down the jar of mashed potatoes on the counter with a thud. "Stop gaping, or you're gonna catch flies with your open mouth. You got a problem with Lauryn Hill?"

He shook his head, a small smile lifting the corners of his mouth. "Not at all. My mom loves that song."

"Where do you think I learned it?" She scooped the jar back off the laminate and into the bag with the rest of Jimmy's stuff: his favorite crackers, some star-shaped pasta. All stuff Matt had at home, but he wouldn't interrupt and risk ruining her good mood.

"If it's not the song—and I *know* it's not my singing—what are you gawking at me for?" She carried the bag over and held it out to him. "Do I look bad or something?"

He hoisted the strap over his shoulder. "No. You look better than I've seen you in a long time." Misfire. "I mean, you look great. Really. Like you're…happy." It let the grip of guilt he felt over what happened between them ease a fraction.

Jimmy toddled over to his mom and wrapped his arms around her leg. She picked him up and propped him on her hip. "You can stop swallowing your tongue, Matty. I get it."

Sighing, she pulled a paper towel off the roll and wiped Jimmy's running nose. "I don't know if I'd say I'm happy, exactly. But I'm not sticking pins in your voodoo doll, if that's what you're getting at."

"You have a voodoo doll of me?" He wouldn't put it past her to commission one from her grandma.

She glanced at the ceiling for a moment before releasing their son back to the floor. "Yeah, well, I've been wallowing in my bullshit long enough. My new job is opening some crazy-cool doors for me. It's not the way I thought I would use my art, but it has my creativity pumping again."

They still hadn't talked about her mystery job. "You never said where you're working."

199

"I'm pulling some shifts at the tattoo place on 5th Street. Everything from answering the phone to scheduling the appointments to taking out the trash. Two guys run the place and one of them just had surgery for a torn rotator cuff. He's going to be out of commission for a few weeks. Steve can't handle all the load on his own."

"Steve?"

She swiped a banana from the counter and pulled down the peeling. "You remember Old Mrs. Peres? The lady down the hall from my mom?"

"The cat lady?" Who could forget all those cats? She must've had a dozen. Patty's mom used to send them down to her apartment with plates of leftovers after the woman's son moved out to live on his own.

"Mmm-hmm," she agreed as she chewed. "Turns out Steve is her son. We'd met a few times over the years before his mom passed. He remembered me from the time they had Christmas at our house."

Oh yeah. The year before the old lady died, Patty's mom had invited her over for a Christmas lunch. She hadn't wanted her to be alone for the holiday. Her son had surprised them all by showing up, hung over and in last night's clothes.

"We got to talking my first day there, about his mom and about art. I did a few sketches for him, and he asked me to bring in my portfolio." She ducked her head as she took another bite and swallowed. "Long story short, he's letting me do an apprenticeship with him now."

From the wonder on her face, apparently, she considered it a good thing, but... "I thought you

200

told me he was kind of a screw-up, the cat lady's son. Didn't he have…" Should he say it? "Um, a drug problem?"

"Yeah. But he's been clean a few years now." She tossed the peel into the trash can, then rubbed her hands over her jeans-covered thighs. "Andrew—the one with the messed-up shoulder—he helped Steve get straight. Let him apprentice at the shop, and now they're partners, in the business, not like they're a couple. Steve wants to pay it forward, help me get my foot in the door. It's really kind of a competitive field."

The idea of Patty, focused on her future, with a good job, a career—it felt fantastic. "Sounds amazing."

"I haven't been so excited about anything in a long time. I want this, Matty. For me. For Jimmy. I'm not going to blow this opportunity." The resolve in her voice reinforced her words.

He scooped their son into his arms. "You have no idea how much I hope this works out for you. If there's anything I can do to help, just ask."

"I will. And maybe we can find a solution to this custody thing." She slung her purse over her forearm and rifled through it until she found her keys. "Time to go." On her way out, she stopped at the door. "It's good to have something to look forward to for a change."

No kidding. He had plenty to look forward to tonight.

The day with Jimmy passed quickly in a blur of building blocks, tummy tickles, and cartoons, making Matt grateful they hadn't needed him at the bar today. Even basking in the joy of toddler kisses and nonsense words, his thoughts kept drifting to what might happen next with Robby, especially after he got the text midafternoon, inviting him over after dinner.

His mom was all-too-happy to babysit, so after a quick shower and shave he found himself on Robby's doorstep, heart beating wildly in his chest. Just as a mild panic climbed toward his stomach, the door swung open and Robby tugged him inside.

Robby gripped his fingers in a firm hold and didn't release them as they settled on the sofa. "I did something important today." Pride shone in those milk chocolate eyes.

"You were going to volunteer, right?" He should've paid closer attention when Robby had told him last night, but those kisses had obliterated any chance of higher brain function.

Those kisses. He shifted on the cushion as the memories cascaded over his body.

"—met the most amazing people."

Crap. He forced himself to focus.

"I really feel like I could make a difference there." Robby squeezed his hand before letting it go.

"Yeah?"

Robby hopped up and loped toward the kitchen. "This kid, Vin, he's in foster care. The parents are garbage." He paused as he rifled through the refrigerator, then popped up with a glass pitcher filled with burgundy liquid. "But he is so talented."

Gripping the handle in his right hand, Robby balanced the base of the pitcher with his left as he carried it back toward Matt and set it on the coffee table. "He's an artist. You wouldn't believe the things he can draw freehand. Brady too."

Matt tried to find the right level of encouragement. "Sounds…cool."

Robby swept back to the kitchen and returned with two glasses. "But Vin's real passion is graphic design. I want to help him. Make sure he graduates. Gets some training. Talent like his shouldn't go to waste."

Reaching for the pitcher, Matt made a small noise of agreement.

Robby put a hand on his arm. "You should come."

"What?"

"To the Q-Center. You should come. Meet everyone."

The idea of meeting new people never sounded exciting. More like nerve wracking. "I'm not great with people, Rob."

"I know you feel that way." Robby's hand slid back and forth over his forearm. "For what it's worth, you're great with me."

Not so great Robby felt comfortable enough to tell his whole story.

Stop looking for trouble. You're letting your own insecurities play with your head.

He shook it off. "It's different with you." Was it too soon to start kissing again? He eyed Robby's bottom lip.

"Hey." Robby snapped his fingers. "Eyes up here." He gestured to his own eyes. "I'm serious. These kids—well, they're not all kids. Some of

203

them are maybe, nineteen or twenty. But they need people who they can trust. People who don't want anything from them. We can change their lives."

Matt returned his attention to the pitcher and filled the glasses. He sniffed his drink. "What's in here?"

"Fruit punch. My own recipe. Sugar free, but it tastes delicious." Robby tipped his glass back and took a healthy sip.

Okay. Matt sipped from his own glass and let the flavors roll over his tongue. Fruity, he could parcel out some orange juice in there and, for sure, some cherries. "Not bad."

Robby beamed. "I feel so good right now. Like I found what I'm supposed to be doing. I've got so many ideas. And Paul, the guy who runs the place, says my only limit is my imagination." Taking another gulp, Robby drained his glass and set it down before scooting closer. "Tell me you'll come with me tomorrow."

No way did he want to take the hopeful look off Robby's face. "I have to work at the bar tomorrow, and I have Jimmy this week, but if the offer still stands, I can come by next weekend."

He wouldn't have thought Robby's smile could grow any wider, but somehow, it did.

"Thank you."

"Sure." He sipped the punch and let the liquid roll down his throat.

Robby's hand wrapped around his and guided his drink to the table.

Matt balled his fists into his lap. "I—I'm not sure what I'm supposed to do." He whispered, "I don't want to mess this up."

Gently, Robby lifted his right hand and pried his fist open before kissing his palm. "You're not going to mess it up."

The kiss, chaste as it was, sent his internal temperature skyrocketing. "You don't know that. I don't either. Last night, I almost sent you running for the hills."

"It wasn't you." Robby kissed the tip of his thumb, then did the same with every finger on his hand. "My past is complicated."

Shut down again. He wanted to press for more, learn how to avoid a repeat of last night's mistake. But he liked Robby's mouth on him, and with conversation, especially serious conversation, the kissing might stop. The man's lips had moved up over his hand to the inside of his wrist, obliterating coherent thought.

"Tell me you want this," Robby murmured against his skin.

He could only nod. Plead with his eyes.

"You want me to take the lead?" Robby's eyes darkened as Matt nodded again. "You want me to go slow?"

Definitely not. He punctuated his grunt with a short shake of his head, and Robby flashed a knowing smile.

"You got it. Just tell me when it's too much."

Too much? Right now, nothing would be enough.

His frustrated groan must've pushed Robby's buttons, because in an instant, his slow kisses, his languid exploration, gave way to insistent demand.

Robby surged closer, putting them chest to chest as he rained fiery kisses over his neck.

Unsure where to put his hands, Matt held them inches away from the other man. Until Robby's attention moved to his mouth.

Then, he didn't have to wonder what to do. Instinct guided one hand to Robby's waist, while the other gripped his neck. Their tongues met in a tangle of wet heat. The taste of their sweet drinks gave way to something bolder, headier.

True to his promise, Robby took the lead, questing a hand down over Matt's collarbone. Squeezing his left pec. Kneading him through the fabric of his shirt.

"Take it off." Robby's voice came out an octave lower as he untucked the T-shirt from Matt's pants.

Holy shit. The gruff sound wrapped around his dick like a caress, coaxing it harder.

Robby tugged again. "Off."

He scrambled to pull it over his head, and his nipples pebbled against the cool air.

"Lean back against the side of the sofa," Robby purred, then knelt on the floor. "Stretch out. Let me see you."

Yes. Yes. Yes.

He did it in a heartbeat. Who knew a demanding lover could be so damn sexy?

For a moment, Robby didn't move. But his gaze traveled from the top of Matt's head, down his bare torso, then rested on the erection bulging in his pants.

Matt knew it wasn't possible, but he would've sworn the man's stare held a weight so heavy, he could actually feel it. Just the idea of a touch on his rock-hard cock forced out a moan.

The sound snapped Robby's attention back to his face. "Put your hands over your head. Hold onto the arm of the sofa." He moved closer. "Don't let go until I say so."

Just as his hands gripped the furniture, Robby settled on top of him, their bodies flush against each other. And for a glorious moment, the length of his erection pressed against Matt's own before he slid downward.

Despite the kisses Robby trailed down his neck, he couldn't hold back a whimper when the pressure disappeared from his dick.

"Trust me," Robby crooned. "I'll make it good for you." He followed his words with a slow lick over one nipple, then the other. His tongue swirled around the peak. Once. Twice.

What he wouldn't give to tangle his hands in those thick brown curls. But he dug his fingers deeper into the sofa instead, holding himself rigid and tight.

His reward came in the hot slide of Robby's tongue down his abs, teasing him just above the button of his fly.

"Do you know how many times I've thought about your body?" Robby's finger roved over the skin just above his waistband. "Fantasized about what you have hiding behind all your buttoned-up clothes?"

He lifted his hips. An invitation. Soon he might beg.

"I want to unwrap you."

Goddamn. The husky note in Robby's voice was going to make him come in his pants. "Do it," he ground out.

And the plea was all Robby needed. Unbuttoning the khakis, tugging them down and completely off—he did it in seconds. Robby licked his lips, his gaze devouring the straining erection in front of him. Then he wrapped his hand around the base and squeezed.

"Your cock is so fucking perfect."

"Oh, God." He'd never heard Robby swear. Ever.

"You like that." Robby ran his hand up to the head and back down again. "Dirty talk."

He nodded hard and fast. He'd never been so turned on in his life.

"I'm going to take you in my mouth. Lick you. Suck you." Another pump up, then down his length. "You want me to suck you, Matt?" He didn't wait for an answer. Instead, he held firm at the base, then licked up the side of his dick.

Matt's hands and feet planted firmly, the rest of his body arched up. Breaths escaped his parted lips in quick, panting gasps for air.

"You taste so good, baby." Robby's tongue circled the tip. "Yes, give me a little bit of your come. Let's see if you can give me more." It was the only warning before he took Matt's dick to the back of his throat.

Nothing he'd ever experienced in his entire life had felt so good. The welcoming heat of Robby's mouth enveloped him with pleasure. The suction started slow and gentle but ramped up quickly, growing urgent and demanding.

No longer able to talk dirty, Robby's mouth now made wet, sucking sounds as he bobbed his head. His hand followed in a slippery slide, working in tandem with his lips and tongue. Then, he took him all the way down…and swallowed.

The working muscles of Robby's throat massaged the head with exquisite pressure. And Matt's hips surged up, seeking more. Robby hummed against his dick as he pumped into his mouth. His balls pulled up tight as he thrust and thrust toward the most perfect fucking feeling.

And when his orgasm finally ripped through him, he shouted Robby's name loud enough to leave the neighbors no doubt what was happening here tonight.

Robby waited, letting him savor the moment, before releasing his softening length and crawling on top of him. "That was even better than I imagined it would be."

He finally released the side of the sofa and wrapped his arms around the man who'd just utterly blown his mind. "Better for who? I think I got the sweet end of the deal." For crying out loud, Robby was still completely dressed.

Here he was, naked as the day he was born, spent and satisfied. All Robby had gotten out of it was a mouthful of jizz. "Tell me what I can do for you."

Robby looked up, a satisfied smile on his lips. "You let me do what I wanted to do. You trusted me. And everything about it was real. It's hard to explain. But I promise, it was good for me. We've got all the time in the world to trade places. To go further."

Matt tensed. Amazing as what they'd just shared had been, the idea of going further kind of freaked him out.

"Or not," Robby soothed. "We don't have to do anything you're not comfortable with. I'm just happy to be with you."

"This. Tonight. You—were amazing. I have never felt anything like it before. I've never wanted anyone or *anything* so much before. There's still some stuff I need to figure out. But how you made me feel tonight? I don't have any questions about that."

Anxious or not, he'd do whatever it took to hold on to this feeling. And this man. Robby was damn near perfect. Sweet. Giving. Responsible. He could trust him while he worked it through in his head.

"I'm glad." Robby kissed his chest and lay his head back down. "We'll figure the rest out together."

CHAPTER NINETEEN

Robby

Robby ran his hand over the top of his head, still in shock at how short the barber had cut his hair. True, the man only did what he asked, but he couldn't remember the last time he'd worn it so short.

One thing's for sure. I don't look like a kid.

He'd hidden behind those long, wavy locks in more ways than one. They'd covered his eyes when he didn't want to see or be seen. But they'd also kept him soft-looking, disguised the harder parts tucked away underneath. Without them, he looked his age, if not a year or two older.

He'd also traded his ill-fitting khakis for a pair of bootcut dark jeans, a thick white cotton long sleeve T-shirt, and a casual blue tailored jacket from H&M. To top it all off, he'd only shaved under his jaw this morning, leaving a dusting of stubble on his cheeks.

The pretty blond barista flashed him a saucy smile as she handed him his coffee. "I don't think I've seen you here before. My name's Kelly."

Chuckling, he returned the grin without engaging her. He'd been buying his coffee at this little donut shop at least once a week for nearly a year, though usually in the morning. It was pushing two o'clock in the afternoon now. With his impromptu trip to the mall, his day had been too busy to get here sooner. And he still had his visit to the Q-Center to go to next.

Kane waved him over from the booth where he sat with Brick. "Holy shit, brother. I almost didn't recognize you."

He lifted his shoulder before sliding in on the vinyl seat beside Brick. "I figured it was time to stop hiding behind my hair. I guess you could probably relate."

Kane's hair used to hang down to the middle of his back, but he'd chopped it down to a more traditional length just before he got married.

The ex-biker barked out a laugh around the beignet he was chewing. "Baby's got bite! New look and a new attitude to match."

"I like it," Brick rumbled. "You look— confident. It agrees with you."

Yes. Confident. Last night had been a revelation.

A first for him in as many ways as it had been for Matt. Because in all the years he'd had relationships with other men—all the times he'd had sex, and there had been a lot—he'd never been the one in control.

He'd played at it. John loved dominance games and every so often he'd pull Robby's strings to act out some tableau. But there'd been no doubt, John called the shots. So had any other man who'd taken care of him, which was the trade-off. He was meek, pretty, young, and most of all, malleable.

But last night, Matt belonged to him. Not in some kind of power play, but because he trusted him to guide their course. Even better, Matt wanted Robby the man, not the kid.

"It was long overdue." Robby sipped his coffee.

Another great thing? He had no doubt whatsoever the guys at this table would be happy he'd figured all this out. They had his back in every way. Which was why he'd called them here.

"Kane, do you think you could set up a meeting for me with Amanda?"

"Mandy?" Powdered sugar clung to his five o'clock shadow. "You don't need an appointment. Just come over to the apartment."

Robby straightened his spine, drawing his shoulders back a fraction. "I have a business proposition to discuss with her. I didn't think it would be right to trade on our friendship and spring it on her out of nowhere."

Brick wiped at his own chin with his thumb in an exaggerated motion, but either Kane didn't see it or he didn't get the message.

"You're family, Robby. You don't have to worry about shit like that. Our door is always open to you." Kane bobbed his head from side to side. "If you don't mind dealing with some pregnancy hormones."

213

Relaxing back against the seat, he thanked his lucky stars for leading him to Cooper Construction and the men beside him. "Thank you."

"Now, are you going to tell us who prompted this make-over?" Kane bit back into his French donut. "Cause I've got to say, it's weirding me out."

"Me. I wanted my outside to match my inside."

Kane snorted. "Can the kumbaya bullshit. I know there's a guy."

His smile barely quirked, but it was enough to make Kane whoop in victory.

Brick shifted, raising one eyebrow in his imperial way. "You want to share with the class?"

"Not yet," he lilted. "But soon."

Draining his coffee, he saluted his buddies and stood to make his exit. On the way to the door, Brick's voice carried over the scattered conversations from other diners.

"—and would you wipe your fucking face, for God's sake? You look ridiculous. You didn't have this much trouble feeding yourself when you had an Opie beard."

"Stop bringing up that fucking show!"

At least he didn't have to worry they'd spare his feelings about his new look. Puffing out his chest as he walked, he sent up a quick prayer of thanks for Brick and Kane, for Matt and the center, and for the confidence to finally show his real face to the world.

***

Matt wrinkled his forehead in an expression

Robby found both confused and completely adorable as he looked around the stacks of books surrounding them the next night. "Tell me again why you wanted to meet at the library."

Robby rubbed his fingertips over the smooth, familiar surface of the wooden table. "Because— A—I love the library. When I was really low on cash, I would spend hours here at a time. They always had heat in the winter, A/C in the summer, computers with access to any information I could ever want or need. And books. Entire worlds of stories within arms' reach whenever I needed an escape."

Matt propped his elbows on the flat surface. "And B?"

"B—I needed a place where we could talk alone, where I wouldn't be tempted to strip you down, tie you up, and have my wicked way with you."

Matt mouthed the words *tie me up* and blinked rapidly.

Robby barked a laugh loud enough for the librarian to shoot him a death glare. Properly chastised, he ran his fingers over his lips like he was closing a zipper. "I'm kidding. Mostly."

He reached down and dug a manila file from the duffel he had on the floor. "I need some of your architecture smarts."

"I don't have any architecture smarts, Rob." Despite his words, Matt eagerly took the file Robby offered.

"The Q-Center needs to expand. They've got some space to use here." Robby gestured to the rough sketch of the building. "But we need a way to make the most efficient use of it. Every hundred square feet could give someone a safe place to sleep."

Matt shrugged. "What do you need me for? This looks like an adequate open space for bedding. Maybe you can add a partition to separate men and women."

"No. This needs to be individual sleep space. An open plan invites all kinds of opportunity for abuse. No one can police that sort of arrangement all night. We need walls and doors with locks. Each room can be tiny. They need to be. But they also need to be secure."

"You have a pencil?"

Robby pulled one out of the bag and placed it on the table.

Matt grabbed it and started sketching right away. "I think you've got some really solid bones here. And you can probably do it for under ten thousand dollars. But where are you going to get so much money? Fundraising?"

"In a way." Robby smiled. "I've got an idea."

***

Later in the week, Robby leaned back on Amanda's loveseat, watching Kane fuss over his wife like she was Cleopatra on a throne, rather than a modern woman sprawled out on her sofa in a pair of sweatpants. "You want me to make you an Arnold Palmer, babe? I bought you some decaffeinated tea from Trader Joe's and the Minute Maid you like."

Amanda waved him away. "Sounds good. Make one for Robby too." She rolled her eyes as her husband bustled to the kitchen. "We had another ultrasound today, and he's had the dial turned to eleven ever since."

Robby eyed her stomach, which barely boasted a bump. "This ultrasound would tell you what you're having, right?"

Nodding, she leaned forward and lowered her voice. "We found out we're having a girl."

"Is it a secret?" he whispered back.

"No." She smirked. "It's just, every time Kane hears it, he freaks out all over again." She modulated her voice down an octave, in a dead-on impression of her spouse. "What the hell do I know about raising a daughter? I'm going to fuck this up."

"I *am* going to fuck this up!" Kane called out from the kitchen. "She'll end up in therapy, with stories about the time her dad busted some dude's kneecaps for trying to get to second base." Loping back into the living room, he placed Robby's drink on the table and put Amanda's in her hand. "I won't be sorry about it either."

It would've been funny if his friend didn't look so serious. "You'll be a great dad."

"How would you know?" Kane groused as he settled beside his wife.

"Because you're a good man and a good friend." Robby wouldn't find a better segue than this. "Not everybody is lucky enough to have someone like you in their lives."

Skepticism poured off Kane in waves.

"You know I had a rough time of things when I

first got to Atlanta."

"I know your family tossed you out."

"Yeah." He was not in a place to delve back into all the details. The revelations he'd shared at the Q-Center a few days ago had opened enough old wounds to last a lifetime. Besides, the people there were different. They'd lived through the same things. No one else needed to know the details. They'd never look at him the same way. "There weren't many resources around here back then to get me on my feet, at least none I knew about. But a friend introduced me to a gay youth center, and I volunteer there now."

"Is that what we should thank for the new spring in your step?" Amanda sipped her drink, then wrinkled her nose and set it away. "I love the new look, by the way."

Though the latest additions to his updated wardrobe were running low, he'd worn at least one piece of new clothing every day this week. Most of the compliments focused on the haircut. Matt, especially, made it clear he was a fan.

"I told Kane I had a proposition for you. It's about the youth center." He cleared his throat. "I'd like Cooper Construction to be a corporate sponsor."

Kane and Amanda exchanged a look he couldn't read.

"I'm not looking for an answer right now. I know you need to talk it over with your brother, since you guys are partners. And, I guess, the board too. But hear me out. Sponsorship could help the Q-Center expand. Right now, the space allows up to about twenty people inside at one time, and it's great, but there is only enough sleep space for two."

"You're trying to turn it into a shelter?" Amanda didn't sound dubious, exactly, but she wasn't jumping for joy either.

"More like a…halfway house. Criminals, recovering addicts, domestic violence victims—those people have residential environments to give them a chance to get them on their feet. And the Q-Center can do it for queer people on a very small scale, but what if we could do more? It doesn't need to be fancy, just four walls and a roof over their heads. I have a plan."

Amanda lifted her drink to Kane. "Please go get me some real tea. This decaffeinated stuff is disgusting."

Scowling, Kane stomped off with the drink.

"Go on," she prompted.

"The guy who owns the building is willing to lease out the neighboring space to the center for only a nominal addition to the rent. He's been a member of Paul's—the pastor who runs the place—his congregation for, like, twenty years. What I'm suggesting is for Cooper to donate the manpower to open up some space between the two rentals and help us fashion it into living space. Nothing fancy. I was thinking six bedrooms and a small bathroom with a toilet and standing shower."

"Six bedrooms?" Kane stuck his head out of the kitchen. "How big *is* this extra space?"

"Not big." He laid out Matt's sketches on the table. "Less than fourteen hundred square feet, but the rooms would be small, something like a hundred by a hundred-fifty feet each. Enough for a bed and a small dresser. It's not supposed to be the Four Seasons. Nobody's looking for luxury. They just need a place where they're not afraid to close their eyes. Where they'll still have their shoes when they wake up. And they don't have to pay for it with their bodies or their self-respect."

Amanda took the mug Kane carried in and sipped as she glanced at the mock-up. Her face twisted, and she spit the offending liquid back into the cup. "What the hell, Hale?"

It had to be bad if she was calling her husband by his last name.

"It's a kale smoothie. The guy at the store said it's full of antioxidants—"

She shoved the cup back into his hand. "It tastes like feet. Just get me a water."

Robby pressed on. "After we get past the construction cost and labor, maybe just a monthly stipend. It doesn't have to be a lot, just enough to offset the additional rent and utilities. Paul's church has money set aside for some general funding. In the meantime, this could be good for Cooper too."

Her focused visibly sharpened. Amanda was nothing if not a savvy businesswoman. She'd grown her stepfather's company since she'd taken the reins, and now they worked in a partnership with one of the biggest developers in Atlanta.

"The owner's husband works in marketing. He's working up a publicity promotion to raise awareness, not only for the Q-Center but for our primary corporate sponsor as well. We're talking a major digital push as well as appearances on some of the local midday lifestyle shows. It's free advertisement, but it also demonstrates the quality of our work through the pictures and videos we'll show of the expansion. And it will give you an opportunity to reinforce Cooper's commitment to giving back to the community."

"It's also a tax write-off," she mused, picking up the sketches. And he knew he had her. "How do you propose we get started?"

***

Matt

The excited energy positively rolled off Robby as they stood outside the community center on Peachtree, and Matt bit back a smile with the glimmer of the old Robby he'd grown to know and love.

Love? He shook his head. It was just an expression.

Over the past week, his friend—boyfriend?—had transformed from nervous and tongue-tied to confident and secure. Like someone had flipped a switch. He was still Robby, of course, but…older.

Either way, the man was hotter than ever. Everything that drew Matt before, but…more. Sadly, he'd had no time to really explore it with daddy-duty all week. Robby had been great about it. Honestly, the guy was great about everything. Still, he was ready to have a free night to himself tomorrow.

"What time is Martin supposed to meet us here?"

Xander looked down one end of the street, then the other, running his hand through his black hair which was seeing more traces of gray every day. The foreman was a pretty chill guy, but he was a stickler for punctuality.

Robby checked his phone. "He should be here anytime now. You know Mr. Hayes?"

Xander grunted. "Sure. Martin and I both go to Paul's church. And Martin's daughter used to babysit my son when he was little."

"It's really nice of him to rent us this space for so cheap," Robby murmured.

"Nice has nothing to do with it," an unfamiliar voice boomed behind him. "This storefront has been empty for months. I'd rather rent it to a friend at a discount than let it keep growing cobwebs. Besides, Paul's a good man. If I didn't trust him and believe in what he's doing here, I wouldn't have leased him the initial space to begin with."

"Martin." Xander reached out and shook the newcomer's hand. "Show us what we're working with."

Mr. Hayes stood a few inches shorter than the foreman, though he had a much heartier midsection. Wheat-colored hair ringed the outside of his mostly bald head, and a graying mustache topped his upper lip. He led them through a nondescript door into an empty space.

Xander wasted no time in starting his inventory of the property. Robby followed, taking notes on his clipboard as Xander rattled off observations about the walls, the electrical, and the pipes.

Matt drew up some bare-bones plans, based on

his initial sketches, showing the placement and dimensions of the bedrooms and single bath. He loved working with plans, taking the pictures in his head and putting them on paper with the idea it could one day be something tangible, a space where people could live or work or just…be.

The entire process only took about an hour. Amanda arrived at the very end to get a report. Jared Berringer, her developer partner, arrived with her.

"It's in good shape," Xander rumbled. "The building has good bones, and we could turn the space around pretty quickly if we put our backs into it. Matt sketched the project out for us."

He stepped forward and held out the plans.

Berringer looked over Amanda's shoulder as she examined them.

"Cost?" She didn't look up as she asked the question.

"Minimal."

Robby tugged on Matt's arm as Xander went through the minutia of the supplies they would need and the structural changes. "They're going to be a while. Come next door with me. I want you to see the place."

Crossing into the empty room next door, Matt's hand brushed against Robby's. He felt the zing of the contact all the way to his toes. The center, itself, was bright and inviting, though quiet inside. Robby gave him a quick tour through the TV area, the computer stations, and the administrative cubicles.

"Back there are the two overnight rooms."

"Where is everyone?" He'd expected to see other

people here.

"At work." Robby shrugged. "School. Usually, there's at least one administrator here all the time, to keep the doors open. But they must've gone to lunch or something, since we were next door." A slow smile crept over his face. "You know what that means?"

"You need more staff?"

"It *means* I finally have you to myself." Robby's hand shot out like a viper and wrapped around the back of his neck and pulled him in for a scorching kiss.

He found himself crowded against the wall, sandwiched between the plaster and a hard, lean body growing harder by the second. His hands gripped Robby's denim-clad hips, tugging him even closer. The press of the other man's pelvis against his own called to the passion he'd been holding back all week.

Robby nipped at his lower lip, then kissed the underside of his jaw. "I can't get enough of you."

"Oooh. Lordy, lordy. No wonder you've got yourself some swagger if a hot slice of toast like him is waiting for you at home." A husky androgynous voice echoed through the room.

Looking over Robby's shoulder, Matt spotted the source, clad in a vibrant red wraparound dress and a matching headscarf.

Robby sighed soundlessly against him before lifting his head. "Come on, Sara. Don't give Matt a hard time."

She shot him an over-the-top wink. "Fine with me. I'd much prefer if *he* gave *me* a hard time. Y'all already know where I live."

When Robby pulled away to face her, Matt felt like he stood naked under the spotlight of an empty stage. His arousal, though steadily shrinking, hadn't entirely subsided, and Sara's gaze locked on it like a laser beam.

"Hey," Robby barked, his hand waving in front of her face. "Eyes over here. I'm serious."

"Whatever," she huffed. "Take away all a girl's fun."

"Robby!" Xander called out from the sidewalk. "I need you."

Robby shot Sara a quelling look. "Behave while I'm gone." Giving Matt's hand a final squeeze, he answered the foreman's call.

Oh God. Was he supposed to talk to her? Talking to strangers rated up there with ant-bites and communal showers. His stomach clenched.

"A shy one, huh? He said your name is Matt?"

He grunted.

"Come sit with me, sweet Matt." She beckoned him to one of the sofas situated on the side of the room, then patted the cushion beside her.

Crap. Easier to just comply rather than argue.

"You been dating Robby for long?"

A single shake of his head.

"He seems pretty crazy about you. I can see a change in just the past week."

"I'm not sure I can take all the credit."

She tsked. "You can't bullshit a bullshitter, doll. You're probably the first man he didn't have to play twink with. Two quiet, submissive types might have a hard time ever getting down to business."

He sat with the idea for a moment. Robby *was* showing a different side of himself. Even if the dirty talk and the gruff voice didn't follow him into the real world, the confidence, the worldliness, obviously did.

"I guess I get what you're saying."

"Forgive me for being so forward, and you can tell me to just go on to hell for nosing in your business, but do you have any idea what you're doing with that man?" She ran her ring finger over her right eyebrow, ghosting over the perfectly drawn arches with the tip of an electric-blue press-on nail. "No offense, but you look like Alice getting her first gander at Wonderland."

He rubbed his eyes, the urge to shrink into himself overwhelming. If only the sofa could swallow him whole.

But.

This could be an opportunity. Someone to talk to who might not judge him for his questions or uncertainty.

"No. I—I have no idea whatsoever." Forcing himself to find some tenacity he didn't really feel, he steeled his spine. "I don't even understand how I ended up feeling this way about him."

"Oh, doll, are you telling me you've never been with a man at all?"

He shook his head.

"Are you bi?"

"I don't think so. Honest to God, I didn't think I was anything before we got together. I mean, I tried to want people. Women. Men. It didn't matter. No one did it for me. Not until Robby. Now, here I am, totally crazy about him, terrified about whatever comes next, and even more terrified I might lose him and go back to feeling nothing."

Holy hell, had he really just spilled his guts to a stranger?

Sara looked unfazed. "You're in the right place, baby. And you're not the first person to need an emotional connection with somebody before they can flick your Bic. Hold on."

She rose to her feet with the grace of a prima ballerina and crossed the room, then returned with a few printed sheets in her hand. "Take this home and read it. There is a whole spectrum of sexuality in the wide world. Yours is just one stop on the ride, and it's just as valid as anyone else's."

He glanced down at the article in the printout titled *Asexuality, Attraction, and Romantic Orientation* from the LGBT Center at UNC-Chapel Hill. Several different categories were listed underneath.

"The labels aren't really important, but I think when you read the article, you might see something of yourself in there."

He folded the paper and slipped it into his back pocket. "Thanks."

"I'm glad Robby's found someone like you. Someone to care about him more than they want to fuck him." She batted her false eyelashes. "Pardon my French."

Did she know things about Robby he didn't?

Something about Sara told him she probably knew a lot about everything. "I think you more than made up for it giving me all this homework to look over."

"You ready to go?" Robby called out from the front door.

He tipped an imaginary hat to Sara, and she waved her index finger in farewell. "It was a pleasure, Miss Sara."

"Oh, honey, a pretty face like yours? The pleasure was all mine."

CHAPTER TWENTY

Robby

The Cooper sponsorship got the green light. As Amanda had delivered the news yesterday, Robby had picked her up and spun her around, prompting Kane to start beating his chest and spouting off about crushing the baby. Paul had signed the lease agreement, and now his husband Chris was here at the center, shooting interviews and video for the website they were working on.

The entire project was coming together in just a matter of days. And to think, it had all sprung from his imagination.

Since he'd been here this morning, Chris had interviewed Sara, Vin, and one of the girls Robby didn't know very well yet. Chris wanted to put real faces on the project. Make it relatable, make people care.

Most of the regulars made it a point to be here to support the center, even if not everyone felt comfortable putting their life stories on display.

They sat in groups of three or four on the various sofas, and a few gathered around the big table, laughing and shooting the breeze.

"Has anyone seen Brady?" Vin raised his voice over the low din.

Robby surveyed the room, but he only saw other people doing the same or shaking their heads. Come to think about it, he'd only seen Brady at the center the day they met, and the guy hadn't shared his story. He resolved to track him down. The idea of the young man returning to the back room at Nitro chilled him to the bone.

Chris beckoned him over.

He walked back to Sara's room where Chris had been conducting interviews. "Have you got everything you need?"

Chris lifted a hanging microphone attached to a long pole and braced it on his shoulder. "The only person left to interview is you."

Gaping like a fish, Robby took a step back. "I—I'm sorry, Chris. I can't talk about the things I've shared with the group. Not publicly." The air in the room felt thinner. He couldn't breathe right. "I want to help, but my dark days are not—I can't—"

"Whoa. Slow down." Chris lowered the microphone and set it on the twin bed against the wall. "You do not have to talk about anything you're uncomfortable with."

No. No. *No.*

A sea of faces flashed through his memories. The men at the shelter. Tex. Harry. Dozens of faces and he couldn't remember all their names. Some of their names he never knew at all.

He couldn't even face some of the things he'd done when he looked in the mirror, much less in the lens of a camera. The ground seemed to tilt beneath his feet.

"—just calm down. Breathe." Chris gripped his shoulder, the pressure grounding him as he lowered himself to the bed. "Robby. I wanted to interview you as a mentor and a volunteer, not as…not to ask you to relive your past."

Squeezing his eyes closed, he swallowed against the lump in his throat, then sucked in a wheezing breath through his mouth. Then another. Lights flashed behind his closed lids.

When the world stopped spinning, and the urge to scream finally fled, he pried his eyes open. Black spots danced across his vision before the room came into focus. He almost wished it didn't.

All the young men and women who had been talking and laughing in the main room now crowded in and around the threshold of the bedroom. Their concern, pity, and fear crashed over him.

Then, thankfully, he couldn't see them anymore. Sara knelt in front of him, her face obscuring everyone else from view. She pressed a water bottle into his hand. "Drink."

Robby didn't think; he just obeyed. The cold water made it easier to swallow and helped restore his calm.

Smile. Make everyone feel better.

He got so far as lifting one corner of his mouth before he realized *he didn't have to*. They didn't need him to be sweet. They needed him to be real.

Holding Sara's gaze, he released the attempt at a

smile and nodded once instead. "Thank you."

Standing, she melted back into the crowd.

"I didn't mean to scare you guys, but I guess if anyone could understand getting triggered with something like this, it would be you."

"I don't." A tiny girl, five-foot-nothing in her shiny Doc Martens, shouldered to the front. Curly dyed red hair, the kind from a salon, not a bottle. She wore jeans, a graphic T-shirt, which screamed Hot Topic, and a bohemian rainbow braided bracelet.

Meggie. She was earning service hours here for her high school beta club.

"Of course you don't get it, princess." One of the guys from the back. "You're only here to earn a badge for your Girl Scout troop."

She crossed her arms at the waist. "Screw you," she muttered. "I've got as much right to be here as anyone. Or does the B in LGBT not count anymore? Are you saying bisexuals aren't gay enough for you?"

"No." The young man, a teenager with a shaved head and long blond bangs, stomped forward. "I don't care who you want to French kiss on your mama's sofa. You don't belong here because you don't need this place. You live in Johns Creek and drove here in a shiny new Kia you probably got for your sixteenth birthday."

"I'm sorry. I missed the sign on the door saying exactly which queer people are allowed. News flash, Pete, a happy home life doesn't exclude me from the gay experience. We're not all the same. Or assholes."

"Okay." Robby held up a hand. "Let's take it down a notch. I'm glad you're here, Meggie, and I'm even happier your home life is a good one. Anyone who *wants* to be here is welcome. I think it's just hard not to envy what you have."

He sent a meaningful look toward Pete, who grunted and stepped back.

"For most of the people here, the center is the only safe space they have. At your age, I didn't have one at all. I don't think back on those years very much because...it hurts. And when I thought Chris wanted me to rehash it all, I freaked out." He shrugged.

Meggie released the hold she had on her arms, allowing them to drop, then clasped her hands loosely in front of her. "I know how good I have it. It's the reason I volunteer. It's why I organized the clothing drive at my school. I wanted to give back. It feels good." She shot a sour look in Pete's direction. "Most of the time."

"It feels good for me most of the time too." Leave it to a sixteen-year-old girl to drill this whole experience down to its simplest terms. "I grew up happy. It was a small-town life...a little place called Sherman. And my mom, gosh, she loved us all so much. Thanked God for us every day. I heard her do it. I felt safe and secure and loved."

"Until you came out."

"Heh, well, I didn't come out so much as get outed, kissing in the barn with one of my brother Travis's friends. And my father kicked me out of the house and out of the family without even giving me the chance to pack a bag. Good old Ephraim

233

Jordan, judge, jury, and executioner. But he was just a product of his environment. I thought Sherman was the problem, a tiny town stuck in the 1950s. So I came to the big city. It was different, all right."

He hummed to fill the brief silence. "I fell asleep on a bench outside the library in Sherman once. Woke up, like, an hour later. No one bothered me. I was safe, and it never occurred to me it would be any other way. When I got here, I was so sure I would find this amazing melting pot and people who would understand and accept me, I never stopped to think about the more fundamental ways it would change my life. Change me."

The rest of the room listened in respectful silence. No one so much as shuffled their feet as he talked.

"I wish I could forget it all. But if I can take what my experiences have taught me and use them to keep even one of you from sinking as low as I did, it's worth it to remember."

From the corner of his eye, he caught sight of Chris moving his mic, leaning the long stick against the wall. "You were perfect, man. I've got everything I need."

"Were you—filming me?" He hadn't thought of the video at all once he started talking to Meggie.

"Mmm hmm. You can watch it back if you want. I won't use anything you don't feel right sharing, but the stuff you were saying right there…how your life called you to this place to help other people…powerful stuff."

He didn't need to think it over. "Use it. If you think it will help with the outreach, use it all." As he stood, he felt at least a foot taller.

The crowd parted as he left the room, head held high. Maybe he made a difference for someone with the stories he shared. But the best thing that came from all this: he'd faced some of demons and came through to the other side.

The past couldn't hurt him anymore. Only an amazing future stretched in front of him. Real friends, a chosen family, and an incredible man who just might give his hopeful heart a home.

He texted Matt to meet him at the apartment after his shift at the bar, and by the time Robby had showered and changed, the doorbell rang.

The man on the other side of the threshold took his breath away. A pair of black slacks hugged Matt's lower half in all the right places, and a red, soft cotton button-down contrasted beautifully with his rich, dark skin. He held a bouquet of flowers in his hand.

Robby tugged him inside, heart beating a riot in his chest. This gorgeous, delicious man was *his*. And maybe he couldn't keep him forever—no one stayed forever—but he would keep him as long as the good Lord let him.

"What are you grinning at?" Matt gave him the side eye. "I'm not sure I've ever seen that look on your face before."

"This face?" He spun his finger in a small circle around his mouth. "*This* face says I am looking at the *finest* man I've ever contemplated kissing."

Matt brushed the flowers over his cheek. "If you're still thinking about it, I must be doing this wrong."

An invitation if Robby ever heard one. He palmed both sides of Matt's face and drew him forward until their mouths met.

The flowers fell to the floor.

Somehow, they skipped all the niceties, the soft, closed-mouth kisses, the tentative touch of tongues. No, this kiss shot from one to one hundred in less time than it took Matt to drop the bouquet. Their bodies locked together at the mouth in a wet, hot exploration, which shot Robby's body temperature through the roof. And he welcomed the burn.

Sliding his hands down to grip Matt's arms, he stepped backward, pulling them toward his bedroom. They didn't break the kiss. It went on and on, growing bolder and more aggressive with each stroke.

"Clothes off." He could barely grit out the words. His higher functions threatened to abandon him entirely as the back of his knees came in contact with the bed, and he yanked open Matt's shirt before it was completely untucked from his pants. A half dozen buttons scattered across the floor.

Matt sucked in a breath, and it shuddered back out as Robby latched his mouth to one of his nipples. His fingers lightly pinched at the other, and both stiffened beneath the attention. With his other hand, he cupped the erection tenting Matt's pants, and a groan rumbled from the perfect, muscled chest in front of him.

"Tell me." He squeezed at the thick length in his hand. "Tell me you want this."

"Yes." Matt panted. "Give me everything. Show

me how."

With nimble fingers, Robby unfastened Matt's pants and freed his cock from the confines of his black boxer-briefs. Lord above, the man's body was perfect.

"Do you trust me?" Robby whispered, his grip firm and sure.

Matt wrapped his own hand around Robby's, both of them now circling Matt's erection. "Body and soul."

Oh yeah. Matt was in for the ride of his life.

CHAPTER TWENTY-ONE

Matt

"Finish stripping down and lay on the bed." The lust in Robby's eyes hit Matt like a drug.

He almost swayed on his feet. "Let me see you first." He reached to untuck Robby's shirt, but before he could grip the fabric, his quarry had moved out of reach.

Something passed over Robby's face he couldn't quite put his finger on. It only lasted a moment before Robby slipped further away to close the door and block out the living room light. It left the bedroom drenched in grey shadows.

"You can look another night," Robby rumbled. "Tonight is all about feeling."

"But I—"

Robby's silhouette surged closer. "You said you trusted me." Movement, then the gentle rustle of clothes falling to the floor.

Warm skin caressed his own as he felt Robby's bare chest rub against him for the first time. A delicate brush of fingers played across his cheek, followed by the ghost of a kiss. "Get on the bed, love." The gritty urgency in Robby's voice gave way to something gentle and coaxing. "We'll start with a massage and go from there."

He didn't argue. Robby clearly knew what he was doing in the bedroom; where he led, Matt would follow.

Besides, a massage would put Robby's hands all over his body. Matt crawled on the bed and settled on his stomach. The rasp of a zipper and some rustling in the nightstand filled the long thirty seconds before Robby joined him.

The weight of the other man's body rested on his back. "I'll stop anytime you want." Robby's hot breath in his ear broke out his skin in goose bumps.

Then, the press against him vanished, taking the heat of another body along with it. But a heartbeat later, warm liquid drizzled over his back and strong, sure fingers began kneading his skin.

Robby focused first on the expanse between his shoulder blades, his thumbs rubbing the slick oil into the spaces on either side of his spine. "Don't think. Just feel." For a time, one thumb would circle harder, then the other would take the lead.

He didn't think anything could feel better, until Robby put down the heels of his hands. They made brief circles over the area where he'd concentrated first, before sliding down along the columns of his back. Up and down, the glorious pressure moved, the muscles relaxing further with each pass.

Every so often, Robby would drizzle more of the oil onto his skin, the wetness dripping a little lower each time to smooth his path. He attended Matt's lower back for a while, mostly with the flats of his hands, before sweeping down to the globes of his ass.

Even the muscles there must've carried some tension because as Robby's capable fingers smoothed and slathered over, they loosened beneath his touch.

He was boneless by the time the oil dribbled into the valley at the center. A little anxiety spiked as Robby's thumbs teased the seam between his cheeks for the first time, but just as quickly, his hands moved away. Then slid back. It felt...good.

Without even thinking, he widened the spread of his legs to give better access. Robby rewarded him with another swipe of his thumbs. Then, more oil. Then, all his attention trained on one spot.

He wasn't sure what he'd expected, but it wasn't the slow, deliberate exploration of Robby's questing fingers. At first, they just rubbed over his asshole. Slipping, sliding.

What would it feel like to have something inside him? The question that had made him so anxious before only titillated him now. He lifted his backside, just a little, and the tip of Robby's finger breached his hole.

Why wasn't he pushing in deeper?

He lifted his ass more, but Robby slapped his rear. "Stop trying to top from the bottom."

He relaxed back into the mattress, and more oil slipped between his cheeks. Robby's middle finger pushed a little bit deeper, then retreated. Pushed deeper again, repeating the motion over and over until his finger was completely seated.

God, he wanted to move. He'd been worried about this? Hell, if people knew it felt this good, no one would ever leave home.

Robby fingered him in earnest for a minute, maybe two, before withdrawing entirely. "I'm adding another finger," he murmured. "You think you can take it?"

"Yes. Yes. Yes."

Robby chuckled and gave him what he craved.

This time, he felt the stretch, but his lover advanced as carefully as before. He moaned softly as the two fingers pumped inside of him and eventually moved apart, widening his hole even more.

"Almost there, baby." Robby's fingers pulled out, and a blunt pressure pushed against him. "It's a toy. I bought it special for tonight." He swept the slick rubber over his opening. "I'm gonna fuck you with it."

The lusty rasp was back in Robby's voice, and it pushed aside any reservations. "Do it."

The stretch he'd felt before had been child's play. Still, Robby moved the rubber toy with infinite slowness past the ring of his muscles. No pain, but a slightly uncomfortable fullness.

"Lift your ass now for me, baby. Face down, on your knees."

The new position changed the feeling entirely. More oil dripped down as Robby kept his promise, fucking him with the dildo. It hit something inside of him and made him shudder.

But in a good way.

"You like it?"

He could only whimper.

"Take your dick in your hand."

Oh Christ. Robby's slick fingers joined his, slathering the oil over his cock. The dildo's torturous, exquisite slide continued from behind as more pleasure assailed him from in front.

"You could come this way," Robby crooned.

Soon. Matt groaned.

"Or you could come with my cock inside you."

Could it feel any better than this?

He imagined the slap of flesh—the way his body would rock, filled to bursting—Robby thrusting in mindless pleasure.

"Yes," he moaned.

"Yes, what?" Robby kept the movement of the toy agonizingly slow. "Say the words."

"I want you inside of me." No shame. No embarrassment. No doubt.

Robby licked the shell of his ear. "You just keep working your needy dick, love. Soon, you won't know where you end and I begin."

Matt heard a rip of foil before Robby pulled the toy away, and while he thought the dildo could prepare him for the sensation of another man inside him, it was a pale imitation. The fullness, the stretch finally reached the level of pain, and he clenched against the invasion.

Robby stopped inching forward but didn't pull out. "Jerk it. Just focus everything on your dick…on how good it feels. Imagine my mouth on it. I loved the taste of you, baby. It's like your come was made for my tongue."

With every dirty word and thought, Matt's attention zeroed in on the slide of his hand.

More oil. Movement behind him. Then Robby was fully seated in Matt's body. His lover reached around and circled his length. Played him like a violin. Then pumped his hips.

"Fuck," he groaned. He couldn't tell if it felt good or not.

Robby pulled away and flopped onto his back beside Matt. "Climb on top of me."

His brain couldn't follow the words. Too many sensations bombarding him at once. "Huh?"

"You'll have more control this way." Robby tugged his arm, and he settled on top as commanded.

Robby reached behind him, slathered more oil on his dick, and pointed it at Matt's opening. "Slide down slowly."

He didn't think…he just moved. Robby held completely still, except for the hand gliding over his shaft. And it was so much better. In this position, the fullness didn't hurt.

He swiveled his hips, and the feeling rocked him to the core.

"Yes, baby. Take what you want."

And he did. Leaning forward, he blanketed Robby's body with his own, his slick dick sandwiched between his stomach and Robby's. Twin points of pleasure sent his body into overdrive, his frenzied movements stimulating his own cock while swallowing Robby's inside him.

He burrowed his face into Robby's neck, breathing in the smell that was uniquely his. "I'm gonna—"

Robby clutched his thighs, slamming himself upward. Hitting the perfect spot. Once. Twice.

He shouted as he came, and in just seconds, Robby's body went rigid beneath him, signaling his own orgasm. Collapsing into a heap, he lay on top of the other man until he realized he was probably crushing him. He only managed to slide a few inches to the right to curl up next to his lover's sweat-soaked skin.

Robby kissed the top of his head, and within moments, Matt fell into the oblivion of well-earned sleep.

***

Robby

As Matt's spent body curled against him, Robby granted himself five minutes to bask in the joy of the moment before sliding out of the bed. He yanked off the condom, tied the end, and dropped it into the garbage can just inside the bathroom.

He waited until he closed the door before he turned on the light. His skin was sticky and his body sore in all the right places. It had been years since the last time he'd flexed some of those muscles. Though if he was lucky, he'd be using them again very soon.

Flipping on the spray, he stepped into the shower, hopping back when he realized the water wasn't heated yet. But the warm up happened fast, and soon, the hot stream enveloped him.

As he hung his head forward, water sluiced over his short hair, down his neck, and over his chest. He grabbed the soap, turning it over in his hands, and built a lather he spread over his skin. Thankfully, the massage oil he used was water-soluble, so it washed away without too much scrubbing.

Matt would need to shower too.

His heart thumped in his chest as he thought about the trust and responsiveness his partner had shown him tonight. Every order obeyed, every request between them, honored.

Except one.

He sighed. Sooner or later he'd have to face that demon, but not tonight. Matt would have too many questions, and the answers would lead nowhere good.

It was bad enough he knew about the addiction. It would only be worse when he knew the reasons for it.

Of course, he'd have to share the details of his history with Matt at some point. The broad strokes he'd offered had seemed to be enough, but Matt deserved to know everything. The only problem...no one who really knew him ever wanted him for long. And there was no one who knew *all* of his secrets. He should've considered this before now, but he'd really never let himself believe they could be together this way.

Fantasies were one thing. In fantasies, he never had to worry about getting triggered by fingers in his hair or who knew what else he had lurking beneath the veil of his subconscious. In fantasies, he never had to worry about what he looked like naked when the lights were on or whether he'd have the nerve to answer hard questions with the truth if Matt ever thought to ask them.

Tonight, he kept things as close to the perfection of his dreams as he could. And hands down, it had been the best sexual experience of his life. Not because Matt let him top; he'd topped before. It was no guarantee of control. To be sure, his partner had all of the control tonight. One word from him and everything would've stopped or changed course to please him.

No, he loved the experience because Matt let him worship his body. And Robby did it because he wanted to. It wasn't a transaction or exchange. He needed absolutely nothing in return.

Oh, but he *wanted* plenty. He wanted more kisses. More bouquets of flowers. More opportunities to see the desire and easy affection in Matt's eyes when he looked at him.

He wanted to dance in the man's arms. Slow dance, not the bump and grind stuff he did at Nitro.

He wanted to snuggle together on the sofa and watch scary movies on Netflix. Unwrap presents together on Christmas morning. Hold hands in the park at sunset.

The longing for it all overwhelmed him.

But for those things to happen, he had to give Matt a chance to make an informed choice. As amazing as this night was, he'd taken a shortcut to get here. Until he bared his secrets, the best he could get would be for Matt to fall in love with a lie.

He climbed out of the shower, dried off, and crept back into the bedroom to slip on some cut-off sweatpants and a white long-john shirt.

Matt mumbled something in his sleep, and he caught himself staring at the lithe strength in his torso and the dark liquid silk of his skin.

No way around it. He'd have to tell Matt the truth for the wishes of his heart to ever be a reality.

But he wouldn't spoil tonight.

Climbing back in the bed, he kissed Matt's forehead, breathing in the lingering smell of sex and massage oil.

Maybe tomorrow.

Sometime soon. What could waiting a few more days hurt?

CHAPTER TWENTY-TWO

Matt

Matt woke up sticky, crusty, sore, and more than a little shocked to find himself stark naked next to another man. Of course, Robby hadn't exactly needed to twist his arm to get him here. A couple of kisses and he was ready to roll over and beg for every drop of the guy's thorough, careful attention.

He chanced a glance at his bed partner, who had changed into his pajamas and now snored lightly, curled around a pillow on his side. He couldn't see Robby's entire face, but his clear, pale skin damn near glowed pink at his cheeks, and his tousled hair paired with his soft, relaxed expression made him look like a freaking angel.

Thanks to the sun's rays, seeping in through the blinds, he could see the bedroom for the first time. A small space, not much bigger than the double bed where they'd slept, with a single tall dresser made out of particle board. A framed photo graced the top, featuring a smiling Robby flanked by Brick and Kane, both grim-faced and possibly poised to kick someone's ass.

Such an unlikely trio. But somehow, they fit. Just like he and Robby fit.

Biting back a groan, he levered himself off the bed. Thankfully, he didn't disturb Robby's sleep.

He trudged to the bathroom and made quick work of cleaning himself in the shower. It sucked a little he'd missed his chance to do this with Robby, but they'd have other opportunities, right? And he couldn't begrudge the man the chance to clean off all this crap before it dried. Thank God, he kept his body mostly hair free or it would be exponentially worse.

Bathing complete, he toweled off, sparing a glance at himself in the mirror. Stubble coated his jaw, but there was no help for it. A shave would have to wait until after he finished up at the bar. As it was, he was going to have to double time it to run home and grab a clean shirt before his shift.

His red button-down may not have raised any eyebrows if it was still in its original condition. Minus buttons? A whole different story.

Creeping back into the bedroom, he swiped his discarded clothes from the floor, then tugged them on. He kneeled beside the bed and shook Robby's shoulder gently. "Rob."

Nothing.

He tried again. "Babe. I've got to go to work."

Robby cracked one eye open. "Hmm?"

"I've got to—" His breath left his body in a rush

as Robby yanked him down to the bed into a bear hug.

"Stay."

If he didn't need his second job so much, he'd stay in a second. Snuggled up to Robby, his lower half flush against the other man's thigh, at least one part of his anatomy would have happily sold his soul for the chance. His other head still made the decisions, though. At least for now. "You could tempt a saint to sin."

He kissed Robby's scruffy cheek. "God knows, you tempt me, but you'll have to settle for knowing I'll be thinking about you all day. I'm opening the bar this morning; I can't flake out." Even if by some miracle, he and Patty could work out custody without the lawyers, he needed the security the money would bring.

"Fine." Robby released him, dropping his arms dramatically to the bed. "I'll just have to console myself with Double Points Sunday playing *Battlefield*."

He reared back. "Without me?"

Robby shrugged. "I do what I have to do to keep the loneliness at bay." Grinning, he nudged Matt away. "Now, you'd better get out of here before my baser nature takes over, and I decide to coax you to stay with the best blowjob of your life."

As far as threats went, Robby was clearly a master. Hopping off the bed, he skittered backward to the door, then leaned against the frame. "Thank you—for last night. I never knew it could be so…"

"Amazing? For me too." Robby sat up. "There's a lot we need to talk about. If things are going to be serious between us."

"Things are already serious between us, Rob. At least for me." His secondary alarm sounded on his phone, warning him his shift was less than an hour away. "I'm working a double. I've got to go. See you tomorrow?"

"I can't wait."

***

A busy day at Closing Time kept him from thinking too deeply on the night he'd spent at Robby's, but the resulting unfamiliar physical sensations kept it on the periphery of his awareness. As a result, by the time he got home at the end of the night and tumbled into bed, his face hurt from smiling so damn much.

His grin finally retreated when he faced the Q-Center Monday morning. It wasn't the place. Actually, he was excited to help make Robby's vision a reality there.

He didn't worry about facing Robby either. In fact, he couldn't wait to wrap his arms around the man and kiss him senseless. Only, he couldn't really give into the temptation—not at work. Could he?

Did Robby tell the other guys they were, what, dating? *Were* they dating? They'd never talked about labels for it. It sure felt like they were dating.

Part of him wanted to grab a megaphone and tell the whole damn world that Robby Jordan was spoken for and completely off the market. The other part? Scared shitless.

For multiple reasons.

Obviously, his high school memories had something to do with it. The other guys had hit him hard before Patty stepped in, calling him queer and names far worse. Some had threatened him straight out, saying they were going to kick his ass or something equally lacking in creativity.

He didn't worry about Brick or Kane thinking less of him for being gay—which, hey, guess those high school pricks were right after all, at least in a way—but he wasn't quite so sure about the other guys on the crew. Brick and Kane never seemed to judge Robby, but he had no idea how Will, Cyrus, or Evan would react.

Kane and Brick presented a different problem entirely. Those men treated Robby like family. What if they thought he wasn't good enough for their friend? What if they warned Robby away?

Maybe Robby would have his own reasons for keeping things low-key right now. *You know what they say about assuming.* He didn't want to make an ass of himself or anyone else...and Robby wasn't always an open book.

Okay. So, a hello kiss was off the table. Should he just nod? Pat Robby on the shoulder? Text ahead?

"Yo, Matt. You waiting for the seasons to change, brother?" Kane elbowed him lightly on the arm. "Get your ass in gear. We've got a lot of shit to do and not a lot of time before we need to get back to the Sandpiper Development. Berringer is cool with our community service, but we can't get behind on his houses."

Kane linked their arms at the elbow and dragged

him through the door of the newly leased portion of the property. The rest of the team was already inside. Cy and Evan pulled up the carpet while Brick and Will marked the walls in the places where they planned to add sheetrock.

Robby and Xander had their heads together, looking at some papers on a clipboard. Before he had a chance to plan his move, his lover looked up and flashed a sultry, secret smile, scorching him to the bottoms of his feet. And no one noticed.

Bashful as a blushing-freaking-bride, he smiled back, and nearly tripped over his own feet when Kane stepped in front of him.

"Where do you want us, Xan?"

The foreman glanced up at Kane's question, then gestured back to the front door. "You and Matt can start hauling in the posts from the back of my truck."

Well, then, no need to sweat their reunion at all.

The day moved by quickly as they worked efficiently, putting up the wood bones of the bedrooms. Basic pipes already ran to a toilet and sink in the back, but they had to call in plumbers to set up the line for the shower and add a tankless hot water heater. The setup wasn't fancy; the narrow stall would only allow for one person to turn around in and get clean, but Robby swore it would be a godsend to someone. Or several someones.

By quitting time, his back and shoulders ached, and he damn-near swayed on his feet. The energy generated from his sub sandwich at lunch had abandoned him hours ago.

Brick and Kane waved goodbye as they hit the

exit together. Cy and Evan followed two steps behind. Other than Robby and himself, only Xander and Will remained, and they chatted over plans in the far corner of the room.

"Wanna grab dinner with me?" At least the hard work had effectively snuffed out any residual nervousness. Matt leaned against the wall, fighting gravity.

"You sure you're up for it?" Robby raised one eyebrow in a move Matt was sure came from Brick.

"I can't bear the thought of a TV dinner tonight, and I'm too tired to cook. Señor Patrón is right down the street. We can grab some tacos or something. Their bar service is pretty quick." His mouth started watering as he thought about the seafood enchiladas.

"Sure. Go grab us a couple of stools, and I'll meet you there after I wrap up with Xander." Almost every day, Robby managed to be the first person in and the last person off the job. The guy was as sure as the sun, basically the antithesis of Patty this past year.

A short walk later, the familiar arched ceiling greeted him. He didn't get to eat out too often, but he couldn't always fight his soft spot for Mexican food. When he allowed himself a treat with his money, it either went to a used PlayStation game—or here.

Snagging a padded wooden chair at the bar, he settled in and placed his keys on the seat beside him for Robby. He ordered two glasses of water from the bartender and zoned off, staring at the rays of a rising sun painted on the far wall.

He nearly jumped out when Robby whispered in his ear. "This seat taken?"

Robby's smile took his breath away. Matt transferred his keys into his pocket and gestured for Robby to sit. "I'm starving. Do you know what you want?"

Robby opted for queso quesadillas while he got the enchiladas he'd been craving. They kept it light as they waited for their meals, chatting mostly about the build at the center and whether guacamole counted as delicious or disgusting.

Delicious, obviously.

When the food did come, talking stopped altogether for a few minutes, and the calories fortified him enough to venture out of neutral territory. "Saturday night was…amazing."

Robby blushed in the freaking adorable way he always did. "For me too." He said it looking at his dinner, but it still counted as a win.

"I, um, wanted to ask you some questions, and I feel…" He swallowed. "I feel kind of awkward, but—"

Robby's gaze shot up and his shoulders tensed like he was preparing to run a gauntlet. "Ask."

Well, shit. He hesitated. The need to avoid the strained, rigid look Robby now wore was the reason why he kept so many questions to himself.

"Ask."

"What are we to each other?"

Robby tilted his head to the side and set his fork on his napkin. At least he no longer looked ready to take a punch.

"It's stupid—and I'm not trying to put you on

the spot—but I've never really been with anybody. I mean, I've never been in a relationship with anybody before, you know, if we're in a relationship right now."

Oh God. He might be sick.

Robby blinked. "Are you asking me if I'm your boyfriend?"

Stomach now churning in earnest, Matt covered his mouth with his hand as he nodded.

"Hey. Just breathe." Robby put a hand on his back and rubbed in slow circles. "I would love to be your boyfriend. In fact, I can't think of a single thing I would love more. But only if it's what you want too. I can't tell if you're freaking out because you want to be a couple or because you don't."

Matt closed his eyes and silently counted to ten, willing his anxiety to step down a notch. It helped a little. "I do," he whispered. Unsure what he'd see in Robby's expression, he chanced a look at his face.

Praise be. A smile. It calmed him better than trying to wrestle his fears under control. "When I got to the center this morning, I realized I didn't even know how to say hello. Obviously, I know how to say hello, but everything feels different now, you know?"

Robby's hand stilled but didn't leave his back. "Different good or different bad?"

"Different good." He turned to face Robby fully, their knees bumping together between the chairs. "I am all-in, Rob. If you're in this too, you can stamp your name on my forehead if you want."

"And ruin your gorgeous face? Not in a million years." Robby's right hand, the one closest to the bar, squeezed his thigh. "When you say you didn't know how to say hello…how did you want to say hello?"

He laughed a little. "Honestly, I wanted to touch you. Not like in some grand, passionate…whatever. Well, maybe a little, but not just a wave or a nod. But I didn't know if you wanted the same thing or even whether you wanted your friends to know about us. Or if we're supposed to be different at work." None of this was coming out right.

"Brick and Kane will flip their lids when we tell them." Robby chuckled.

Why was it funny? "It's not funny," Matt groused. "They're your best friends. I thought they liked me, at least a little."

"They do like you." The megawatt grin Robby sported should've been illegal. "They're gonna flip because they've known about my inappropriate, almost stalker-level crush on you for months now."

Matt gaped.

"They tried to let me down easy. Gave me tons of pep-talks. Ha!" He slapped the bar beside his empty plate. "I should just plant a fat kiss on you right in front of Kane to watch him swallow his own tongue."

Smiling despite himself, Matt sipped his water. "I'm not sure if I'm ready to go full-tilt PDA. Some things should stay private, I think."

Robby fluttered his hand in the air. "I'm just playing about the kiss. They're going to be happy for us, though. I promise. And you can tell me hello any way you want. I still can't get over the fact you *want* it to be something special. You

257

wanting…me…at all blows my mind."

"Stop it right now. You're the best person I know."

"Hardly."

Gripping Robby's hand, he interlocked their fingers. "You are smart and kind and giving and patient. Anyone would be lucky to have you in their life. I'm lucky, and I need you to hear it and believe it. Know you deserve special hellos and flowers at the front door and probably a hundred other good things I haven't even thought of yet."

"I didn't thank you—for the flowers. No one's ever—It was the first time I've ever gotten flowers."

"The first time I've ever given them." He kissed the back of Robby's hand joined with his own. "Also, the first time I've ever been in love with someone. A bunch of firsts with you, Rob."

Robby's fingers tightened around him, but he didn't say anything; he only nodded to himself for a while, like everything was sinking in. Matt wanted to stuff the words back into his mouth.

Before he could break the tension with some awkward backtracking, Robby spoke. "I like that. Being a bunch of firsts for you. I'm not sure I have many firsts left for me. I've, uh." He let out a breath. "I've done a lot…of stuff. But it's never felt like it did with you. Not with anyone else."

"Good." Not as good as an *I love you too*, but Matt would take it.

"I want to meet your son."

"Jimmy?" Matt probably should've thought about it before. If this was going to be the kind of relationship he thought it would, he couldn't keep one part of his life separate from the other.

"Yeah. I know he's the most important thing in your life. I respect the fact you're a package deal, and I want to get to know him." Robby shrank back a little. "Unless you don't want me to."

"No. I do. I have to talk to Patty, though." Matt tilted his head back and stared at the ceiling. "Our conversation should be interesting." Who knew how she would react? Would it make her ditch the offer to talk about custody? God, he hoped not.

"Okay."

Matt released Robby's hand long enough to put two twenties on the table. "C'mon. I'll walk you to your car. Since I didn't give you a special hello, I need to make sure you get a special goodbye."

CHAPTER TWENTY-THREE

Matt

As much as Matt looked forward to giving Robby an exceptional greeting the next morning, he settled for a soft smile. Like he'd said before, public displays weren't high on his to-do list. Besides, he and Robby had dinner plans at Brick's Thursday night. Well, Robby had plans. Hopefully, no one would mind him crashing the party.

Tuesday night, he went to his computer class, then went home and finished his final project. He'd need to decide soon if he could spare the money for a summer session.

But it was a question for another day. Tonight, while Robby went to the Q-Center, he'd tackle a different problem: Patty.

He'd hoped to talk at her apartment, but when he called, she told him she was working. So, he'd kill two birds with one stone, checking out the tattoo parlor she loved so much and break it to her about Robby at the same time. No telling if she'd be livid or heartbroken or maybe even a little happy for him. Only one way to find out.

Fantasy Ink took up one space in a glass-fronted strip mall, not too far from Closing Time. A neon sign sporting the name of the place hung next to the door, surrounded by colorful hand-drawn dragons, eagles, and snakes, amid a lush, verdant landscape, and a jewel blue painted sky.

The door brushed over an old-fashioned bell, which tinkled as he walked in. Not one person looked his way. A young white couple sat with their heads together, flipping through a book of designs. A Hispanic man with muscular arms, sleeved in tattoos, fiddled with a needle gun over the shoulder of a slender woman with skin the color of milky tea. Patty took notes on a small pad, a cordless phone crammed between her ear and her shoulder.

He walked through the modest, open lobby type area, needing less than a dozen steps to reach the small desk and computer area where Patty stood.

"Yes. I've got all your information. Like I said, Steve is pretty booked up, and the kind of work you're looking for is going to take a while. He's going to have to call you back to set something up." She set the notepad next to the computer. "Yes, sir. Y—yes. Okay. Bye."

Hanging up the phone on the wall mount, she groused under her breath before she looked up and caught Matt's eye. "Never expected to see you here. You must really want to talk."

She motioned him to follow her toward the tattoo

area, where only one of three stations had a customer. "Steve, I need to take five."

Her boss grunted and kept working.

Patty motioned for him to sit on the one of the chairs, and she pulled up a stool in front of him. "So, where's the fire? Is this about Jimmy?"

Straight to the point as always. Patty looked good tonight, her hair pulled back in a tight bun and just a hint of make-up coloring her cheeks. She also looked impatient, keeping only one eye on him as she checked her phone and swiped her thumb over the screen.

"Sort of." He took a deep breath. "I'm seeing someone."

She dropped the phone, and it bounced once on the emerald green tile. Thank goodness she had a case on it, or it would've been a goner. "Seeing? As in, dating?"

He couldn't read her voice. "Yes. I am dating someone. A guy I work with. It's serious."

Patty retrieved her phone from the floor, then turned it over slowly in her hands. "What does this have to do with me?" Her voice was guarded…and cold.

"You're always going to be part of my life. Even if we can't make it being friends again, we'll always be Jimmy's parents." He wiped his sweaty palms together. "Robby is going to be a part of my life too. I want him to meet my son."

"Our son," she snapped.

No. This could not go downhill, not so quickly. "Of course, our son. It's why I'm here. I want your blessing to introduce them."

Her left thumb tapped against her leg as she blinked her eyes rapidly. "What's so special about this guy? Robby." She seemed to catch her nervous hand movement and gripped her leg instead. "I've known you, what, eight years? You never so much as looked at anyone. But with this guy, it's serious? What does the word even mean for you?"

"It means I'd like to keep him around long-term." The red vinyl chair creaked as he tried to get more comfortable. Though to be fair, his discomfort had little to do with the furniture. "As for what's special about him?" He shrugged. "Everything."

She produced a fingernail file, seemingly out of nowhere, and suddenly grew very focused on shaping her stubby nails. "He's in construction? A roughneck, then. You know, they say the musclebound guys all have little dicks, but maybe you don't want to pack too much meat up your ass."

With her overloud declaration, every person in the room swiveled their heads to stare in their direction. Everyone, including Patty's boss, who growled low in his throat. "You want to take it outside, guys?"

"Sorry, Steve. We'll keep it down." Patty clenched the file tightly in her hand before stuffing it into her back pocket. "I shouldn't have said that. It was a knee-jerk reaction."

Matt leaned toward her. "He's not part of the crew. He's the foreman's assistant. I get this is hard for you, but you don't need to take it out on him. He's a really nice guy. Tries to help other people. Volunteers. The kind of guy I hope you can find. Someone I'd be proud to introduce to our son."

She folded her arms across her chest. "He doesn't meet Jimmy until he meets me first."

For Pete's sake. Who knew what she would pull if she met Robby face-to-face?

"I'm his mama. As much as you'd like it to be otherwise. You want Jimmy around your boyfriend—you want to keep this whole custody thing out of court—you'll do what I ask."

Steve approached them, his customer presumably gone. "This the famous Matt I've heard so much about?"

"In the flesh." He stuck out his hand, fully prepared for a brush off, but Steve took it in a firm grip and shook.

"My mom spoke highly of you. You and Patty both were always nice to her. It was a time in my life I'm not very proud of, so I appreciate you guys were around when I wasn't very much." Steve shot a reproachful look at Patty. "You need to stop giving him shit about the guy he's dating."

Patty huffed. "I have a right to know the people he is bringing around our child."

"Is it about his partner being a stranger or about it being another man? Because you know I don't tolerate bigoted bullshit in my shop, no matter what kind of history you have with my mother."

"You know I don't have a problem with you being gay, Steve."

Matt laughed darkly. "You just have a problem with *me* being gay. Hell, woman, you've said it yourself for long enough. Or were you just trying to get under my skin?"

"It's hard, okay? To think about you with

264

anyone. I said I'd meet him, though, and I won't be an asshole. All right?"

"All right." He climbed out of the chair and headed for the door. The couple returned their attention to the design book so quickly, he almost missed their shameless eavesdropping on the conversation. Almost.

"Hey, Matty."

He turned and looked over his shoulder.

"I want you to be happy."

Despite the way she lashed out at first, he let himself believe her. Even a gamer-geek, single dad with two jobs and a terrible track record with love deserved a shot at a happy ending. Right?

***

Robby

Robby squeezed Matt's hand, hoping to calm the nervous clenching and unclenching of his fingers as they stood on Brick's front porch, waiting for someone to answer the bell. "Take a deep breath, hon. We're not entering enemy territory. These are our friends."

"They're your friends," Matt murmured. "They barely even know me."

True, but Robby hoped to change that, starting tonight.

Liv opened the door before he could continue his pep talk. She flashed a welcoming smile, then lifted her brow at their entwined hands. "I didn't know you'd be joining us, Matt, but I'm glad you're here.

Please come in. We have plenty of burgers."

Matt returned his squeeze, then let go to follow her into the house.

Brick came into the kitchen from the back door on the other side of the room, a plate full of steaming burgers on a big plate. Kane stood over the counter, salting a platter of French fries. Amanda laid out a tray filled with lettuce, tomato, and onion.

"I hope it's okay I brought a date."

Everyone froze in place, except to whip their heads in his direction in a move so synchronized, it looked rehearsed.

Kane snapped out of it first, chuckling as he positioned the fries next to the hamburger fixings. "You may want to watch how you phrase things, brother. You're gonna give people the wrong idea."

"Or the right one," Matt murmured.

And they froze again.

Robby snapped his fingers in the air, three times in quick succession. "Guys. Hey. Wake up. I'm trying to tell you I've got a boyfriend. The customary thing to do would be to congratulate me."

"Holy fucking shit!" Kane whooped.

"Not exactly what I was going for, but I'll take it." Robby laughed as Kane gripped his right shoulder and shook it.

"I'll be damned," Brick murmured. "Congratulations. To both of you."

Liv pulled an extra plate from the cabinet and quickly added a place setting to the sixth seat at the table. "I, for one, think it's long overdue. I saw the way you both looked at each other the night we went to Moe's." She glanced at the three incredulous faces around her. "What? Are you guys blind? Matt was looking at Robby like he was a prime rib."

Matt made a choking sound, and the rest of the table relaxed into laughter as they filled their plates.

"How are you feeling, Amanda?" Matt changed the subject. "You're in your, what, fifth month now?"

"Almost, yeah. I'm doing great, actually. I've finally got some energy again."

Matt smeared some mayo on his bun. "For sure. I remember, in Patty's first trimester, she said it felt like Jimmy was sucking all the life out of her like a high-powered hose. Plus, she had terrible morning sickness. I think around her twentieth week, she got her second wind."

Though Matt seemed oblivious, Robby noticed the awkward silence following the reminder Matt had a Baby Mama somewhere out there in the world. Kane opened his mouth and closed it, then did it again, his better angels apparently stopping him from whatever he wanted to say.

"Go ahead and ask." Better to get it all out on the table.

Matt looked up from assembling his hamburger, eyebrows furrowed.

But Kane knew exactly what he meant. "What's the deal with her? You said Patty's her name? I've got to say, this seems like a change of pace for you, going from the whole nuclear family thing to getting freaky-deaky with Robby here."

Kane's wince and flinch away from his wife made it clear something happened under the table. "Or not, dude. It's cool."

Amanda cleared her throat. "Forgive my husband. You don't have to respond to his interrogation."

"Actually," Brick put both his hands down flat on either side of his plate, "I'd like it if you would." He scooted his chair back and stood, his big frame towering over everyone. "Kane's manners may be for shit, but he's not wrong, and maybe it makes me an asshole too. So be it. Robby is family, and we look out for our own."

Aw crap. What was Robby supposed to do with that?

The only way to meet it was head-on. He held out a hand, holding off Matt's reply, then stood to face his best friend. "I don't need you to look out for me. Not this time."

Brick opened his mouth, but this was too important to let him interrupt.

Robby hardened his voice. "I love you. We're family, and it means everything you want to slay dragons for me. But I don't need protection from this. Even if you don't trust Matt, you have to trust me and accept my choice. Respect *me* enough to show *him* some respect."

His friend silently returned to his seat.

"Damn, Robby." Kane whistled. "When did you grow such a big set of balls, brother?"

"If you want a look at my balls, *brother*, all you have to do is ask." He cocked his head and lifted his chin in challenge.

It was Amanda of all people who broke the tension with a bark of laughter, and her mirth spread like wildfire. In a matter of seconds, everyone at the table was laughing.

Everyone but Matt. When Kane coughed out his last chortle, he spoke up. "I get it. You guys don't know me very well. To be real, sometimes, I'm not sure I know myself. I do know I'm not looking to hurt Robby. I'm in this one hundred percent."

Matt looked at Kane, then Brick. "I'm not with Jimmy's mom. I never have been. We were friends who gave it a one-time shot at something more. It didn't work out, but it gave me my son, so I am never going to regret it. Patty may always be in my life, but she isn't my future. Robby is." He sat up ramrod straight. "I'd love your blessing, but we're going to be together whether you give it or not."

Both big men gaped, but Brick recovered first. "Does he make you happy, Robby?"

Happy? His heart could burst right now after Matt's little speech. "Yeah. He does." And he planned to keep him as long as he possibly could.

"Good enough for me. Now somebody better start eating these hamburgers before they get cold. No way I'm letting all this fucking meat go to waste."

Kane waited until Robby took a bite and started chewing before he leaned forward. "Just for the record, I don't want to see your balls, bro. I'm sure they're nice and all, but my own nuts are more than enough to behold every day."

His wife nudged him with her shoulder. "You just keep telling yourself that, baby."

And this time when the laughter started, everyone joined in.

CHAPTER TWENTY-FOUR

Robby

Tonight would be the night.

Robby ran his hand over the stubble on his jaw and nodded resolutely at his reflection in the mirror. It was time to drop the last of his walls. One by one, he'd shed the layers he'd built to insulate himself from the outside world.

He'd cut the long bangs and ditched the thrift store Oxfords that made him look like a teenager taking his grandma out to lunch.

He'd stopped smiling when he didn't mean it. Stopped agreeing with everything. Stopped hoping for people to fight his battles.

And with every new side he exposed of himself, he'd given the people he loved an opportunity to turn away, to reject him. Only, they hadn't.

Brick had said he liked the haircut and clothes right away. He'd said confidence looked good on

271

him.

Kane had laughed when he stood up for himself and made a crack about his balls.

And when he'd lost his mind a little with the cameras at the Q-Center, no one batted an eye over the fact he couldn't bring himself to smile. If anything, being real had brought them all closer.

Now all he had left to reveal were the dark, oily secrets writhing beneath his skin…and the scars they'd left behind. He couldn't hide them forever. It had been a miracle he'd managed this long.

Besides, their acceptance pumped like a drug through his veins. The more he got, the more he craved. With every smile, every hug, every touch, he got a little closer to flying. God wouldn't bring him this far only to get rejected in the end.

No. This time someone would see him—all of him—and want him anyway.

He dipped his hand in the running water from the faucet and ran it through his hair, making it stand up in short spikes. With one last satisfied look in the mirror, he left to join Matt at the tattoo parlor.

Finally, he would meet the infamous Patty, which he both dreaded and looked forward to in equal measure. On one hand, she'd been the best friend Matt had ever had. She was a window into his history, and Robby hungered for every new piece of the man available to discover.

At the same time, though, she might hate him on principle. She'd wanted the kind of relationship with Matt he had. Could she be happy for them? If she wanted to, she could keep him away from her son, which could draw a wedge between him and

Matt in a way he might never overcome.

He shut down the bubbling anxiety as he parked the car in front of the shop. Either she'd like him, or she wouldn't.

Though a short prayer never hurt anyone.

A quick petition to the Almighty later, he threw back his shoulders and strode inside. Matt waited in the seat immediately to the left of the door and popped to his feet when the bell sounded overhead.

"You look great, Rob." Matt gave him a shy smile before tilting his head toward the woman at the counter. "Let me introduce you to Jimmy's mom."

Patty's eyes narrowed as she caught sight of him. Men—and women too, he supposed—had taken his measure many times in his life, but he'd never felt the weight of their assessment the way he did hers. Her gaze catalogued every inch of him, from his barely styled hair, to his blue V-neck shirt, all the way down to his navy jeans and brown knock-off Helm boots.

His initial assessment of her from Closing Time held up fairly well on closer inspection. A red cloth headband held back her short brown hair. It brought out the rich color of her dark skin and matched the shade of her lipstick. She wore a black Alicia Keyes T-shirt and sported at least six green and red fabric bracelets with various designs on her right wrist.

Suppressing the urge to blind her with one of his sunshine smiles, he kept his face neutral as he approached.

Matt broke the ice. "Patty, this is Robby. Rob, Patty."

He wasn't sure she would accept his hand, but he offered it anyway. Her grip was cool and firm. It warmed him she accepted the peace offering, but he wouldn't fool himself; a handshake was a far cry from a sign of approval.

"It's really great to meet you. Matt says you were the best friend he had growing up."

She gave nothing away with her silent shrug.

"I respect you wanting to get to know me before accepting me in your son's life. I want you to know I take it very seriously. I grew up in a family and an environment where children were cherished and lifted up by the community." As long as they didn't make the mistake of ending up gay. "I've spent a lot of time around kids, and I love them. I'm sure I'll love your son too."

Patty's face softened a little. "Did you grow up around here?"

"No. A small town, not too far away."

"So, you're still pretty close with your family."

Why had he brought up his family? Stupid. "I was. Until they found out I was gay. They…couldn't reconcile who I am with who they thought I should be. I've been on my own ever since."

She leaned forward, resting her elbows on the counter. "Your family sucks. My mom's always been there for me, no matter how much I've fucked up."

Matt bumped her shoulder gently with his own. "When you love somebody, you don't stop loving them just because they disappoint you."

They shared a meaningful look.

A beat later, her gaze shot back to Robby. "What's the deal with you and Matty?"

"Pat—" Matt tried to interrupt her, but she shooed him away.

"Because he's right. I didn't just stop loving him because he didn't love me back the way I wanted him to. And maybe I don't have any right to nose into what's happening between you, but I'm asking anyway."

"The deal is…we're together. We fit." He chanced a look at Matt, and the smile he found fortified him to continue. "I love him. Not as long as you have, but it doesn't have to be a competition. I'm not trying to replace you in his heart. There's room for both of us there."

"What kind of man are you?"

"I'm loyal. Faithful." He swallowed. "I work hard. I believe in God. I'm grateful every day for the friends who have become my family. And want to spend every day loving Matt…and hopefully, one day, your son too."

"He already has two parents who love him." She stood straight, folding her arms and lifting her chin in challenge.

"I don't think anyone can have too many people who love them."

Patty released her arms, but her chin didn't drop at all. "I'll think about it."

"I appreciate it. I'm sure this is weird for you. It probably sucks. So, thank you. For meeting me and for hearing me out." Robby didn't offer his hand again. Instead, he ducked his head and turned toward the door.

Matt rested a hand gently on his back and followed him out to the car. "You said you love me."

"You said it first." He leaned against the car, with a smile part flirt and part tease.

"I did, huh?" Matt put both hands flat against the roof, caging Robby's body between them. "Remind me when this happened."

"At the restaurant. You said this was the first time you've ever been in love with someone. Did you think I missed it?" To the contrary, it had rattled around in his head in a near-constant loop ever since.

Matt sucked on his bottom lip. "It's not like you said anything, and I *was* acting pretty needy, so…"

Advancing a fraction of an inch, he poked a finger at Matt's chest. "Stop right there. One." He held up a finger. "You were not acting needy. You had questions, and they deserved answers."

A second finger joined the first. "Two. I didn't say anything because—" He sighed. "I didn't trust myself to handle it the right way. No one has ever said they loved me before, and it's like I just froze up for a minute. Then, I didn't say it back because what if you thought I was just saying it to say it?"

Stupid as the words sounded to his own ears, he could only imagine how dumb they seemed to Matt. Inadequate.

"And even after all my overthinking, I still didn't do it justice." He cupped the other man's face in his hands, feathering his thumbs over the clean-shaven skin. "I love you, Matt York. Not just the best parts of you. Not just the idea of you. You."

276

Matt dropped his hands from the car to grip Robby's hips at the first brush of their mouths.

The intimacy threatened to drown him. Still, he pressed for more, his tongue licking at Matt's lips, a plea for entry. When the kiss finally deepened, he felt it all the way down to his toes.

Matt pulled away first. "I love you too. God help me, I don't know what it is you see in me or how I got so lucky, but I'm not going to question it. I'm holding on, you hear me? I'm holding on and I won't let go."

Every dream Robby had ever had was coming true. A family. Friends. A calling.

And love.

"Matty." The light from inside the shop framed Patty as she stood in the doorway. "We need to talk."

"Coming." Matt stole one last chaste kiss, then stepped back. "I'll meet you back at your place in a bit?"

Robby rubbed at the warmth in his chest. "I can't think of a better way to spend the night."

In fact, this might just be the best night of his life.

***

Matt

It took every drop of his self-control to walk away from Robby when all Matt really wanted to do was get to the apartment and get skin to skin with the man he loved.

Love.

A little shimmy crept into his walk as he replayed Robby's confession outside of the car. It seemed inconceivable for him to be the first person to ever tell Robby he loved him. The guy couldn't have been closer to perfect. Not only was he gorgeous, he was kind and smart and…good.

Maybe all of his paranoia about Robby's mysterious past was just that—paranoia. Robby dedicated himself to other people and carried his faith close to his heart. Not to mention the amazing things he could do with his body.

Matt's pulse picked up. Who knew what amazing things Robby would show him tonight? Maybe he'd finally get a glimpse of the rock-hard body his lover kept hidden under all of those clothes.

Oh yeah, he needed to wrap things up with Patty as quickly as possible. Maybe pick up another bouquet of flowers on the way to Robby's place. He didn't know whatever happened to the first cluster of daisies, but they'd meant something to Robby, and nothing else mattered.

When he got back inside the shop, Patty stood with Steve and a slender blond man he didn't recognize. Something about the guy made the hair stand up on the back of his neck.

"Are you sure he's the same person?" Patty wore the intense, pinched expression she usually saved for a visit from her ultra-conservative Aunt Karen.

"I'm sure," the blond guy responded. "I've known Robby for years. Could describe every nook and cranny of him, if you need me to."

He did not like the direction this was going. "Excuse me, but who are you?"

Steve looped an arm around the man's waist. "This is my new boyfriend, Parker."

The blond pressed a kiss against Steve's cheek. "I was in the back when you brought Robby in. I couldn't believe my ears when I heard my buddy out here."

"Why didn't you come out and say hello, then?" Something felt off. Maybe it was the way Parker didn't look him straight in the eye or the conspiratorial tone in his voice.

"Seemed like a private conversation."

"But not too private for you to eavesdrop."

Parker's features tightened. "You want the skinny on your boy or not?"

"From you? No."

Patty waved her hand. "Excuse me, but I *do*."

The smaller man smirked. "Robby Jordan is the dirtiest, sloppy bottom I've ever met in my life. The dude can suck cocaine back like a Hoover, and he whored himself without shame for years."

"You're lying." Matt didn't even have to think about it. This guy had sleazebag written all over him, from his skin-tight jeggings to the pink harness he wore over his white T-shirt.

Parker stuck out his bottom lip. "It would be easier for you if I was, I'm sure. But if I didn't know Robby, how could I describe the little birthmark he has an inch away from his dick? How he doesn't make a sound when he comes?"

He had no idea whether the birthmark was a real thing or not, but he'd never admit it to this asshole.

"Are you trying to insinuate you've had sex with my boyfriend?"

"Not at all." Parker stepped out of Steve's embrace and glided toward Matt. "But I've seen him get fucked a million ways from Sunday." He dropped his voice like he was sharing a secret. "At the parties, you know. And, of course, in the home movies."

Patty advanced. "You said something about drugs? Matt? You know what drugs did to Shawn."

Parker fanned his face with his hand. "Oh yeah. I can't tell you everything he did, because I wasn't there for all of it, but he did mountains of coke when he lived with John. I mean, really, he'd put anything up his nose."

John. The ex who showed up at the work site.

Still, Matt refused to let doubt trickle into his heart.

Parker shot him a knowing look. "Ah, you've heard of John. Amazing in bed, you know, though he didn't do all the freaky shit Robby did with other guys." He fluttered his lashes at Steve. "Couldn't hold a candle to you, though, sweetheart. Still, our Lambchop broke his heart when he left him in the middle of the night. How could you abandon someone after so long together?" Sighing for maximum effect, he lifted his shoulder. "He found some greener pastures, I guess. Though the little apartment he has now leaves something to be desired."

Matt hardened his heart against the picture Parker painted. "Even if all of what you say is true, and I'm not saying I believe it is, you're talking about ancient history. Robby broke up with John years ago." And he refused to believe this douche had seen the inside of Robby's apartment.

"True." Parker blinked. "But I saw them together at Nitro not so long ago, and they looked awfully cozy."

"John wants to get him back. And?"

"He had his hand in Robby's pants, sugar. Plus, Robby came back again just a few Saturdays back. We did shots in the party room. He got so drunk, I'm still stunned he could walk out of there."

The day he showed up at Closing Time. Dread pooled in his stomach at the pinched look on Patty's face.

"The party room? At Nitro?" Steve thundered. "You hang out there? I am not okay with that, Parker. The cops need to shut the place down."

Wait. He'd been in Nitro, himself, a few weeks ago. Nothing there stood out as anything immoral or illegal. "I don't understand."

"Sex. Drugs. Underage boys." Steve gritted his teeth. "It's disgusting."

"I didn't see anything of the sort, and I've been there in the past month."

Parker soothed Steve, petting his arm. "I didn't stay, darling. And you didn't see it, because you didn't go to the VIP room. Older men, young boys. If you don't believe me, I'll take you there myself. See it with your own eyes, and then ask your precious Robby if he was there. Decide what you can live with once you've got all the facts."

"Fine. Let's go." He'd show Patty the place wasn't so bad. Surely, she wouldn't find fault with

Robby just dancing and hanging out with some friends.

"No can do." Parker tsked. "Back room is only open on Saturdays. I'll take you there tomorrow, though. Meet me at five, and I'll help you take your blinders off."

"Whatever," he growled.

Patty grabbed his arm as he turned away. "If even half of this shit is true, you know this freak is going nowhere near my son. And if you're with him, neither are you. I get that you care about Robby, but don't even try to come back to me making excuses if what Parker says pans out."

"I don't know what he's talking about, Pat, but I'm going to prove to you, Robby is a good man. And Parker is nothing but a liar."

His phone buzzed.

Robby: A friend of mine has an emergency. I need to help out. Rain check on 2nite?

Locking his jaw, he considered a dozen different responses. But this was not a conversation they could broach over text.

Matt: Can we get together afterward? I really need to see you.

Robby: I've got to get to the hospital. Tomorrow?

Matt: Fine.

Hopefully by then, he'd have put all of Patty's worries to rest. And he'd be one step closer to the family he'd always wanted.

CHAPTER TWENTY-FIVE

Robby

Robby woke up close to noon on the sofa at the Q-Center, his heart still aching over what had happened to Sara the night before. At least now, she was safe and sleeping soundly in her own bed.

He thought about calling Matt but decided against distracting him during a shift at the bar. Besides, he needed to fill in Paul on what had happened.

Willing his tight muscles to move from the couch, he stood and spotted the reverend and his husband peering at a laptop on the wooden table.

"Hey, guys. Why didn't you wake me?" Robby slid into the chair beside Chris.

"Figured you must've had a late night if you crashed here." Chris turned the computer at an angle so he could better see. "Look. The website is up and running."

The homepage had a clean look with THE Q-CENTER centered in white text at the top over a navy-blue header. What looked like two hand-drawn LGBT rainbow flags flanked the words on either side. Drop down menus offered an About Us page, Directions, Services, Donations, and Testimonials.

His finger hovered over the mouse pad for a second or two before he took the plunge and clicked on the Testimonial tab. The first video box featured a still image of Sara, and as he scrolled down, box after box showed a thumbnail of one of the kids who looked to this place for help. Marshall, Vin, Meggie.

From there, he clicked on the services tab and found pictures of the new addition, the bathroom, an inside look at Sara's room. The new bedrooms didn't have beds in them yet, but he'd bet his last dollar the private floor space would beat the shelter experience for some folks any day.

"If you want to watch the video-clip I took of you, it's part of the About Us section." Chris pointed to the screen. "I know you were nervous about it, but it's really good."

His stomach protested just thinking about it. "Pass. Thanks, though. I'm sure you did a great job; everything about the site looks amazing."

Chris puffed out his chest at the praise.

He pushed the computer away, dreading what he needed to say next. "Did anyone tell you what happened last night?"

The reverend shook his head. "Does this have anything to do with why you spent the night here?"

"Someone hurt Sara. A guy she met at a bar. He, uh, didn't realize she was trans." Robby rubbed at the hard knot in his shoulder. "She's pretty banged up. Her arm's fractured. She called me from the hospital last night."

Paul sank into his chair. "What kind of world are we living in?"

It hurt to see the bleak expression on his face. "I thought maybe we could do some outreach today," Paul continued. "Send some of the kids to the parks and libraries, hand out some cards."

Chris responded. "We'd asked Sara to help us out with intake for the new wing, kind of serve as a den mother for any new young people looking to bunk down for a while. I think we'll need to find some temporary help while she recovers."

"Probably a good idea. In the meantime, I'd like to help with the outreach today too. I could check out a few places I used to haunt. Spread the word." Staying busy would help keep his mind off what had happened to his friend last night.

Paul slid a few cards his way. "You're doing God's work, son. I know He brought you to us for a reason."

The words turned over in his head as he left the building. Awful as his early years in Atlanta had been, maybe something good could come out of them.

He hit the a few of the tent cities beneath the interstate on-ramps. In the middle of the day, there weren't too many people around, but he'd learned early, if you had to sleep on the street, it was far safer when the sun was out.

In three stops, he only gave out one card. The slight man was probably younger than eighteen, but if he had any sense, he'd lie to anyone who asked. The guy had firmed his jaw and planted his feet at Robby's advance, but he took the card. Only time would tell if the kid had enough trust or desperation to seek out the center at nightfall.

The guys he really needed to find probably weren't on the streets. They'd be holed up with men like John or Harry. Or in the clubs.

Dammit.

He never wanted to set foot in a place like the Nitro party room again. Just thinking about it made him queasy. Then again, the easy path wasn't always the right one.

Ten minutes later, he forced himself into the front door of the club's public area. No one and nothing inside could distinguish it from the last time he'd visited or any of the times before.

He didn't recognize the sentry posted outside the VIP room, which meant no way he'd get in. Instead, he approached the bartender—the good-looking one with the beard. What was his name? Larry? Lucas. Hopefully, the guy had a better memory than he did.

"What can I get you, gorgeous?" Lucas leaned forward, elbows on the bar.

"I'm looking for Parker." *If all else fails, go with name recognition.* "Have you seen him around?"

"Can't say I have."

Robby pushed a twenty across the bar. "You mind if I go look for him in the back?"

Lucas lifted an eyebrow, then swiped the bill and stuffed it in his pocket. "Sure. Tell the Terminator

287

over there I said to let you through."

He passed over a second twenty, which prompted a grin and wink from Lucas. Who knew when it would pay off to be in the bartender's good graces?

No one in the thin crowd stepped in his way as he approached the back door, but the big guy in the tight black jacket dropped his arm menacingly across the entryway when he made it back. "Private party."

"Not according to Lucas." He ran an exaggerated gaze over the bouncer's bulging biceps. "I see why he calls you the Terminator."

The bouncer scoffed. "Why the fuck can't he pick something hotter than Schwarzenegger? How about Jason Momoa or something?"

The man looked nothing like Jason Momoa or Arnold Schwarzenegger, even in his younger days. He was more beefy than muscular, and his short, dark hair was visibly thinning on the top.

But the guy's appearance didn't matter. Robby wasn't here to find a date; he only needed to get in the back room. "Sometimes people can't see what's right in front of them."

The bouncer shook his head in a cross between irritation and disgust, but more importantly, he stepped aside to leave the doorway wide open.

No more wasting time.

Robby stepped into the back room, and the change in atmosphere hit him like a ton of bricks. How had he not noticed it instantly when he came in here before?

While the dance floor had a distinct sexual

energy, out there, he'd felt exhilarated, liberated, and carefree. Out there, the men owned their sexuality, whether they showed it through sweetness, swagger, or a shy smile.

In here, the air felt heavier, stickier. Debauchery and desperation dripped from the dark velvety curtains and clung to everything like an oily sheen.

He shuddered against the pit in his stomach and scanned the crowd for anyone who might want to get out. Though most could hide it, Robby felt like he'd be able to sense any true desolation. Like calling to like.

Almost immediately, he zeroed in on a slight redhead, maybe nineteen or twenty years old, with deep purple bruises creeping above the collar of his tight emerald-green glittery shirt. The guy leaned against the bar, his gaze trained on the floor, but he snuck glances around him every few seconds. Submissive, but aware of his surroundings.

Robby approached him from the side and stopped with about three feet between them. He didn't look at the guy directly, instead facing the bar when he spoke. "I don't expect you to believe me. When I was you, I wouldn't have, but I'm telling you the truth. There's a way to get out of here. Out of this place, out of this life."

Setting the card on the bar between them, he lifted his hand for the bartender and ordered a bottled water. The redhead made no move to take the card.

"I volunteer at an outreach center on Peachtree. It's not like the community shelters. We have individual rooms with doors and locks. You won't have to share. You don't have to pay, not in any way."

He passed a five-dollar bill to the bartender as he accepted his drink. "We don't have anything fancy, but we can give you four walls and a roof over your head. We'll help you find a job, help you get on your feet."

"And what's in it for you?" the guy rasped. "Are you wanting me to believe you're just saving souls out of the goodness of your heart?"

"I'm trying to make peace with what happened to me." He turned to face the young man for the first time. "I didn't think I'd ever get out, but I did. Nobody rescued me. Thing is, though, a stranger gave me a chance, gave me a job, when I needed one. If he hadn't put a hand out to me, I don't know how long I would've lasted before I ended up right back where I started. I'd be dead right now. One way or another. Someone would've killed me, or I would've killed myself."

He gave the bar his back. "I hope you take the card. I hope you visit the center, but you've got to make the choice to save yourself first. You are worth saving; you just have to believe it."

Of course, he wanted to say more, to plead with the guy to believe him and take what he offered, but he knew if he pushed, he'd only sabotage any progress he'd made. Instead, he walked away.

Trying to look casual, he sipped his drink as he passed one booth after the next. Even before sundown, men filled the seats.

At the first table, a forty-something Hispanic man jerked off, watching the trans woman standing naked—save for red heels—rubbing her breasts and getting a blow-job from a guy kneeling on the floor. Robby couldn't tell if all the players really wanted to be there, but he couldn't justify interrupting to find out. His stomach roiled as he moved on.

A group of five men crammed in the second booth, apparently halfway through a game of strip poker.

In the third, a couple kissed ardently as though they were the only two people on earth, a half-eaten plate of skewered shrimp on the table in front of them.

Then, the world stopped when he turned to the next tableau and locked eyes with the last person he'd ever wanted to see at a place like this ever again. A pinched-face older man gripped a shirtless Brady by the back of the neck and shook him.

"Do I have to remind you of the rules?" he hissed.

"No, sir," the boy choked out.

"If feel your teeth one more time, I'll knock them right out of your mouth."

Robby didn't think; he just reached to the table behind him, grabbed a skewer, and lunged, digging the tip into the older man's throat. "Let go of the kid right now, or so help me, I will fucking end you."

The man released his grip, and Brady stared at him with wide eyes.

"Grab your clothes, Brady, and stand up."

The boy scuttled from his seat, and Robby pulled the metal stick away from the man beside him. A dot of blood welled in its wake. "Get out of here, asshole. If I ever see you again, it will be the worst day of your life, you understand?"

He stepped back to give the man room to escape, which he did quickly, his hand cupping his neck as if he might bleed to death rather than just drip on his collar. Dropping the skewer on the table, Robby turned to Brady.

The boy's body shook, his thin arms wrapped around his bare midsection. At least a pair of white shorts covered some of his bottom half. "He's going to tell my boyfriend about this, and I'm going to lose everything. I know you were trying to help, but—" He took a stuttered breath. "I don't have anywhere to go now."

Robby took off his lightweight jacket and hung it around Brady's shoulders. "You're wrong. Come on." He steered him toward the door. "We're going back to the Q-Center."

***

Matt

Matt stood outside of Nitro at exactly five o'clock, trying to ignore the smug look on Parker's face as he pranced up the walkway in a pair of skin-tight jeans and a form-fitting T-shirt.

"I wasn't sure you'd really come, dove." The blond looked around in an exaggerated motion Patty would've called extra. "I don't see your lovely lady friend. She seemed very interested in what I had to say about Robby."

"Patty's working," he gritted. She'd been pissed about it, had wanted to see what Parker had told her

292

about firsthand, but apparently, Steve had booked a ton of appointments and said he couldn't spare her help. "Just show me what you came to show me, and let's skip the small talk."

Parker dropped his fake smile. "Okay. Follow me." The man led him into the club, past the dance floor and straight to a door in back, guarded by a balding guy wearing all black.

The bouncer—or whatever he was—didn't even blink as Parker opened the door and breezed inside. The flashing lights and pounding beat melted into a dim yellow cast and a slower, more sensual soundtrack. The lingering scent of piped-in smoke mixed with some kind of incense and sex.

The shadows hanging over the room kept him from taking in everything at once, but as Parker led him to the far right near the bar, more details took shape. Like the sweaty, pudgy man kneeling on his seat with his dick in hand, coming on the tits of a woman who was…getting a blowjob?

"You took me to a sex club?" he hissed.

Parker chuckled. "Where did you think you were going? Narnia? I told you, Robby's not the saint you think he is." The asshole gripped his arm. "See the kid over there?"

A tear leaked down the cheek of a redhead, a very *young* redhead. A man crushed the side of his head against the paneled wall, as he fucked him from behind. Matt's stomach gurgled, threatening to cast his lunch on the floor.

"Kids like him, guys like the one doing him— they're the bread and butter of places like this. You asked me how I knew so much about Robby's sex

293

life; it's because I've seen him, just like this. And those were on the tame nights. Other times, he got downright kinky. The more drugs he did, the less he cared. I saw him take on two at once. Oh, and I hear he gives a hell of a blowjob." He cocked his head. "Is it true?"

Shaking his arm out of Parker's grasp, Matt tried to put distance between them. "Screw you."

"But don't pull his hair. Right?"

He stopped in front of a table of naked guys playing cards and spun back to look the blond viper in the eyes. "I don't believe you. No matter how many disgusting details you throw at me. No matter how you try to get under my skin."

Robby would never come to a place like this. At least, not the back room. He couldn't. He wouldn't.

No. Parker was just using tiny truths to convince him of lies.

Flexing his fingers, he tried not to ball his hands into fists—and failed. "Obviously, you've got some ax to grind with Robby, but you're wasting your time trying to poison me against him. He would never be a part of this sordid garbage."

"You sure?" A wicked gleam shone in Parker's eyes.

Matt lifted his chin. "I'd bet my life on it."

"Yeah? You might want to rethink that bet." Parker smirked and looked pointedly over Matt's shoulder. "Your paragon of virtue is right over there, and it looks like he's not leaving alone."

Following the direction of Parker's gaze, his heart stuttered, then shattered into a thousand tiny pieces.

Robby guided a teenage boy through the room, the kid wearing nothing but a pair of shorty-shorts and Robby's distinctive new H&M jacket. As they turned toward the door, the kid reached back and grabbed Robby's hand.

"There has to be an explanation," he whispered and moved forward to get it.

Or tried to. Parker gripped his arm. "It doesn't matter."

"Of course it matters." He tried to shake off the other man's grip, but Parker's fingers dug in like a bear trap. "Maybe not to you, but to your baby's mama. I know a dozen guys who'll happily tell her all about seeing Robby here. One or two might be willing to testify to it in court."

"Why?" he asked hoarsely. "What difference does all of this make to you?"

Parker released Matt's arm and ran his hand over his hair. "Maybe it's because Steve matters to me and Patty matters to him. Or maybe I just have a soft spot for children. I wouldn't want your little boy wrapped up with someone as fucked up as your boy Robby."

Bullshit.

Matt took in the debauchery all around him. The smell of sweat and lube. The wet slapping sounds. And something cracked deep inside of him.

Why had he ignored his own intuition? Why had Robby been with men like John? What kind of secrets did a man have to bury in a hole to live with?

Because he was hiding something he thought was unforgivable.

And while he knew, without a shadow of a doubt, Robby would have an explanation for all this—the man he loved was good and kind and true—he knew, just as surely, this could be the wedge Patty would use to take Jimmy away once and for all.

Matt had already put aside dreams to which he'd come so close. Of becoming an architect. Of finishing college. And he would do it all again a hundred times over for his son. His heart beat for his little boy. He would never abandon him. Never give up fighting for him.

Honestly, he'd never imagined he'd ever fall in love. Find a person who filled his heart and made his body come alive. That dream had seemed a million miles away, but with Robby, it had become a reality. And now, like he had with his other dreams, he would have to let it go.

Because he wouldn't—he couldn't—lose his little boy. He wouldn't abandon Jimmy the way his father had abandoned him.

Even if it meant ripping his heart from his body.

Matt didn't move, didn't speak.

A full minute passed as he stood there, reeling. Then, he threw up all over his shoes.

CHAPTER
TWENTY-SIX

Robby

Robby squeezed his clasped fingers together as he knelt on his living room carpet and sent up a prayer of thanksgiving. Not only had he gotten Brady into a room at the Q-Center, at least three other rooms had occupants when he left tonight.

He'd barely rose to his feet before a battering knock shook his front door. His first thought, even after all these years, was maybe John had finally found out what he'd done and had come to collect. It rooted him to the floor.

"Robby!" Matt's voice echoed from outside.

Some of Robby's tension eased, and he drifted over to answer.

Matt's shoulders hunched forward as he stepped into the living room. His hands were crammed deep into his pants pockets.

"Why didn't you tell me?" An emptiness swirled

297

around the words as Matt forced them out.

"What are you—"

"I met Parker this weekend." Matt bit his lip. "Old friend of yours?"

Robby sank into a chair. "Yes." Where was this going? It couldn't be good.

"He said some pretty awful things. To me and to Patty." Matt pulled his hands from his pockets and flexed his fingers at his sides. "Did you have sex for money?"

The question hit him harder than Matt's fist ever could have. "Not exactly. I mean—"

The sad shake of his lover's head stopped him mid-sentence. "He said you fucked people in front of an audience, Rob. Went to sex parties." His voice grew duller with each word. "He talked about the cocaine. I guess it was your drug of choice."

Robby buried his head in his hands. This couldn't be happening. "I can explain. It all happened a long time ago. I *told you*."

Matt dropped down to the sofa and laced his fingers together. "You told me *you've been through some stuff*." He kept his voice low even as his words betrayed his distress. "I thought you meant you had an asshole boyfriend or two, like the guy who showed up at the site. Or maybe you had to live on ramen noodles for a while. I had no idea it was anything like this."

He squeezed his eyes closed. "I knew about the drugs, or at least your struggle with addiction. But the sex club I didn't see coming." When he blinked, his haunted gaze locked with Robby's. "I don't care about your past. I love you no matter what, but he was talking about you snorting up and tag teaming guys in front of Patty."

Tag-teaming? The only time he'd ever done anything like that was when John had sent him out with Harry for the night. When Harry had invited over a group of his friends, all as single-mindedly focused on their own pleasure as their host, all as happy to treat Robby like a fuck-toy to use and discard.

Even high as a kite, it had been the worst night of his life and the last night of Harry's.

Well. Here it was. At the end of it all, Matt was just like everyone else. He saw the real Robby and wanted nothing to do with him. He only wanted the idea of him. The construct. Or at least, he needed a different kind of guy to parade in front of his ex.

Robby wouldn't let it hurt. No.

No one—nothing—would have the power to hurt him again.

Rage bubbled hot beneath his skin and he sprang to his feet. "You want to know if I've fucked more than one guy at a time? Yeah, Matt, I did. Though you don't have to worry. I've been tested, and I'm clean. I wouldn't have screwed you otherwise. I fucked for money, though, and food and a place to sleep at night. I did enough coke to give myself nosebleeds."

Years of fury shook him to his core, and in long strides, he crowded Matt back against the wall. "You want to know what else I did, you perfect fucking bastard? I slit a man's throat. I prayed to God to strike him dead, and when He didn't, I did it myself, and I've never regretted it a day in my life."

Matt reeled back, like the words struck a physical blow. "You don't mean that." He shook his head, banishing the idea. "This isn't you. I *know* you. But Patty doesn't. And you were back at that awful place tonight. *Tonight*, Rob."

"I was doing outreach for the Q-Center."

"She won't care. She'll take Jimmy, Rob. I can't live without my son."

"I'd never ask you to." Robby faltered then, the reality of what was happening nearly taking him to his knees. "You're breaking up with me."

"I don't want to. God knows, I love you. But—"

"Just go." He wouldn't beg. He'd done enough begging for scraps in his life; he would never do it again. Broken deeper than he ever believed possible, he turned his back on the man he thought he finally found forever with. "I won't even make you say the words. I know what your son means to you. But I need you to leave now. It hurts too much to look at you."

***

In his bedroom, Robby waited until he heard the slam of his front door before he pulled his shirt over his head. Woodenly, he tugged open the drawer to his nightstand and dug out the shiny silver blade singing to him with promises of peace.

In a way, he could thank Parker for this. After all, it was the very razorblade he'd left on the table at John's place the first time he'd brought over cocaine. And Harry.

After what he'd endured that night, the icy hot

sting on his arm had barely hurt at all. It grounded him, entranced him, comforted him.

He turned the blade over in his hands, remembering the last time he'd made a cut with a razor *just like this one*. Not on himself, but on Harry. There'd been so much blood. And by some miracle, the cops called it a suicide. No one—not even John—even considered the possibility Robby could've ended the bastard's life.

Just a little of Harry's own GHB in his drink. A cut to the throat and to both wrists. He'd bled out in less than five minutes.

Robby packed up his things and moved out of John's apartment the same night, and no matter how scared or hopeless or alone he felt, he'd never cut himself again. He'd never even taken it out of the drawer once he put it inside. Not once. Not until now.

***

Matt

This can't be happening.

Matt stared at the steering wheel of his car, willing the events of the past twenty-four hours to unmake themselves. Nothing he'd ever felt could compare to the hope and pure joy coursing through him in the parking lot the night before.

He finally knew what it meant to love someone and to be loved in return. The soul-deep connection they wrote songs, wrote poetry about. The kind of love that made you stand outside someone's window with a fucking boom box playing a Peter Gabriel song.

But can you love someone you don't even know?

The answer stuck in his throat as Robby's words about killing a man echoed in his head. He shut the memory down, wrenched his body out of the seat, and stomped the short distance to the apartment door. He knew Robby, even if he didn't know every detail of his past. But it didn't matter.

He knocked with desperation, sending pain radiating through his knuckles.

The door flew open, and he stumbled into Patty, wrapping his arms around her and burying his face into the crook of her neck. The scent of her favorite soap grounded him in familiar comfort.

She allowed the embrace for a moment, even returning it briefly before she pulled him inside and onto the couch. "Aw, Matty." She held both of his hands in hers. "I'm so sorry."

The truth of her words echoed in the sincerity of her voice and the sadness in her eyes. It pulsed through the connection they'd shared for so many years. All she'd had to do was look at him, and she knew he needed her.

"Everything Parker said was true, Pat, about the club. It was as awful as he described—and Robby was there." He choked on the last words.

Patty nodded her understanding. "How long ago?"

He pulled away from her and covered his eyes with the heels of his hands. "Tonight. I know it won't matter to you...I know this looks bad, but Robby's a good guy. The stuff he did before? He's

302

different now. He's clean."

She pulled his arms down to reveal his face. "You can't know that. I told you, no excuses. I just can't have that shit around Jimmy. Drugs killed Shawn. Finding him like you did…what if Jimmy ever stumbled on something like that?"

"Oh, I know." He laughed darkly. "I'm still not over it. I won't get over this either, losing Robby. But I deserve it, right? After the way I hurt you."

Patty groaned. "It's not the same thing." She sighed. "You didn't lie to me, Matty. I lied to myself. And when I didn't get what I wanted, I acted like a spoiled child. I hurt you. I hurt myself. I see it now. This isn't about hurting you, though. It's about protecting him."

He could only stare at the growing resolve on her face.

"I am so…deeply ashamed of the way I've treated you. I'm sorry. I'm so sorry." A tear trickled down her cheek. "I know it doesn't seem like it, but I'm really am over the idea of us, together. I just want to be your friend again."

"You'll always be my friend," he murmured, wiping the moisture from her cheek with his thumb.

"I got all jealous over the idea of your guy meeting Jimmy because I was afraid I'd waited too long to get my shit together—and maybe the two of you would end up wanting to raise Jimbo without me. I don't care if you're gay, but I hate seeing you so hurt right now."

He pulled her into his arms and hugged her tight. "When I saw him tonight, the things he said—"

He was hurt…lashing out.

"I broke his heart, Patty. Broke my own." His eyes burned as Robby's viscous words replayed in his head.

Words he would take with him to his grave.

Even from the man's own mouth, he couldn't believe they were true.

He wanted to beg Patty to see Robby through his eyes. To believe Robby was clean. But Parker's threats were too damn effective. The guy would just trot out his so-called witnesses to destroy any inroads Matt managed to make. And he'd lose his son.

So instead, Matt embraced his misery and let the magnitude of the loss sink in. He wasn't only losing his lover, but his best friend—at home and on the job.

"How am I going to face him at work? It hurts so much." Patty's hair tickled his cheek as he rested it on the top of her head. "I need this job. The bartending thing won't be enough to make ends meet."

They sat in silence a moment before she spoke. "Talk to your boss. See if you can get on another crew. It's a big company, hon. You've got nothing to lose."

True. It already felt like he'd lost everything.

***

I've got nothing to lose.

Saying the words in his head didn't calm his anxiety as he waited in the lobby of the company's main office the next morning. He'd arrived at the same time as the receptionist, hoping he could get in early for a face-to-face with Mike Cooper. Though he knew the man's sister better at this point, Amanda would have more questions about Robby and their relationship than he wanted to answer.

Mike probably had no idea they'd even started dating. Maybe. Hopefully.

"Matt, what a surprise to see you here." Amanda stood over the uncomfortable chair where he waited. Jared Berringer flanked her right side.

Shifting in his seat, he nodded to the developer before answering. "Just waiting to talk to Mike."

She wrapped her hand around his forearm and pulled him up. "Sorry. My brother is home with a sick baby. Come back to my office. I'm sure I can help."

He hesitated a moment but then allowed her to pull him toward the back. Explaining why he didn't want to talk to her would only make things worse. When Jared took the seat beside him, though, he reconsidered once again.

Amanda faced him from behind her glass and chrome desk. "I think I know why you're here."

One look at her face ruled that out immediately. If she knew how things had gone down with Robby, she would not be smiling.

"Robby talked to us already." Jared folded his hands on his lap. "I honestly wasn't sure about the suggestion at first, but he did make some good points."

He could only blink in confusion.

Amanda flashed an encouraging smile. "I had no idea you were even interested in architecture, but I thought about it, and it could really serve Cooper in the long run to have a dedicated architect on our team."

"What did Robby propose…exactly? You know I don't have my degree yet—"

"He showed us some of your sketches and designs. Impressive," Jared said briskly. "He said you only have two classes left. If they really are just electives like he told us, you should be able to get the internship applied to those credits."

"I'm sorry. What internship?"

"Aww." Amanda exchanged a look with the developer. "Was this all a surprise?" She chuckled. "When Robby showed us some of the plans you've been drawing up on the builds, he told us some of your situation. He proposed an internship for you with Berringer. We'll continue to keep you on payroll here at Cooper, while you intern with Jared's team over the summer."

"Once you have your degree in August," Jared confirmed, "you'll work with us on your IDP."

He couldn't get his license without getting through the Intern Development Program. More than five thousand experience hours to help put what he learned in school to practical use.

"Cooper will pay a portion of your salary, and you'll also be a liaison between the companies while you're there." Amanda dug a small stack of papers from a manila folder on her desk. "Of course, you'll have to sign a contract. This is a big commitment for all of us. Do you need some time to think about it? Do you have any questions?"

A dozen. When had Robby planned this? How

could the man be so thoughtful and wonderful and so completely impossible to have in his life?

How could he keep going without seeing his smile and kissing his lips?

So many questions. But in the end, he only asked one. "When can I start?"

CHAPTER TWENTY-SEVEN

Robby

The next few days passed like a foggy bad dream. Xander hadn't blinked an eye when he'd agreed to allow Robby's last-minute request to take the week of vacation he'd earned.

Of course, he didn't tell his boss the truth about why he needed the time, or at least, not the whole truth. He said he wanted to focus on his volunteer work and some personal stuff.

For sure, he did go to the Q-Center every day and N.A. meetings every night. Sometimes, he stayed, drinking burnt coffee with Thomas, until he could barely keep his eyes open. Anything to avoid the emptiness and the shadows at his apartment.

Just being at home brought his awful confrontation with Matt back into focus, and that night had done enough damage already. So, he tried to be useful to other people. By picking up some beds with Paul for the new recruits. By helping Vin study for finals. By convincing Brady he didn't need to crawl back to his ex and beg forgiveness.

It kept the demons at bay.

His phone chirped, and though he wanted desperately to ignore it, he tugged it out of his pocket and checked the screen.

Brick: We miss you at work. Come by the house tonight for dinner.

Nope. He couldn't face them yet. Couldn't explain why his grand love affair was over before it barely had time to start.

Robby: Can't tonight. But I'll be back before you know it.

Brick: Still celebrating Matt's big news? I get it. Just don't forget about us.

Big news? The pull to ask warred with fear he should already know.

Brick: Why didn't you tell us he was going to work at Berringer? Liv would've thrown him a party or something. She loves any reason to celebrate.

Ah. The internship. He'd forgotten about his pitch to Amanda and Jared last week. Damn. Was it only last week? It felt like a lifetime ago. At least he wouldn't have to look Matt in the eye when he went back to work.

Robby: I'm at the center. GTG. See you soon.

He sank on the sofa, grateful the place resembled a ghost town this afternoon. The idea of facing anyone while he felt like this—well, maybe God was finally giving him a reprieve.

"I know Robby's working today." Paul's voice echoed from the other side of the door, linking to the new add-on.

Who would be here to see him?

The answer slapped him across the face.

Paul entered the room with two men following behind him. Two men he never expected to see again for the rest of his life. Ephraim and Travis Jordan. His father and big brother.

As he caught sight of Robby, Paul greeted him with a wave. "Hey, son, these folks say they're here to see you."

Seeing his family knocked the wind out of him. Years of conditioning had him scrambling to his feet as his father approached.

"You couldn't just stay dead and buried, could you?" Disgust dripped from his father's voice, almost exactly as it had the last time they spoke. It burned like acid, even after all this time.

"What are you doing here, Dad?"

His father stopped his advance and squared his jaw. "Don't you call me your sire, boy. You're no son of mine."

"Wh—what's going on?" Paul stepped forward, but no one was paying attention to him.

"Fine. Ephraim. What are you doing here? Obviously, you're not interested in a family reunion." And while it hurt, the man's malice almost made it easier to disengage his emotions.

"A video of you, sent on the computer, to of all places…*my church.* I go to visit Reverend Green to talk about Bible Study, and he shows me this *interview* with you, telling everybody you're queer and about the sh—shameful thing you did in my barn. You used my name!" He sputtered and flung his arms around as he worked himself into a frenzy. "Haven't you done enough to this family?"

The more hateful words his father flung at him, the calmer he felt. Almost like when a blacksmith dipped hot metal in cold water. Robby grew harder with each passing moment. "I've done nothing to you."

"As soon as we saw your disgusting video, we called your brother—" He shook his head. "—my son, and he said Jerry Connor's boy had found it on YouTube. It was on an official church channel— they called it 'outreach.' Can you believe a church would sanction such sinfulness? Travis got me here with the map function on his phone."

The most shocking part of the whole rant was the fact that his father knew what YouTube was. "I'll ask you again. What do you want?"

"Take the video off the internet. Stop embarrassing my family. Have some dignity."

He huffed out a breath. "Dignity? How much dignity did you show when you threw a child—your child—out on the street? How long did you think I would last without any money or any help?"

"Your hardships are not my doing. They're your own."

"I was a child!"

"Bull spit." His father crossed his arms. "I got married at seventeen years old, became a father a year afterward. If you weren't ready to take responsibility for yourself, maybe you shouldn't have disregarded the will of God while living under my roof."

"Robby," Sara's husky voice broke into his father's tirade. "You didn't tell me we had company, darling."

"What the hell are you supposed to be?" Travis contorted his face into a grimace so exaggerated, it would be comical if it weren't so offensive.

"We're just leaving, Sara. Please cover the desk for me." He didn't ask his family to follow, but he knew they wouldn't stay in the center without him.

"I'm so sorry, Robby." Paul sounded stricken. "I didn't know who they were."

Of course, he didn't, but Robby would have to absolve the reverend some other time.

He made it half a block down the street before his father grabbed his arm. "Don't you make me come back to this disgusting place, boy. You fix this, before your mama catches wind of it."

Looking down at his father's grip, Robby peeled Ephraim's fingers away. "I don't have a mama, remember? I don't give a *shit* if you are embarrassed by what I am doing. You threw me away, and when you did it, you lost any say in how I live my life."

He turned to his brother. For as long as he could

remember, Travis had loomed tall and strong over him. Now they stood as physical equals, and in one glance, he knew his brother would fold under the threat of hard living. "Take your father and get out of my city. If I ever see you again, it will be the worst day of your life." He threw the parting words his brother had given him back in his face, and this time, Travis was the one to withdraw.

His brother took their father's arm. "It's not worth it, Dad. Let's just go. We never have to see him again."

"But you'll remember this," Robby vowed. "And one day, maybe on the day you finally greet the Lord, you'll realize which of us committed the graver sin. I hope you take the knowledge with you to the hereafter. God might forgive you, but I never will."

***

Matt

Matt scowled at the unfamiliar number blowing up his phone. The same person had called him close to ten times in the past hour. He'd just sat down on the sofa after a long day, and he didn't have time to deal with a telemarketer. Not with all the papers Jared had sent home with him to review.

The man had worked some kind of magic, getting all of his paperwork in order at school so he could get credit for his internship, and with Amanda overlapping payroll with Berringer for the summer, he had just enough to pay the university fees.

He hadn't set foot back on a construction site, which meant he'd avoided Robby entirely. A blessing for his tattered heart, but it didn't escape him that he wouldn't have this opportunity without Robby's interference.

Only the late-occurring thought of Patty trying to reach him from a stranger's phone made him finally swipe open the line. "Hello?" He infused the single word with as much irritation as humanly possible.

"Matt? Is that you, doll?" Even if anyone else in the world had ever called him doll, he'd still recognize Sara's throaty voice anywhere.

"It's me. What's going on?"

"I need you to get down to the Q-Center ASAP. Please. Hurry." She disconnected before he could ask any more questions.

For a minute, he thought maybe Robby had put her up to the call, but he dismissed the idea as quickly as he had it. Sara didn't strike him as the type to play games, and the last time he'd seen Robby, the guy seemed more than happy to be done with him.

He swiped the keys off the coffee table and speed-walked to the car. When he'd had questions and needed someone to talk to about his feelings, Sara had been there for him. Busy or not, he wouldn't let her down when she needed him.

Riding the accelerator hard, he made the normally fifteen-minute ride to the center in ten, even in the dusky tail-end of rush-hour. He did a quick scan for Robby's car when he pulled up to the curb, then breathed a sigh of relief because it wasn't there.

Sara waited for him inside, seated with her elbows on the big wooden table and her scarf-covered head cradled in her hands. A cast covered her right forearm. She jumped to her feet at his approach.

"Hey. Where's the fire, hon?"

She reached out and grabbed his hand. "You need to find Robby."

He pulled out of her grasp. "Did he ask you to call me? Things between us are over." He didn't ask about her black eye, though he suspected she was the friend Robby had visited in the hospital.

"What?" The confusion on her face looked too authentic. "When? Why?"

"Because I can't keep him and keep my son."

She frowned. "I don't know what you are talking about. Robby Jordan is one of the best men I know. He's been through hell and back, and he's still more worried about looking out for other people than himself."

"It doesn't change the things he's done—or that my ex can't see past it."

"So…what? You don't love him enough to fight for him?" a soft male voice answered before Sara could.

Matt almost swallowed his tongue at the sight of the boy he'd seen Saturday with Robby. "You." The kid looked so different, now wearing a pair of Levi's and a *Star Wars* T-shirt.

"Yeah. Me. Robby got me out of a nightmare situation and brought me here. He's been helping me get my head on straight ever since." His glare could strip the paint from the walls. "And if you won't fight for a future with a guy like him, you never deserved him to begin with."

He fought to keep calm. "It's not so simple—"

"Are you fucking kidding me?" The kid advanced on him like a bull in a China shop, but Sara gripped his shoulder, stopping him in his tracks.

"Enough, Brady."

Matt rubbed at the back of his neck and tried again. "We're talking about my son. I can't give him up."

"No one is telling you to. But if you love Robby, fight for him. Fight for your kid too."

"It's more than just the club." Matt shook his head. How could he explain? "You don't know the things he's done. The things Jimmy's mom heard about him."

Sara released Brady, her lips pursed. "You would let her judge him for what happened to him when he was Brady's age? You say he did things as if he had a *choice*. You think a teenage boy can give consent when his next meal depends on the man who keeps him off the streets?"

Sara didn't give him time to think it through. "Those men abused him in the worst possible way, and he took it because he had to. I don't even know how he got out because he sure as hell didn't have any help."

Robby's words barreled into his brain with a vengeance.

"I prayed to God to strike him dead and when He didn't, I did it myself."

His stomach turned over. Suddenly, the words

stopped feeling like a lie.

Robby had killed someone.

Holy fuck.

The air in the room felt thinner as he sucked in a breath. Why hadn't he pushed for more? He'd been so focused on his own heart breaking, he didn't ask any real questions—and when Robby lashed out, he never really tried to understand. He'd only thought about losing Jimmy.

"And now, his fucked-up family," she lifted her fingers in air quotes, "is here to deliver one more kick in the head."

"His family?" he echoed, his brain still firing frantically over his revelation.

"It's why I moved heaven and earth to track down your number, Prince Charming. His dad and his brother showed up here, raising hell, calling him a sinner and an embarrassment."

Her words dragged him back into the moment. "Where are they now?"

She shrugged. "I hoped you'd be able to track him down. Make sure he's okay. Of course, I didn't know then you were capable of throwing him away just like everyone else ever has."

Sara squeezed her eyes closed and drew a deep breath before opening them again. "I'm not saying your boy shouldn't be your first priority. I think a lot of us would be better off if our parents cared so much. But you can't just throw up your hands and let Robby go without a fight. *Did* you fight for him? At all?"

"No," he breathed. Had anyone ever fought for him?

The answer dropped like a lead balloon.

Not until now. Not before Brick and Kane and…him. He *would* fight for Robby. He would meet Patty's challenge head-on. Make her understand. For once in his life, he would stand up and fight.

If Robby killed a man, he did it to survive. He'd never hurt someone for pleasure or for personal gain. Matt knew it as sure as the sun, and he'd make sure Robby knew it too.

Heat crept up his neck. It wasn't too late, though. Was it?

"You did the right thing, calling me. No matter how much of a fool I've been, I won't make you regret it." Though Robby probably regretted ever laying eyes on him after he walked away with the man's heart still on the floor. "I should've trusted we could find a way to make things work. I want to help him now, though. See if there's anything left to salvage."

And see if there was any chance Robby might trust him enough to finally tell him the whole story.

CHAPTER TWENTY-EIGHT

Robby

The splash of cold water on his face helped ground Robby amid the rioting emotions sparked by his family's surprise visit. Leaning against the bathroom, he closed his eyes and focused on the sound of the running faucet.

His father didn't deserve to occupy his thoughts. He'd written the entire lot of them off a long time ago. But the derision in his father's voice brought him back to the night his entire world fell apart. He needed to stuff it all back inside the little box in his head.

The doorbell rang and his breath caught. Surely, they hadn't followed him home, not after he'd sent them packing so spectacularly. His father did what he wanted, though. Always had.

Fine, then. He'd just tell him to go to hell all over again.

The bell sounded a second time before he could get his hand on the knob. "Wasn't I clear enough—" The words died on his lips at the sight of Matt on his doorstep. He'd honestly never expected to see the man again.

He hardened his expression when he realized his jaw had gone slack. "I think we've said all we needed to say, don't you?"

"Sara called me." Matt bit his bottom lip. "She said your dad showed up. Are you okay?"

"Okay?" He scowled. "Yeah, Matt, I'm *okay*. I've learned how to live with disappointment."

"I'm sorry," Matt murmured. "Can I—Can…I please come in?"

Robby turned his back, but he left the door open as he walked into the living room. Crossing his arms, he leaned against the wall.

Matt shuffled in behind him. "I handled everything wrong the other night."

Robby cocked his head. Waiting.

"Steve's boyfriend overheard us talking to Patty at the tattoo place. He said he knew you. Told us all kinds of horrible stories about your past."

Sinking onto the sofa, Matt dropped his head into his hands. "I didn't believe him. I called him a liar and told him to go to hell. So, he offered to take me there—to the club—and I saw you."

"I wasn't there for kicks," Robby growled. The very idea made him want to be sick.

"I know. I didn't go there to catch you doing wrong. I was trying to prove to Patty it was all a lie." Matt lifted his head, his gaze searching. "I met Brady today. He and Sara set me straight on a lot of things. I was a fool not to fight for us. There's so much about you I didn't know. Why didn't you just tell me before?"

He planted his feet and dropped his arms. "You make it sound so easy. Tell me, when exactly was the right time to bring up my past? When we met? When we became friends? How about when you found out I went to N.A.? Brick doesn't even know the stuff I've done." Though he realized now his friend would never judge him for it.

Neither would Matt. Even after everything went down, it was never about Matt judging him.

"I planned to tell you. Once we—" Made love? Screwed? "—slept together. I knew you deserved to know, but I never got the chance. Or maybe I just put it off because I didn't want to face it. We're talking about the worst thing that's ever happened to me."

"I told you everything going on inside of me. I kept waiting for you to tell me whatever it was you were holding back, and you never did." Matt shook his head, his hand hovering over his mouth. "I was afraid to ask." He dropped his hand and lifted his chin. "But I'm asking now. Please tell me."

"I'm not trying to take anything away from the stuff you've had to work through." Robby needed to make him understand. "But the problems I had with my exes weren't like the ones you had with Patty."

Untucking his long sleeve T-shirt from his jeans, he pulled it over his head and dropped it at his feet. Slowly, he turned, giving Matt a full view of the crisscrossed path of scars across his back, before he faced him again. "You think I ever wanted you to see this?"

Matt's eyes shone as he gritted his jaw. "Who did this to you?"

Robby shrugged. "Mostly a guy named Harry. He was a friend of John's, and sometimes, they used to trade. Me for Harry's boyfriend, Parker."

Matt sucked in a breath. "Steve's boyfriend, the one who took me to the club."

"We used to be friends, sort of, but his life went one way, and mine went another. I got out, and he didn't. I don't know if he hates me for it or what. But, yeah, Harry was pretty sick, a sadist. He didn't think of us as human. We were just things. To screw or to hurt or humiliate. The guy was dead inside. We were like ants burning under a magnifying glass. He got off on making me cry, bleed, hurt. I only went to him a few times—Parker lived with him for months. Who knows what that does to someone?"

"This guy, Harry, is he the guy you were talking about? The one…"

"I killed? Yeah." His body shook as he said the words out loud, but Matt didn't shrink back this time.

He'd never admitted what he'd done to anyone. He couldn't even bring himself to pray about it. "I did a lot of drugs by then, just to get through it all. The night it happened, though, Harry had invited a bunch of guys over, and I was there as a party favor."

Robby sank down onto the sofa next to Matt and stared at the floor. "I'd coked up plenty before I went, but it didn't help much. It was like having four Harrys all at once."

The memories bubbled close to the surface. "I knew he roofied me sometimes, and it was a blessing really because at least I don't remember everything. I know there were videos he posted online. They're probably still out there somewhere."

Matt tried to take his hand, but Robby pulled away. The idea of anyone touching him right now made him physically ill. "That last night, I think our drinks got switched or something because I remember everything. But when it was all said and done, and the other guys had gone, Harry was practically unconscious."

He relived the events as he recounted them aloud.

Every part of him hurt. The cold trickle of blood dripped down his back from the flogging. He'd be shocked if his ass wasn't bleeding too. Even his own prep couldn't prepare him for taking on so many men at once. They were all gone now, except for him and Harry.

Every move was agony. It hurt to swallow, a reminder of the guy who choked him when he came. It hurt to sit, to walk.

He pulled a bag of cocaine and a razor blade from the back pocket of the jeans he'd discarded on the floor.

Then, Harry laughed.

It was a drunken, filthy, and cruel chuckle, and it broke something inside of him.

He looked at the stocky, hairy, smelly bastard, reclining naked on the sectional couch, and all he could think of was making it all stop.

Clenching the blade, he strode forward, leaned over, and sliced. Everywhere he knew the blood would run quickest.

Harry was dead before he could even think about what he'd done. When it finally sank in, he carefully wiped his prints off the razor with a paper towel, then pinched it in Harry's own hand.

He scrambled into his clothes and left the bastard in a pool of blood rapidly sinking into the upholstery.

"I went back to John's, packed a bag, and never looked back."

A lone tear trickled down Robby's face before he swiped it away. Apparently, he was still capable of crying. "It took me a while before I could stop thinking about the coke all the time, especially when the memories got bad. But my meetings made all the difference. I haven't gotten high since, and I haven't cut myself either, no matter how bad it gets."

"Cut yourself?" Matt's voice remained even, but judging by the look in his eyes, it cost him.

Robby took a deep breath, then held out his arms. The shiny, silvery-white lines chronicled his last few months as John's item for trade. "I never wanted you to see. Every day I look at these, I'm reminded how weak and pathetic I was back then."

"Bullshit." Matt's sharp tone cut him off. "Your scars don't prove you were weak. They prove you were strong enough to survive."

"The cutting gave me some control at a time

when I didn't have any. Just like the coke, I knew I was hurting myself, but I didn't care. Now I do." Reminding himself he'd broken his shackles gave him the strength to finally throw the blade away the night Matt walked away. He refused to reenter the cycle of self-harm.

Still…

"I understand if you can't look at me the same, knowing what I've done. Sometimes, I can barely look at myself."

Matt's intense stare softened. "God, Rob, none of this was your fault. You've been through hell. And I won't judge you for what you had to do to pull yourself out. I love you."

Something hard inside Robby yielded, but it didn't change the reality of what had happened. "I believe you, and I love you too, but I'm not sure where we can go from here. You didn't leave because you didn't love me. You left so you could keep your boy—you can't just will the problem away. And I kept things from you. Things you deserved to know if we ever had a chance at a life together."

"It doesn't matter anymore. I understand why you didn't tell me."

He chuckled softly. "Liar."

Matt gripped his hands and scooted closer. "You were ashamed. Afraid. Even if you did have a choice, and I don't think you did, your past is behind you. Patty has no right to judge you for it. I won't let her keep us apart. There has to be a way to hold onto you and Jimmy both. Please." His voice cracked. "Please let me try."

He wanted to. Oh, how he wanted to. But he'd unloaded a lot on Matt tonight. What if he decided one day the truth was too much? What if the next time Robby's past popped up, it tipped Patty right over the edge?

"I think we both need a little time. A little space."

"But Rob—" Matt sunk to his knees on the floor. "I'm ready to fight for us. Let me."

Robby slid his hand over Matt's cheek. "I need you to go. I'm not saying forever. But I am asking, for now. If you love me, respect me enough to do what I'm asking. You need to think about Jimmy. You'll never forgive yourself if you lose your chance to be his father."

Matt took a deep breath. He covered Robby's hand with his own for a heartbeat, then released it and stood.

"I'll go." Head down, he started to leave but stopped with the door open. "I'm not giving up on you, though. As long as there's a chance, I'll keep coming back, until I can prove to you I'll never walk away again. I'm going to find a way to keep you and Jimmy in my life."

CHAPTER TWENTY-NINE

Robby

It felt surreal going back to the construction-site without Matt there, knowing he'd probably never return. In a way, though, it freed them both. There was no room on the job for love or the loss of it. Whether he and Matt ever worked through their issues, Robby needed to keep a clear head at work.

At least it was what he told himself.

"You've been ducking my calls," Brick rumbled as he stepped into the trailer where Robby sat behind Xander's computer.

"Mine too," Kane groused, closing the flimsy door behind him.

The two men settled on the small sofa against the long wall, their big shoulders taking up all the space. They mirrored each other, arms folded, jaws tight.

"This isn't just a honeymoon period for you and

327

Matt, is it?" Brick cocked his head. "Something's going on."

Robby thought about lying. About smiling and saying everything was fine. But it wasn't. And if his best friends in the world—his brothers—couldn't handle the truth, well, they weren't the men he thought they were.

"I've never really told you a lot about myself."

Brick blinked. "You said your family tossed you out when you were young."

"Sixteen. I went from living in a tiny backwater town to downtown Atlanta. I had no idea what to do to get a roof over my head." Steeling himself, he continued, "I tried a shelter. Lost my virginity there in the worst way you could imagine."

Kane nodded subtly, but Brick went stock still.

"I figured out really fast I'd rather deal with one guy—any guy—for a place to sleep, rather than four or five at a time."

Brick shot to his feet, but Kane pulled him back down with softly spoken words. "It's come and gone, brother. Let the man tell you his story."

"Kane's right." Robby came from the behind the desk and leaned against the front of the scarred wood. "It can't hurt me anymore."

From there, he told them about his first trips to the bars. About finding men to take him home. John. Parker. Even Harry. And his escape. "I never thought I'd have it in me to kill somebody, but I can't bring myself to be sorry for it. Not even now."

"Course you're not," Kane growled. "Some people deserve to die."

Robby gripped his hands together. "I'd

understand if you looked at me differently."

Brick let out a heavy exhale. "At least you've only killed someone who deserved it. I've killed plenty who didn't. Do you look at me differently?"

Of course not. "That was the old you."

"And all this—everything you just told us—that wasn't the old *you*?" Brick pressed. But he didn't wait for an answer. "Does Matt know?"

Kane rubbed his chin. "It's what this is all about, am I right? Your disappearing act? The radio silence? It went bad."

"I wasn't honest." Robby swallowed. "He found out about it all in the worst possible way. And so did his son's mother."

"Do I need to break his legs?"

"No, Brick." He had no doubt his friend would do it in a heartbeat. "He could lose his little boy over this. This could give Patty ammunition in a custody fight, and Matt's baby is everything to him—as he should be. We need to work this out ourselves. Just—be my friend. Can you do that?"

"No, man." Brick stood, his six-and-a-half-foot frame towering over him. "We're not friends."

Kane stood beside him. "Not friends. Family."

Brick nodded. "Forever."

It felt like a hug-it-out moment, but a tap on the trailer door interrupted them.

"Um. Hello? I'm looking for a Rob Jordan." A tinny voice leaked into the room, followed by another knock. "Is anyone there?"

Eyebrows drawn together, Brick pushed open the door.

A skinny, balding delivery guy held out a spring

329

bouquet. "Mr. Jordan?"

Brick swiped the flowers out of the man's hand and held them out to Robby before digging some cash out of his pocket for a tip.

Flowers. He didn't have to read the card to know where they came from. Still, with shaking hands, he tugged the small, thick square from the envelope.

You deserve a lifetime of flowers.

I love you.

Not just the best part of you. Not just the idea of you.

I will love you until the end of time.

Robby held the card and the flowers to his chest, and before he could wrap his head around the unsigned card, his phone buzzed in his pocket.

Matt: I'm sitting outside your apartment. With a grand gesture. I'll wait. As long as I have to.

"I need to go," he murmured.

Kane dropped a hand on his shoulder. "Go work it out, brother."

He fought the urge to drive a hundred miles an hour back to his apartment. He went ninety-five at the most. Surely, the police would understand.

Thankfully, he never had to explain.

His mind spun, wondering what Matt would consider a grand gesture.

He didn't have to wonder for very long. As soon

as he pulled up, he found his front porch covered in flowers. Colorful carnations, daisies, tulips. Sunflowers, lilies, begonias. Pansies, lilacs, and some blooms he didn't even recognize.

And in the center of it all sat Matt, leaning against the front door with his eyes closed. He startled and jumped up when he heard Robby's approach, the daisies clutched in his hand. He held them out, helplessly. "Th—these are for you."

Robby accepted them, his gaze sweeping across the porch then locking on Matt's face. "I figured."

"You told me once—your favorite part of a romantic movie was when the guy—"

"I remember." He swept as many flowers as he could into his arms. "Help me bring these inside."

Matt grabbed the last few arrangements and followed him in.

"You didn't have to do all this. You don't have the money to waste on this."

Matt dropped the flowers on the table, then spun to face him. "A waste? Is that what you think?" He advanced. "You could never be a waste."

Matt cupped his cheeks. "You are worth anything—everything to me. I love you, Rob. With all I have and all I am. And I hope you're willing to try again, but if you're not ready, I'll wait, but I won't give up. I'm willing to do the work. For as long as it takes. Until you believe—until you know. You. Are. Worth. It."

The still-wounded part of him fought against it, but Robby's heart could not deny the truth right in front of him. "It's a lot easier to forgive you than it is to forgive myself. You think maybe you could help me there?"

The answer didn't come in words. Matt leaned in for a kiss. Tender, just a gentle sweep of his lips. But it was enough.

The emotion—the connection—threatened to overwhelm him. The kiss answered prayers he hadn't dared to give voice to. The man he thought he'd never get back held him in his arms now shared his breath. He'd offer up his soul right now if Matt wanted it.

But he had to be sure; he had to ask one more time. Fighting his deepest instincts, he pulled back and held Matt at arms' length. "I want this. More than anything, I want a life with you, but I need to know you're all in. I'm not sure my heart can take having you, then losing you again. Maybe you need to take some more time to think about what you really want."

"No. I already know. I was miserable without you. Even with the best possible future in front of me—a future you made possible, by the way— nothing felt right. Somehow, my world is only complete with you in it. I don't need more time; I just need you. Trust me, I'm not giving up on a life with you or my son."

***

Matt

Matt could see the second Robby accepted his words as the truth. Those gorgeous brown eyes, so full of vulnerability, softened, along with the tight lines bracketing his mouth.

And words were no longer necessary.

Robby took the lead, leaning in first for the kiss, but they met somewhere in the middle. It was a tender joining, a brush of lips. Matt's hands glided up his lover's bare arms, the scars imperceptible beneath his fingertips.

Gently, Robby's kisses drifted to the column of his throat. "Be with me tonight."

Matt could only moan his consent, but it was enough. They rose together, headed toward the bedroom, dropping their clothes like breadcrumbs in their wake. This time, the light stayed on.

Finally, he could drink in Robby's beauty, and oh, was he beautiful. A light dusting of hair covered the center of his slim but defined pecs. It vanished over his tight stomach and reappeared in a trail below his navel leading down to the trim patch around his half-hard cock. Indeed, he did have a small birthmark.

Matt wrapped his hand around the ruddy skin, growing empowered as it hardened further in his grip. "Let me make you feel good tonight."

No way he could work the same kind of magic Robby had for him, but damn he wanted to try. "Say yes."

"Yes."

His heart raced. "Lie down."

Robby climbed across the bed, giving him a quick flash of his marked shoulder blades and firm, round ass before settling on his back.

Matt couldn't help but stare at the beautiful, defined lines of Robby's body. "I want to taste you."

"Yes."

Moving slowly, he climbed up Robby's legs, resting with his face just inches away from the now full-on erection. He grasped it at the base, as Robby had done for him, then licked the underside with the flat of his tongue.

His lover shuddered beneath him.

Emboldened, he swirled around the tip, then swallowed as much of the length as he could. Sucking, he bobbed his head up, then down. He knew right away he wasn't coordinated enough to use his mouth and his hand in tandem. Not yet. Instead of striving for the near perfection Robby had delivered, he took his time learning what touches, licks, and movements made his partner moan, groan, and downright beg.

Robby undulated beneath him. "Stop. Please. I want to feel all of you against me."

Yes.

Matt slid himself up so his body pressed flush against Robby's. Their dicks slid against one another, slick from the moisture his mouth had left behind. Every inch of him tingled where they touched, and he ached for Robby to fill him the way he had before.

"Get me ready," he breathed against Robby's warm, damp skin. "I want to feel you inside of me."

Robby stilled. "Are you sure? You can top if you want."

"Not tonight. Will you…make love to me?"

With a groan, Robby reached for his nightstand and pulled out a small bag. "Switch places with me."

No need to tell him twice. Once he was on his back, Robby dropped his head, but instead of going for his cock, he dipped lower. Hooking his hands under Matt's knees, Robby pulled his legs apart. His tongue swirled expertly around, then inside of Matt's opening.

Exquisite. Matt let his knees fall outward to give better access. In and out, his lover's deft tongue coaxed and massaged, and Matt's tight muscles relaxed under his ministrations. Using his thumbs, Robby widened the hole to allow him to delve deeper. The tip of one thumb edged inside, played and teased.

Pulling back to sit on his heels, Robby bit his lip. "I love you. I'm going to spend this night showing you exactly how much."

Matt already knew.

Unzipping the bag, Robby deliberately pulled out the lube and coated his fingers with the clear liquid. "The way you look at me. No one has ever looked at me that way before." His gaze locked on Matt's and didn't waver as he slid the first digit inside. Robby moved as slowly and carefully as he did their first time, and he was just as thorough. One finger became two, and just as the sting made way to pleasure, he gripped Matt's cock with his other hand. The laser-like focus of his stare made the experience even more erotic.

Without thought, Matt swiveled his hips and the sensations skyrocketed.

"Yes, baby. You are so sexy, working my hands," Robby whispered. He thrust his fingers faster.

"Give me more," Matt pleaded.

"I'll give you anything."

The absence of Robby's hands left his body crying out for more touch. A rip of foil and a heartbeat later, the familiar pressure of Robby's erection pressed for entry.

"Do it. Do it," Matt pleaded. "Show me I'm yours."

And in one thrust, Robby gave him what he asked for. "You are mine. Only mine. Tell me you want this. You want me."

He ran his hands over the cheeks of Robby's ass. "Please. I want it. You. So. Much."

Robby pulled out leisurely and slid back in. "Tell me you love me."

Matt clenched his lover's hips. "I love you. Please, Rob."

The next deep plunge cut him off, and Robby took him, strong, steady, and sure. Pleasure drowned out the little wisps of pain.

Robby grabbed the lube, dousing his erection again in a moment between thrusts and spreading the wetness over Matt's cock too.

He didn't wait for Robby's instruction; he gripped himself, his hand making quick work, escalating his pleasure.

"I'm not going to last, Matt. Come with me. Fly with me, baby."

The slap of Robby's pelvis against his ass, the driving pressure, and the slick slide of his hand, along with the gruff edge of the words drove him over the edge with a shout. As his eyes rolled back,

Robby went silent and rigid…then let out a heavy breath.

The world stood still.

Then, Robby rubbed a hand along Matt's arm. "Don't move."

Matt mourned the loss the fullness as Robby pulled out and stepped over to the bathroom. His body might never feel complete again without the other man beside him—or inside him. Thankfully, his lover returned quickly with a warm washcloth he ran over Matt's stomach and below, taking care of him yet again in his tender way.

By the time Robby turned off the lights and settled in beside him, exhaustion had wrapped him in its grip. He fought it as long as he could, determined to appreciate the moment and the man snuggled up in his arms. What if something snatched this happiness away and he'd wasted a perfect part of it by drifting off?

Robby must've known, or maybe he felt it too. "Sleep," he whispered. "I promise, we'll still be together when we wake up."

He held the vow close to his heart, allowing him to let go and drift off into a content and peaceful oblivion.

CHAPTER THIRTY

Robby

Robby floated through the next day on Cloud Nine. Though he'd hated saying goodbye to Matt this morning, the knowledge they'd be together again tonight, maybe every night, made it much easier.

Sitting at the big, wooden table at the Q-Center that afternoon, he flipped through the loose-leaf journal pages he'd collected from his work clipboard. Most of his early entries chronicled his loneliness, but over time, he could see the infusion of hope in his ramblings.

Nowhere did he document explicitly when Brick came into his life, but the paragraphs he wrote about friendship and family announced it as clearly as a neon sign. As he read through his self-affirmations, his scribbles about sunrises and happy ever after, he could see the journey he took falling in love.

The stack of papers had to be two or three inches thick. The pages had served as a friend and confidant when he didn't have one. Given him a place to unburden his heart when no one else cared to listen. They'd kept him sane.

And now, he didn't need them anymore.

He scooped the pile into his arms and fed the loose-leaf into the shredder. With the destruction of each page, his heart grew even lighter.

Now, he had people who wanted to hear what he had to say, and just as importantly, he was no longer afraid to say it. They'd love him no matter what. Smile or no smile. Docile or obstinate. He could be happy or angry or sad, and they would never throw him away.

Smiling, he bagged up the shredded remains.

"They got you on trash duty now, doll?" Sara leaned against the doorframe to her room. The hesitation on her face told him it wasn't the question she'd really wanted to ask. He hadn't seen her since the meltdown with his father.

"Thank you for sending Matt my way and for whatever you said to him. It changed everything."

The tightness in her shoulders relaxed. "And your daddy?"

"Gone. Hopefully, for good." He wasn't sure how to deal with Parker and the trouble he'd tried to make, but right now he had more pressing concerns. "Have you seen Brady? We were supposed to talk about long-term housing." If anyone caught a whiff of an underage kid staying here, social services could get involved.

"I'm right here." The smile on the boy's face transformed him from cute to downright gorgeous. In his jeans and T-shirt, he looked like the carefree teenager he'd probably never had a chance to be.

Paul and Chris, hands joined, stood behind him.

"The housing issue is covered." The reverend beamed. "Chris and I have been approved to foster him."

"So fast?" Robby was no expert, but he'd looked in to doing it himself, and his Google search indicated the process would take months.

"We got licensed a few years ago, and we fostered a little girl, Tammy. She stayed with us for nine months." Chris spoke with the echoes of old hurt. "When they took her back, we needed time for our hearts to heal."

"We're going to get some placement tests done so I can go back to school in the fall." Brady stared at the couple with unabashed wonder.

"We also made a report to police about the back room at the nightclub." Paul folded his hands. "The detective assured me they're going to shut it down. God willing, we can make a difference for some other folks who need it too."

"I'm so happy for you guys." With Paul and Chris, Brady had a chance at a real future.

Chris lifted his shoulder. "We've always wanted a son. This could be the miracle we've all been praying for."

Matt could use a miracle too.

Robby glanced at the clock. It was worth a shot.

"I need to go take care of some things. Sara, you've got the place covered?"

"Go on, doll. I've got this."

***

Robby had his choice of parking spots in front of the tattoo parlor. Not surprising. He wouldn't expect the place to get busy for another few hours. At least he wouldn't have much of an audience if things went south in the next few minutes.

With a fortifying breath, he stepped inside, and Patty's head shot up at the tinkle of the bell. Her brows furrowed together.

"What are you doing here?"

"I'm here to get square with you."

She shook her head. "Matt told me—"

"Matt got some bad advice from a guy I knew a hundred years ago. And I can tell you right now, drugs are not part of my life. I've been in N.A.— I've been clean—for five years."

Parker sauntered into the lobby from somewhere in the back of building. "Look what the cat dragged in. I would've thought they'd run you out on a rail by now."

He narrowed his eyes at his old brother-in-arms. "Is that what you were hoping for? Why? Why are you trying to wreck my happiness? And you can drop the act. Matt knows everything and we're stronger than ever."

"Of course, you are." Parker's pretty face contorted. His perfect features looked almost alien, set in cold, hard lines. "Perfect Robby lands on his feet again. Why do good things only happen to you? It's not fair."

"You know damn good and well my life was no walk in the park." Of all the people to be jealous of, why would Parker choose him?

"I could've taken your spot. John was going to

pick me, I know it. But you left—and between missing you and dealing with Harry's suicide—he wouldn't even look at me again. Said I made him sad." Parker huffed. "Then, after whatever happened with your beefcake bodyguards at work, he left town. He's *gone*." Parker stamped his foot. "I was so close to finally hitting the jackpot, and you ruined it."

"John was not the jackpot." Though he could understand why it would seem so to Parker. "Besides, you don't need someone to take care of you anymore. You're a grown man. Get a job; make a life."

"How? Should I go get a job working a drive-thru somewhere so I can afford to rent a hovel and sleep on the floor?" His old friend bared his teeth. "Fuck that. Even a place like this is better than you're suggesting."

"A place like this?" Steve appeared like magic behind him. "Are you slumming it, Parker?"

"No. No. You misunderstood. I love you, baby."

"You love having a free place to live, more like." Steve ground his back teeth. The emotions flitting across his face vanished into a stony stillness. "Get out."

"But my stuff is at your place. And you know no one else can make you feel as good as I do." Parker reached out, but Patty's boss swiped his hand away.

"Good is the last word I'd use to describe how I feel right now. Get out before I throw you out." As Steve took a menacing step forward, Parker scurried out the door.

Robby wondered briefly if he would be caught

up in the raid when the cops shut down Nitro's back room.

There but for the grace of God go I.

At least he never had to worry about John showing up again.

The bell over the door rang with Parker's exit, then quieted, and the three of them stood in a heavy, awkward silence. Patty spoke first. "Does this mean he was lying about you? To like, get even or something?"

"They weren't all lies, exactly. I did some questionable things to get by when I was a kid. But I'm not a kid anymore. My life is different now. I love Matt, and he loves me."

The bell rang, and Matt strode in. He smiled when his gaze landed on Robby.

Grinning in return, his heart rallied. He drew on the feeling, then turned back to Patty. "I'll take a drug test if you want. Anytime you want. I'm not perfect, but I promise I would never do anything to endanger your son."

Matt twined their fingers together. "You're perfect for *me*." He turned to Patty. "I want peace with you, and it feels like we're finally getting there, but Robby's worth fighting for. I won't give up on him—or on Jimmy."

She looked at their joined hands. "Are you sure, Matty?"

"More than anything."

"And Jimmy will be safe?"

Matt nodded. "I trust Robby with my life."

She stared uneasily at Matt, then Robby, and back again.

"I don't want to be your enemy." Matt ran his hand over her arm. "I love you. You're Jimmy's mom, and no one can take that away. I don't want to fight you…but I will. Please. Can't we just try to be friends again?"

Patty closed her eyes briefly and rested her hand over Matt's. "Okay, then. If my blessing is what you need, you have it. I trust you—God knows, you've earned it. And no matter how much I deserved it, you never gave up on me. You supported me, always, and now I'm going to support you."

She turned her tremulous smile to Robby. "Welcome to the family."

EPILOGUE

Six months later

Robby

A soft toddler's hand, smacking his face, woke Robby up from a sound sleep. "Baba!"

Now that Jimmy could maneuver out of his playpen, he loved climbing into bed with his daddy and Baba on weekend mornings to demand his breakfast.

He pulled the little boy into his arms and breathed in his curly black hair. "Five more minutes, Jimbo."

A wet baby kiss dragged across his cheek. "Cancake."

How could he resist? Leaving Matt snoring in the bed, he hefted Jimmy onto his hip and carried him to his highchair. "Pancakes, huh?" He dropped a handful of Cheerios in front of the boy as he pulled some Eggo's out of the freezer. Not pancakes, but close enough.

Since Matt had moved in last month, and Jimmy stayed the weekends, he kept his kitchen fully stocked. He still wasn't much of a cook, but he made do with what he could cobble together from a box. Jimmy didn't mind, and Matt said he was just happy he didn't force him to eat spaghetti or lasagna. Marinara sauce gave him heartburn. He'd finally broken down and told his mother the night he'd introduced her to Robby.

She was still adjusting to both ideas.

The toaster pinged, and he dropped the baby's breakfast on a plate and cut it into bite-sized pieces. A drop of syrup on each piece would guarantee a mess, but it made Jimmy so happy, he never said no.

Matt shuffled in just as the toddler stuffed the first bite into his mouth. "Do I smell waffles?"

Robby laughed at the lines still smooshed in his face from the pillow. "Sit down, old man."

Since Matt had quit his bartending job, the weekends meant relaxation and quiet family time. Well, maybe not quiet. Jimmy never stopped talking. But the little boy's joyful babble only made life better.

"Are we still going to Brick and Liv's for dinner tonight?" Robby asked, pulling more waffles from the toaster oven. "The guys say it's been too long since they've seen you."

"It's only been a week, babe."

Robby grinned as he piled Matt's breakfast on the plate. He missed seeing Matt at work every day, too, but the internship at Berringer put a light in the man's eyes that made it all worth it. Besides, he saw

346

him plenty at night.

"What can I say, it's hard for anyone to get enough of you."

Matt rolled his eyes. "Hmm. Kane just wants me there for more parenting advice. Having a newborn is freaking him out."

"Can you blame them for wanting to learn from you? You're an amazing father."

"So are you."

Robby froze.

"Don't look so shocked. You are the heart of this family, Rob. I love you. Jimmy loves you. Even Patty thinks you're amazing."

He rubbed his chest against the rising joy and looked around the table. Matt and Jimmy were his everything. He had a family, one who would never turn their backs on him. And a tapestry of human connections from Brick and Kane, to Paul and Chris, and all the kids whose lives he touched at the Q-Center.

Not bad for a throwaway queer kid from Sherman.

Who said dreams didn't come true?

Acknowledgements

The first draft of this book was a far cry from the version that ended up on the page. Thank you so much to Amanda and Joanna for wading through the worst of it. Thanks also to Amelia and Meka for your tough love. I needed to hear your feedback. All of you made this book infinitely better. You are amazing writers and friends, and I am grateful for you beyond measure.

About the Author

Jen started her love affair with romance novels, first as a reader, then as a reviewer and blogger.

She is happily married to her high school sweetheart. Together, they're raising two kids, a cat, and a dog who is afraid of his own shadow.

Jen spends her days working as television journalist and her nights curled up with a good book.

Facebook:
https://www.facebook.com/jen.davis.author

Twitter:
http://twitter.com/redhotbooks

Website:
http://jendavis.net/

Join our Reader Group on Facebook and don't miss out on meeting our authors and entering epic giveaways!

Limitless Reading

Where reading a book
is your first step to becoming
limitless...

LIMITLESS PUBLISHING *Reader Group*

Join today! *"Where reading a book is your first step to becoming limitless..."*